Elisabeth Russell Tayl two Virago Modern Clas She has also written fo articles and reviews. Her stories have been broadcast on BBC Radio 4, and her writing has been translated into French and Dutch. Elisabeth has been awarded a Wingate Scholarship and grants from the Authors' Foundation and the Arts Council. Her writing has been shortlisted for the Mind Book of the Year, the Jewish Book of the Year, and the Jewish Quarterly-Wingate Prize for Fiction. She lives in London.

'A very fine quality of writing' *Financial Times*

'A slim, beautifully written novel that bulges with the grossest inhumanity'
Daily Telegraph

Present Fears
'She writes brilliantly' Elaine Feinstein, *The Times*

'Witty, deadpan language with a bleakness reminiscent of Roald Dahl'
Daily Telegraph

'A sparkling collection of stories, each with a sting in its tail'
Sunday Times

'Taylor mingles the elegant with the grotesque, as if seating Flaubert next to William S. Burroughs at dinner'
Publishers Weekly

'Taylor's elegantly engineered anticlimaxes leave the reader with the disquieting feeling of waiting for the other shoe to fall' *Observer*

'Elegant and witty surfaces break open to reveal the darkness at the heart of these cosmopolitan tales'
Georgina Hammick

Tomorrow
'A haunting, beautifully written lament for the isolating power of love' *Financial Times*

Belated

and other stories

Elisabeth Russell Taylor

Kimblewood Press
London

First published in Great Britain by Kimblewood Press 2014

© Elisabeth Russell Taylor 2014

The moral right of the author has been asserted.

'Les Amants' and 'The Meaning' were originally published
in *The Moth*, and 'The Unexpected Marriage of Vanilla
to the Stars' in *Primal Picnics*, edited by Jennifer Heath.

A CIP catalogue record for this book
is available from the British Library.

ISBN 13: 9781491285312
ISBN 10: 1491285311

www.elisabethrusselltaylor.wordpress.com

Contents

Les Amants

But, oh! as to embrace me he inclined
I waked, he fled, and day brought back my night.
after Milton

The village of Les Amants de Ste Agathe is infamous for being the site of *un crime passionel.* At the time, and it was many years ago, the effects of the crime were not confined to the three families whose lives were most closely touched by it. Questions of fidelity and betrayal haunted the whole population of three hundred souls, and succeeding generations continued to bear the weight of a tragedy that had led to the knifing of one young man, the drowning of his lover, and the death through heartbreak of his wife. Eventually the villagers, in an act they hoped would both consecrate and purge the affair, added the words Les Amants, and the new name was a continual reminder of the past. Even today, when gathered in the Café du Marché, villagers have a tendency to talk as much about passion as about fishing, rising prices or the perfidy of their government.

Les Amants is perched high above a bend in the river Seine, its houses gouged out of the chalk cliffs. At the front of each house small platforms of land provide space for potted plants, a table and a couple of chairs from which to marvel at the spectacular view over the contortions of the river below and the forests and plains beyond.

The road that curls from the banks of the river is steep, with a gradient of one in three, dictated by the altitude of the cliffs and the outcrop of scars round which it had to be cut. In the winter months of snow and ice and the autumn months of dead leaves soaked in rain, villagers look up at the sky, consult old-fashioned lore and contemporary weather forecasts before setting out, for the way is hazardous. The modern road follows the bends of the old lane and makes no accommodation for vehicles to pass.

———

Fleur Cortot, aged seventy, lived at the summit where the exhausted road falls short of the plain. Behind her house, in an orchard of cherry and plum trees where hens pecked, a large barn had been converted to a studio. Fleur had lived in Les Amants since she was eighteen when Léon Cortot, the painter, brought her from Paris to be his model and mistress. Now, Fleur was somewhat stooped, her once flawless complexion the texture of crumpled linen and her once gold-red hair the colour of thin cream. She was tired. She had not ventured down to the river since Léon died; she had not taken *le thé* with her neighbour; she had no appetite to eat alone, and at night she barely dozed. When old friends telephoned, she turned them away. How to invest life with meaning when the heart had been torn from it?

It was so different when Léon was alive: there was laughter and good living. Like Bonnard's Marthe, Fleur sat to Léon in the orchard, at table and in the bath. They walked together, they talked together. Theirs was happiness *à deux*.

Léon worked obsessively. His only recreation was fishing. This he enjoyed in the company of the ferryboat man at Roc. For years the two men sat in silence together, sharing their wine and sausages and their catch. And when Léon needed help in stacking pictures away, weatherproofing the studio, digging the ground or locating supplies, he would turn to Jean, the son of the ferryboat man. From time to time, the old man wondered to Léon whether his son would not have made more of his life had he not felt responsible for his disabled father?

Fleur stood at the kitchen door looking out through the cherry blossom to a corner of the orchard where Jean was sawing rotten branches for firewood. In the past she had taken no notice of Jean, dismissing him as someone merely practical. Since living with Léon she had never bothered with other men. Now she noticed how tall Jean stood, how well proportioned he was, how harmoniously his body and person combined in his labours. He leant into his tasks, working silently, involved in detail most would consider too trivial to consider.

Jean was never inconvenienced by changes in the weather. Rain suited him as well as shine, heat as well as cold. It was not mere indifference; it was acceptance. She wondered whether he had ambitions? Perhaps it would be impertinent, even upsetting to enquire.

He was courteous but taciturn. It seemed he laid claim to nothing. Whereas most young men had some sort of vehicle on four wheels, Jean had a bicycle. Whereas others had gadgets – mobile phone, iPod – and some money, Jean's pockets were empty; Fleur always had to advance him what was needed to buy her provisions and materials to maintain the house and outbuildings. On one occasion, while Jean was reglazing the greenhouse, Fleur offered him a beer. He took it without a word, just a nod of thanks. To break the silence, she asked him whether he had ever been to Paris. He had not. Was there nothing about Paris that tempted him, nothing he would like to see? There was not. He had all he needed to hand: the river to fish, the plot to dig. The odd jobs he did in the village covered his and his old father's needs, and left him time. Time was what he required. 'For what?' 'To think.' Fleur was astonished and felt a little ashamed; it had never so much as crossed her mind that Jean would have needed time to think. She had observed that thinkers were not normally suited to action, yet Jean was always on the go, applying himself physically to one thing and another and often in advance of his being asked to do so. One day she would find an appropriate moment to slide a question to him, imperceptibly, and ask him what he thought about.

One monotonous day followed another. Time lay barren: Fleur felt shackled to leaden hours, manipulated by an unseen force that overlooked her grief and robbed her of her ability to act. She had become an automaton, imprisoned in the past. She was frustrated, she had no more influence over her mind, and her ardent longing for Léon's flesh, his touch, frightened her. She became aware of danger. She knew that disaster lay ahead and that an unexpected disaster would kill her.

The last thing Fleur wished for was visitors. But they turned up unwanted and unannounced during the summer months. They had heard of Léon Cortot and of Les Amants and of its unsurpassed beauty, its unique situation. It would be such a pleasure to combine a visit to the locality with the purchase of a picture by a local artist! And would that not mean they could avoid the gallery's commission?

Then there was Léon's gallery owner, M. Geier. He planned to hold a commemorative show of Léon's work the following year. He was counting on Fleur to select paintings for him to view, to date them and sort out the framing and produce a biographical piece for the catalogue. Now that the painter was dead, there was an excellent chance that the exhibition would be a financial success. M. Geier laid his plans before her enthusiastically. She could have three weeks in which to assemble the work.

She had not opened the studio door since he died. She dreaded entering the studio and discovering dilapidations that her neglect might have occasioned. She did not feel able to confront the work. It was all too personal; she was a part of every picture. She would be reminded too powerfully of the last sight she had had of Léon, a lifeless, waxen effigy, who had ignored her entreaties: 'Come back! Don't leave me! Don't die!'

But she found everything in order. The holes in the roof had been plugged, the floor scrubbed, the old pots of paint stacked in a corner, the brushes cleaned, and the canvases neatly stacked. Clearly Jean had not liked to throw away anything without consulting her, and had gauged that the time was not yet ripe. Files of papers, boxes of photographs, letters and catalogues were ranged on the table that had served Léon as a desk. It all looked as if, just a matter of seconds ago, the painter had risen from his work and slipped out to go fishing.

Fleur felt faint. She dropped into Léon's chair, laid her arms on the table and her head in her arms. She closed her mind. She must not look back; memories should only be revived in happiness. She had not been happy since he died. Her thoughts had been stuck in the featureless wastes of absence.

Jean lifted the canvases from the stacks and slowly, one by one, propped each against the back wall of the studio for Fleur to consider. There, the heavy curtain of willows dipped their elegant branches in the water; there the radiant cherry tree, where Léon listened to the larks; there a laundered sky; a table with a basket of peaches; Fleur and Prune, the cat, at breakfast; barges chugging towards Le Havre; launches at dusk with their lights flickering; Fleur stretched out naked on the chaise longue, a book slipping from her hand. Years of intimacy in paint. She was filled with inexpressible longing. The still atmosphere of death imprisoned her. The work did nothing to fill the void; indeed, it was a calumny. She would be glad to see the back of it all.

M. Geier arrived in full spate and made straight for the studio. 'This road of yours is truly treacherous, my dear. I wouldn't like to have to negotiate it under snow!' He flicked through paintings as if through a sheaf of papers. 'Come, we need luncheon.' Fleur did not need luncheon, although she avoided saying so. She was not dressed for Le Château Vert, but that was where Geier intended they should eat so there they drove. Geier did not notice Fleur's attire; she was no longer a woman in his eyes. He talked and talked, barely pausing for breath and certainly without engaging his guest. 'You do not alter.'

'Oh, but I have.'

'Yes, when Léon died. But not since.'

'That's true. Once love died, my spirit was consumed. I'm in the clutches of something malign.'

'I always wondered why you and Léon never married?'

'We did not feel the need for the town hall in our love.'

'You were very beautiful once, with that red-gold hair, that flawless skin, those curves! But you never so much as gave me a chance.'

'No, I suppose I didn't.'

'Why was that? Am I not a fine figure of a man?' Geier laughed, and when he laughed he seemed to do so in German, a language Fleur did not trust. He muttered under his breath several times and turned his thoughts elsewhere. This old woman was beginning to bore him.

'Now,' he said, wiping his face with the ample damask napkin, 'we must go over the sketch books.' He drove at speed back to Les Amants, continuously complaining about the gradient on 'her' road, the early hour at which he had had to leave Paris, the cost of printing the catalogue and Fleur's lack of conversation. 'I shall put on a *vernissage* to beat all *vernissages*, my dear. *Le tout Paris* will fight to be invited.'

'Thank you. I am sure they will.' Fleur, on the other hand, knew she would not be attending.

———

It was late November. The carters had been and the pictures were delivered to the gallery. Fleur locked the studio door and dropped the key into her apron pocket. How love congeals around ordinary things! Jean would post her letter to Geier with the summary of Léon's life: 'I Belong to No Movement.'

Jean was burning the last of the detritus of autumn. He had recently demolished the chicken run; for the next months the surviving hens would be safest in the shed. A lowering sky hung over Les Amants. Smoke filled the air. Snow was on the way.

During all the years Jean had worked for the Cortots he had never once initiated a conversation with Fleur, so she was astonished when he entered the kitchen and without pre-amble proposed that she could do with a rechargeable battery lamp and some plastic overshoes. She had to make an effort to bring herself back into a world where objects had utility. Now he was reminding her that the electricity lines had been driven down by the weight of the snow last year, and that she had twisted her ankle on the icy path because she was wear-ing unsuitable shoes. She registered Jean's thoughtfulness and thanked him and said yes, she would be grateful if he bought both items for her. She was seated at the kitchen table under a low, overhanging light. She pushed her purse towards him. He took the money he needed and pushed the purse back to her side of the table and turned to leave. He had not dwelt on her face, just brushed it with a glance.

When Jean returned and handed Fleur a lamp and some overshoes, Fleur examined them as if they had been objects for use in some far-flung ritual in which, for cultural reasons, she should express interest. She wondered how a lamp got itself recharged but set the query to one side when it became obvious to her that Jean would know. The overshoes were extraordinarily ugly, the colour and texture of cheap jellies.

She tried putting them on over her slippers but they would not go; Jean told her they would fit over her lace-ups. And then he left the room; he was going to do some draught-proofing at the windows and see that the water tank and one exposed pipe were thoroughly well lagged. The chicken could do with some grain and the log pile needed to be built up.

Snow was falling gently as Jean wheeled his bicycle into the shed. Fleur could hear the chickens complaining. Really, she thought, Jean should go home right away. She called to him but he did not answer. When he came back into the kitchen she insisted: 'You must start for home!' No, he said, he had other matters to attend to in the house, there was plenty of time, she should not worry. However, the blizzard was gathering force and the snow was falling silently and inexorably across the land. When the only light rose from the whited ground, Fleur insisted Jean ring his father and explain he would have to stay the night in Les Amants. She listened to him while he spoke tenderly to the old man. There was no need for anxiety, he would ring again at daybreak and get back to Roc as soon as the road was negotiable. He advised his father on what to eat and recommended that he go to bed, well covered, with a hot-water bottle.

When Jean worked at the house, he generally ate from Fleur's larder as he had done when Léon was alive: he pre-ferred to do so alone, in the orchard or the shed. That night, however, he put out plates and glasses for two, heated soup and piled a plate with sausages and cheese. They ate in silence. After the meal Fleur busied herself unloading the oak chest in the sitting room of blankets, pillows and a patchwork quilt she had made during long hours of sitting to Léon. Jean would sleep on the sofa. She showed him his coverings and advised him to keep in the fire.

She climbed the stairs to the bedroom. She was not aware of anything that disturbed her mind but she registered some sense of half-formed, half-hidden experiences so long past they might have happened in another incarnation, deep as the forces that work beneath the earth at this time of year. From time to time, the silence of the world snow-bound was interrupted by bursts of sparks from the fire in the room below. Obscurely comforted by the sound, Fleur recognised its succour in her unconscious. She might sleep that night. She might even dream.

It was night's high noon. The blackness and the quiet enveloped her and effaced her grief as the snow concealed the ironhard ground. Perhaps he would return? *But if he did, would I hear his steps?*

She sensed a sudden little draught as the covers lifted. A soft, smooth body, wood-smoke scented, slipped in beside her. A hand enclosed her breast. A face pressed against the side of her face and warm breath at her ear formed coaxing words. She was ready. He lifted himself over the length of her body and gently bore down on her, crushing her. She gasped. In due time, they turned together, 'close as two pages'.

Fleur woke to frozen silence. No bird sang in the still air. She was in the grip of a transformed white world in which the evergreens took the weight of the snowfall and their branches bent helplessly.

Charlotte

To be rooted is perhaps the most important and
least recognised need of the human soul.
Simone Weil

'How do you do, Herr Anders? I hope you had a comfortable journey.'

Caspar Anders lifted his pigskin case from the step on which he had rested it and entered the hall. 'It was not unagreeable,' he said.

'Allow me to show you to your room.'

Stairs leading from the ground to the basement floor were steep, and the visitor negotiated them with care. 'Excellent,' he said, entering Rainer's old study.

'We call it the Garden Room,' Charlotte said, handing him several keys attached to a ring.

He was relieved to find the room light, airy and uncluttered. He glanced around. There were book-lined shelves, a desk that filled a bay window overlooking a garden, a swivel chair, a divan and adequate storage space. He opened the door to the shower room, tested the water and found it piping hot. He peered into the lavatory pan. Spotless. He picked up the keys, unlocked the glass-panelled door and stepped on to the path which to the left led round the garden and to the right wound round the house to the front gate and, ultimately, to the road. He would come and go without having to use the front door.

Charlotte had been waiting on tenterhooks, alive to every passing taxi. In her anxiety she had toppled a vase of daffodils on the hall table. Would she need to apologise to the Herr Doktor for the piles of rotting refuse at the corner of Belsize Park? Should she mention at once that there would be power cuts and delays on the Tube? Hardly an auspicious introduction to London. Perhaps it could wait.

As for the Garden Room itself, she was torn. She had preserved Rainer's study as he had left it, lined with the books he read, the files in which he stored his contracts with the BBC and his German publisher, his typewriter and his dictionaries. On the one hand, she wanted the Herr Doktor to understand something of the weight of the man in whose room he was going to work and sleep; on the other, she did not want Rainer's legacy to be overbearing, as if it were sanctified. She'd worked methodically, lining the drawers of his desk with fresh paper and polishing it with beeswax. Three generations of family history attached to the desk's bulk, and as she opened each drawer she caught the lingering scent of cigars. She decided to clear the surface of all but the angle-poise lamp and the telephone. She made a note to buy a copy of the *A-Z*, 150-watt light bulbs, and filters for the coffee machine, which needed a thorough scour. All the while she'd cleaned and re-equipped the room, questions picked at her. What was it that was motivating her to rearrange Rainer's study and introduce a lodger? Since Rainer's death, she had come to savour living alone. What had induced her to agree to an invasion of her privacy? She had taken the decision impulsively and regretted it immediately, but because Mr Handel, the social secretary at Heine House, had been so grateful to her for coming up with suitable accommodation for the visitor, she felt she could not suddenly let him down. However, had Mr Handel suggested landing her with a traveller in machine tools or a buyer of detergents, she might well have dared to disappoint him. Mr Handel had provided few details about the Herr Doktor and the reason for his visit, but he'd made it sound as if the man was cultivated and added that 'the gentleman wished to be out of Berlin for a while – perhaps there is some affair of the heart from which he is fleeing?' He knew that Herr Doktor Anders was promoting an unknown German artist, and believed the English might be more susceptible to the work than were the Germans.

Charlotte was certainly not doing this for the money. But if not for money, for what? Company? Hardly. The Herr Doktor would be out all day and probably most evenings. He would want to avail himself of the theatres and concert halls: there was *The Rocky Horror Show*, Picasso at the Tate, *The Misanthrope* at the National, which had had very good reviews, and Trevor Pinnock was playing Bach Suites at Wigmore Hall. And that was not all. He would not want to hang around in Belsize Park. But between his obligations and his social life, might there not be time to speak together of German literature and painting, of the old philosophical ideas on which German culture was based? Perhaps he played the piano and would try the Bechstein.

Of course, it was not for the money. There was no need; she could manage on what she was earning. Taking in lodgers was not something of which she had experience. Such an occupation had played no part in her family and would have been positively frowned upon, indicating a descent of several rungs on the social ladder. No, she was not becoming a landlady.

What was it then?

She had been living in England for thirty years, twenty-five of which she'd spent married to Rainer. Both were refugees from Berlin. Charlotte's father had been a lawyer, Rainer's a wine merchant who had written a string of books on vineyards and vintages and kept offices in Paris and London. Charlotte and Rainer had met in London in the Grosvenor Square flat of the Baumgartens, assumed to be an immensely rich husband and wife but in fact an immensely rich twin brother and sister. The two floors of the Baumgarten flat had been furnished throughout – from chandeliers to Persian carpets – by the celebrated M. Harris of Oxford Street, purveyors of the finest antique furniture and accessories to the richest and most noble houses in the land. In addition to which Thais Baumgarten herself was decorated in a collection of ancient, oriental jewellery selected for her and regularly refreshed by Moshe Ovid of Cameo Corner. But despite the provenance of their magnificent acquisitions, their couture clothes and handmade shoes, their Sèvres dinner service and crystal – the intrinsic worth and beauty of the objects they bought – the

Baumgartens' ostentation was such that whatever the merit of their purchases, they appeared fake in their possession.

The Baumgartens could afford anything they wanted, and assumed everything could be bought. And so it was frustrating to discover that the route to a title was encumbered. Theo sought advice from a colleague on the stock exchange, who signalled that their path might be cleared by the evidence of 'good works' – particularly those with a lesser royal as patron. The Baumgartens quickly warmed to the idea, and raised a fund for German refugees from monies they badgered from acquaintances and tradesmen rather than their own pockets, and to this end formed a charity in aid of refugees from Hitler. However, the unstinting advice they dispensed regarding the manner in which 'our refugees' should instruct themselves in the English language and comport themselves among the English population in order to equip themselves for gainful employment was more generous than the exiguous sums of money they distributed. But because their salons were lavishly catered by Fortnum and Mason and Berry Bros and Rudd, the opportunity to foregather with scattered ex-prisoners from their Isle of Man days at the same time as eating and drinking well seemed irresistible to those living in cold bed-sits.

Rainer had been coaxed there by Otto Gross, a musician on his uppers. Charlotte had come to know Thais Baumgarten through her work: Thais had become a customer, and although she haggled mercilessly over Charlotte's prices, she nevertheless brought customers in her wake. She would summon Charlotte to Grosvenor Square to have fittings in her bedroom, the windows and four-poster bed of which were dressed in crimson velvet with gold rope ties thick enough to hang a man. Charlotte and Rainer had gravitated towards one another in that peculiar way that happens to people in a crowd, where each recognises at a glance the hunger of the other and knows how it can be met. They left Grosvenor Square together, never to part.

Rainer was then living in the flat in Belsize Park that had belonged to his late father's business. Charlotte had a work-cum-living-room in an artist's house in Hampstead where, with her friend Eva from Prague, she designed and made hand-knits in silk, linen and wool. Although the knitting was time-consuming, tiring and ill-paid, she and Eva were never without commissions. British women were crying out for style and glamour after years of wartime restrictions, and these garments provided both. Just as soon as one client was observed in a dusty pink linen skirt and jacket with a silk rose lolling from the lapel, six women from her bridge club hastened to Charlotte's workroom, and Charlotte found herself having to take on more out-workers to line and make up the garments.

Rainer had been adamant about remaining in his father's flat, improving it rather than selling it and moving on. The rooms were large and difficult to heat and the basement floor, once the Edwardian kitchen quarters, would be expensive to turn into living accommodation, but whatever the limitations and disadvantages, the flat retained for him a sense of homeliness. Not that it had been used for domestic purposes in the past, but its walls seemed to him to have absorbed his father's voice and character and he needed to hang on to both. He had not chosen to find himself in England, had not expected to be summarily ejected from his country and its culture at the time of its dissolution. He, along with many others, had been stormed by bandits who had robbed him of his family, and landed him alone among strangers. The flat was his one place of some safety, a harbour where he tied up fast. And it was close to cafes which kept open from breakfast to well past dinner, where he could find conversation with other refugees who felt the same awkwardness in being foreign. He felt as orientated as ever he could in Belsize Park.

———

Rainer and Charlotte married and Charlotte set to to redecorate the gloomy flat. She organised a workroom for herself on the ground floor and for Rainer a study in the basement, where a battery of cooks and scullery maids had once toiled. The couple always spoke German together, for it was the vehicle of their culture. Both had suffered their losses in German, left without a single family member. But whereas the aberration that was the Third Reich had burnt, pillaged, gassed and murdered in the German tongue, it had not penetrated German cultural roots. Goethe, Schiller and Heine survived safely unmolested, so too Beethoven, Mendelssohn and all the 'degenerate' artists. So too Grunewald, Cranach and Caspar David Friedrich, each of whom may well have wept and beat his breast in the grave, yet survived unhumiliated.

Charlotte was taking a German lodger because she yearned for the Germany she had shared with her parents before the Schoa.

She recalled a letter written by a young English woman to her dead lover, in which she told of how she had been advised to manage her grief by keeping alive the standards and values she and her lover had shared. But, the young woman asked, how might she do so, for she had only kept them for him? Everything had been for him. She had loved life because he had made it perfect. Charlotte recognised herself in this lamentation: Rainer had been her all and she his: *"Twas my one Glory— /Let it be /Remembered /I was owned of Thee—'* Since his death, she had known a surfeit of lonely days and fearful nights. She had no one to whom to lay claim. Sometimes she would make a superhuman effort to bleach out the past, invent a new life, but she discovered that the past is never dead, indeed it is never past. Her need for Rainer was continuous. She felt herself trapped in a deep, airless chasm surrounded by slimy walls on which she could not get purchase. Breathless in the gloom, she would rehearse the details of their life and love as if each were a grain of sand to plaster over the slime and provide footholds. The cloistered night offered no more comfort than the open day: I sleep, I wake, and you are gone again! Perhaps this project is mistaken, she thought. She was not adequately prepared for it. It might produce the semblance of an *entente*, but it would be an illusion of companionship. She turned chill, overcome by widow's shame: unattached and predatory.

———

'Charlotte, darling, Papa and I would really appreciate it if you kept your visit short.'

'Oh, Mutti…'

'Yes, I know, but things are hotting up. Our plans are made and we must keep to them.'

'Are you going to worry?'

'Of course I am.'

'I promise to be back by Friday.'

'Promise?'

'Promise.' And they embraced.

'What are you taking Elis?'

'Some photos of Berlin and a silk scarf.'

'Perfect! And do include a nice snap of yourself. Did you find your climbing boots?'

'I did. And I'm taking Papa's waxed sweater.'

Every spring the Bernhard family – mother, father and only child – travelled to the Breger Hills, under the Blauenberger peaks, for the multitude of bluebells that smothered the fields and rose in homage about the feet of the beech trees which clad the hills. With winter over and their muscles flaccid from the immobility imposed by their sedentary occupations, the Bernhards craved exercise and fresh air. For ten days, they set out each morning equipped with climbing boots and sturdy sticks to amble through the dense, sweetly scented fields and climb the rising ground. They struggled to reach a narrow plateau where the wooded hills met the arid mountains, and settled for a grassy ledge from which to view the valley to one side and the snow-capped peaks above while they consumed the beer, bread and sausages provided by the inn. They chose the isolated Hunters' Inn because in spring it was frequented by real climbers. The accommodation was more spartan than that to which they were accustomed and the food rustic and unfamiliar to their palates, but they put these matters aside for the pleasure of sitting over evening meals with climbers describing their obsession, exchanging tales of peril, and holding councils of war regarding the weather, as if it were an enemy force commanded by Thor.

The inn sounded empty. Of course, the climbers would have headed for the mountains hours ago. Charlotte stood waiting at the bar. Suddenly, the somnolence was shattered by a clatter of saucepans.

'Anyone there?'

Gert Hoffmann, the innkeeper, emerged from the kitchen, a towel slung over one arm. 'Where are your parents?'

'They are not visiting this year.'

'No, I imagine not.' He rummaged through his reservations. 'Same rooms? D'you want back or front?'

'Back, please.'

Hoffmann's manner had never been warm, but Charlotte detected deepened frostiness. She looked around. Nothing had changed: same decorated stoneware ale mugs, same wood carvings of fox and boar hanging sluggishly from the beams. And same smells of herbal tobacco laced with those of ale, sauerkraut and chestnut-seasoned pork. She collected the key from Hoffmann's extended palm and mounted the stairs.

From the open windows, she looked up at the snow-capped peaks. A storm was brewing. She exchanged her shoes for boots and her skirt for breeches. It was past noon; she could hear the farm-workers packing into the bar, raising their mugs, swinging them back and forth in tune to the songs they always sang of the fatherland, of girls and fornication.

The banks that lined the rutted cart track leading to the Steins' farm were yellow with primroses, beneath whose shady leaves white violets grew clandestinely. Such perfection made Charlotte ache, she so wished her parents were along. A dog barked; it must have been the nails on her boots that had alerted him.

'Oh Charlotte, I'm so glad you have come! But where are Frau and Herr Bernhard?'

'My parents were not able to leave Berlin this spring,' Charlotte said, holding out the little packet she had brought with her.

'You never come empty handed!' Elis stowed the packet in her apron; she would save opening it until she was alone. 'Tell me everything you have been doing in Berlin.'

'No! You first. Tell me everything that you have been doing here on the farm.' The two young women laughed as each claimed to go second. They ran to the stone seat set into the wall of the farmhouse. It was traditional for them to unwind their skeins of experience in that place.

For Elis, the highlight of the week was market day. Breger lay twenty miles west and attracted farmers from far afield, so it provided an opportunity for young people to meet. Elis spoke shyly of this and Charlotte was careful not to ask questions. She told Elis about concerts she attended at the Steiner House and described her studies. Elis was not equipped to enquire about those matters. There was no concert hall in Breger and no audience for one. Once she had heard a piper accompany a *schuhplatting* dance, and she always enjoyed joining in the hymns in church, but that was all. As for studies, she had been relieved to forget books since leaving school. But she did want to know about lipstick and what people wore to concerts: did they really have special clothes for such occasions? Charlotte wanted to be told how many litters the doe had produced and on what she preferred to feed. 'You have many more goats this year than last. The little ones are adorable.'

'They are not! They are monsters. They eat everything, including the washing on the line. Father gets furious because they always get to his paper before he does. But the cat's litter is truly adorable.' And Elis jumped from the seat and returned with two tabby kittens pressed to her chest. 'You must have this pair. Take them home with you!'

'But we don't have a garden. They would hate to be confined to the apartment.'

'You don't have a garden? But where do you eat in summer?'

Charlotte refrained from describing summers in splendid hotels on Maggiore, at Talloires and in Grasse, and told instead of the cafes in the parks in Berlin, and cycle rides to Wannsee.

The Steins' farm, like others for miles around, was poor. The family raised chickens, goats and a single pig, and they had a vegetable plot and an orchard with plum and apple trees. Chickens roamed freely, and where the orchard met the hills there were hives. The grey stone farmhouse extended on either side with open-faced buildings where the cart was kept, the horse stabled and the pig penned. The huddle of grey stone appeared dismal until enlivened by the rain, when it glistened. Elis grew geraniums in used tins and settled them wherever she found a flat surface. Charlotte imagined she was responding to the gloom. She took snaps and posted prints to Elis, who could not see the point: what had a poor old farmhouse to offer someone living in Berlin? How might the life of a farmer's daughter have anything of interest to share with someone from the city? After all, Charlotte did new things every year, met new people and travelled to new places; the furthest Elis rode was to Breger. Charlotte did what she could to persuade her friend that knowing one thing well was in fact better than knowing lots of things superficially, but Elis was not convinced. And so she turned to the pleasure she took in coming to see Elis each spring, and that Elis seemed to understand.

'Has anything surprising happened in your area this year?' Charlotte enquired. At the back of her mind she was wondering how far the tentacles of the regime had stretched.

'No, nothing that I can remember.' And then, little by little, as if in an effort to please her friend, Elis said, 'Well, there has been one thing. A dumb derelict, certainly not from around here, has set up home in the forest.'

Indeed, it was surprising, enough to arouse rumour and speculation at the inn and among the charcoal burners, for it was they who had first spotted the man collecting fallen branches. They subsequently discovered that it had been for the thatching of the hut the stranger was building beyond and higher up the hill from their settlement. It must have been from gossip at the inn that Herr Stein came to hear of the vagrant's existence, although it was not much later that the stranger himself appeared at the farm gate for milk and potatoes. Herr Stein dubbed him a simpleton but Elis objected: just because he didn't speak didn't mean he was simple. He could hear all right, and he knew what he needed. He was dreadfully thin but he was sturdy. He walked to Breger and back when he had to. Perhaps sometimes he got a lift from a passing cart, but most times they were full of timber, animals or produce for market.

Then one day when the charcoal burners noticed the vagrant pass their settlement, making for the valley, they took the opportunity to climb to his hut and have a good look round. They had been impressed: the mute turned out to be a true craftsman. His dwelling had a door – unlike theirs, open to the wind and rain – and a lock, not one he had fastened that day. He had tools, and he had made everything in the hut from trees he had felled. There was a bed, a table and a bench. And he had other things besides: a paraffin lamp, a horsehair mattress and some warm covers, items the charcoal burners both envied and despised. 'He must have money. Must have it buried deep, somewhere hereabouts.' How else could be pay for necessities? He didn't make anything to sell. And the so-called necessities aroused added suspicion, for in addition to paraffin he bought soap and sugar. 'Just points to what he wants.' One of the merchants in Breger had asked him his name, in response to which he drew a bird on a piece of paper on the counter. So ever since, everyone in the town had called him Vogel.

'What does he look like?' Charlotte asked Elis.

'Thin, very thin. His cheeks are sunken. He looks like the picture of Jesus in our church. I wonder: could he be Jesus?'

'I don't think so,' Charlotte said.

'No, you're probably right. Anyhow, Hitler's our saviour nowadays. Father says the people love him. Best. He's cut out his photo from the paper and put it up in the kitchen.'

Frau Stein called to Charlotte and Elis to come inside. The kitchen was dark, and it took a moment for Charlotte to locate the picture of Hitler pinned to the wall. Frau Stein placed bowls of goat's milk on the table, and chunks of rye bread.

'I've been listening to Herr Goebbels,' Frau Stein told Charlotte. 'He's very clever, you know, and he speaks quite quietly, not like the Fuhrer – he's noisy. Oh dear, I shouldn't have said that, should I? Herr Stein says Hitler's a great man and a great orator. Do you get to see much of him in Berlin, Charlotte?'

'Not a great deal, but I do sometimes catch sight of him when he is being driven in an open car to one of his rallies.' Charlotte prayed she would not be asked her views on the great man.

'Charlotte tells me that Austria belongs to Germany now.'

'Really?' And Frau Stein turned to stir the soup.

Charlotte ate dinner with the climbers, some of whom she knew from previous years. When the drinking got going in earnest, she retired to her room and despite the laughter and the singing below she slept until before dawn, when a cock crow cleaved the dark.

———

The climbers were having breakfast in the bar. As Charlotte entered, two of them pushed apart to make space for her. Noticing that she ordered only coffee, they rebuked her folly and told her she must eat heartily before taking to the hills. They pelted her with advice.

'You will need it, especially in this changing weather. It's going to be tough. There's a storm brewing. Keep to the paths you know and start your descent before you want to. You must be back before dark.'

Charlotte listened and took their advice: it would have been her parents'. She got to her feet and went to the kitchen door and called to Hoffmann to serve her a climber's breakfast. She lingered over the fat ham, the hard eggs and potato pancakes before picking up the packed lunch of bread and sausage with her name scrawled across it, and gathering her rucksack and iron-shod stick. And then she made for the track she knew.

She walked west. The sullen cloud suspended over the crown of beeches had lain the blue of the sky in massed flowers, the bells of which rang out with scent. The silence was dense. The trees themselves kept their vow of noiselessness while breathing the scented air and slaking their thirst on invisible mountain melt. *Mutti, Mutti, how you would love it!* The sun was sealed behind unvarying cloud and in the distance, Charlotte thought she heard a roll of thunder. She must press on.

The route she took was the one the charcoal burners trod, leading to their encampment, recognisable for the little piles of wood and others of worked earth stacked at intervals along its length. As a child, Charlotte had been frightened of the charcoal burners. Simple, dirty individuals living outside the company of women, they seemed unnatural. The fire they built to produce the charcoal demanded such continuous vigilance that the men slept in shifts in shelters open to the wind. It kept them alert, and carried away the carbon fumes that would otherwise have killed them. Their possessions lay scattered. An iron pot hanging from a tripod was the sole upright under which lay unwashed bowls and spoons. They had slung their garments over low-hanging branches, together with headless chickens and rabbits. Only their boots attracted respect and stood lined up under cover. One worker nudged his fellow and uttered a few words under his breath while pointing at Charlotte. She did not understand what he was saying, for he spoke in dialect.

'*Guten Tag*,' she said, forcing a smile while continuing uphill at an unaltered pace. Further on her way, she could hear the men laughing. They made her feel uneasy, but they did not follow her.

The weather was improving. The sun signified noon. Shortly, she would reach the turfy bank on which she and her parents used to rest and admire the view. The beech trees had thinned out and in one direction provided a view of the valley and the outline of the church at Breger; in the other, gnarled pines protected by the mountain face and over-hanging outcrops rose tall and menacingly thick. The Bernhards had never explored that route.

The incline was still gradual – manageable – but the way was littered with crumbling shale, which dislodged itself under her feet and rolled noisily downhill. What if the charcoal burners heard, supposed the dislodgement precipitated by wild boar, and took shot? All was silent.

She climbed on. A wind was coming up, churning the upper branches of the trees. Crystal rain drops fell one by one, as if from a broken chain of beads. And then the gentle drops coalesced and turned to relentless downpour. Charlotte sheltered from the onslaught at the entrance to a cave.

This might be the last time she would climb these hills, and although there were finer ranges in Switzerland, nothing would replace the Breger forest or the Blauenberger in Charlotte's heart; the whole region was steeped in love and memories. She wondered how her parents could bear not to take leave of it with her? But they were understandably anxious, for most unauthorised attempts to escape Germany failed. Up to now, their professional status and non-Jewish friends had protected them from molestation, but they knew that time was not on their side. They were constantly fearful that they might have omitted some essential detail from their plans, and daily went over their itinerary. They would leave the flat separately, as they always did after breakfast, as if on usual business. Neither the neighbours nor the police would have reason to register any change in their routine. They would conceal their papers and their train tickets in their undergarments so that were they stopped and searched in a casual manner, their pockets and briefcases would give nothing away. They had transferred money a year ago and Cousin Pierre had accommodation for them in Lausanne. But had the transfer of the money and the letters to and from Pierre been intercepted?

Prior to deciding to make this last visit, Charlotte had closed her mind to the possibility that the virus of Nazism could have spread to Breger and infected the people she knew. But now that she had been confronted, she must face facts. There were questions to be answered. Did Herr and Frau Stein really believe that the Führer would bring them lower taxes, a higher standard of living, more fertile land to till and better breeds of animals to raise by killing the Jews, the gypsies and the homosexuals? It is likely that the only Jews they had encountered were the Bernhards, whose visits they welcomed and of whose Jewishness they were unaware. Had they stopped to consider how mass slaughter would change their lives for the better? As for Elis, was she going to trade eighteen years of love of Jesus for that of Hitler? And in her simplicity, might she not feel she was being short-changed?

The rain fed the sweet smell of earth. The few beech trees surviving at this altitude were pushing out new glistening leaves. And there was birdsong. Poised on the edge of chaos, life had rarely seemed sweeter.

———

It might have been frightening to find herself unwound from the sapling to which she clung by a silent stranger, but somehow it was not. Elis had been accurate in her description of the vagrant who named himself Vogel. She recognised 'Jesus'. Had she not stumbled, it was unlikely that she would have come upon him. He had concealed his shelter in a circle of tenebrous pines, which created an atmosphere Charlotte feared. Even when the sun alighted on their tops, it never discharged its light and heat on the lower branches or the ground.

He lifted Charlotte to her feet, retrieved her rucksack and stick, and led her towards his hut. He motioned her to sit and undo the lacings on her boots. Not a word passed his lips, but his movements and his aura were eloquent, and Charlotte understood that he was concerned she might have broken a bone. He pressed the flesh round her ankles while he watched her face for signs of flinching.

'I am not in pain,' she said.

Charlotte was in a quandary. She needed to continue her descent but felt it would be rude to simply rise and leave. Without access to language, Vogel had none the less communicated his humanity.

He was painfully thin, with arms like broom handles; his clothes were threadbare. Yet he was not the caricature vagrant, an unkempt, foul-smelling, incoherent alcoholic, but a man in flight who had taken to the hills. That image had made itself contemporary, one with which Charlotte was all too familiar: everyone who was not a fascist was taking flight to save his life. She wondered from what particular circumstance Vogel was fleeing, but propriety prevailed. It was not a question she could pose, and in any case, how would he answer? Was he really dumb? He was certainly not uncomprehending, and he did not have that unfortunate manner of the dumb of trying to speak and making ugly sounds.

While Charlotte laced her boots, Vogel turned to his bench and from a pile of papers extracted a drawing which he placed by her side. It was about six by eight inches – an interpretation rather than a representation of the hut in the pine grove – made by marks like hieroglyphics. Charlotte examined the drawing closely before holding it out to return it, but Vogel indicated that it was for her. She undid her rucksack and, having placed the sketch carefully between the leaves of her map, removed the little volume of Heine's poems she carried with her, with its dedication 'To my beloved Charlotte, from Mutti'. She held this out to him, 'in exchange', she said. And not wishing to embark on what would be a monologue, she left.

The encounter with Vogel seemed to have meaning, but not one of which she could make sense. He had given her what he had made, and she had given him a precious possession, one she would not have passed on to anyone else. In other circumstances, might they have made friends? It looked as if he had settled in the forest, that if he had a home, it was not one to which he was going to return. And what of relatives and friends? And if he was fleeing from Hitler's men and the police, would the farmers, the charcoal burners and the folk of Breger not give him away? She would talk to Mutti about him and show her the drawing.

———

Rainer had been seized by panic when the knock on the door came and he was escorted to the Isle of Man to be interned with other 'enemy aliens'. A pall of fear and humiliation would imprison him for the rest of his life. He had experienced the British at their most crass, unable to distinguish between victim and oppressor, and when he was released he had no wish to practise law in England, even if he were able to muster the energy to requalify.

When he and Charlotte married, Rainer took whatever work he could find: tutor at a north London grammar school, translator of business letters, coaching the German accents of English lieder singers. Eventually he was offered work in the German sector at the BBC, and something of his sense of worth was restored. But the question of his worth would not on its own have restored him. That would be for Charlotte to acknowledge and support. For whereas Rainer had been disfigured by experience, Charlotte had turned it to purpose.

Rainer's forays into a city he experienced as dirty, cold and foul-smelling were undertaken solely in pursuit of work; otherwise he kept closely to Belsize Park. At Libris, a short walk from the flat, he could find the books he needed for his research, and at Cosmo and Dorice on the Finchley Road, he could be certain of schnitzel and strudel and the opportunity of exchanging a few words with Canetti. He kept to those shops and cafes where the owner and the clientele spoke German, Polish and Hungarian, where foreign roots were taken for granted. He did not want to parade to strangers that status to which he felt he had so ignominiously sunk. He dismissed Charlotte's attempts to retrieve him from his withdrawal by introducing him to the friends she made. But even the footsteps and the susurrus of her clients in her workroom above his study were too much of an intrusion, and she was obliged to rearrange her business by keeping her workroom for design only, and have clients meet at Eva's workshop in Daleham Mews.

Despite her outgoing nature, Charlotte's needs were met in her relationship with Rainer. She enjoyed an intimacy verging on conspiracy. They shared in a contaminating sorrow, but dealt with it differently. Whereas Charlotte diluted it, Rainer fortified it. They combined in their commitment to German culture, wanting nothing better than 'the three Bs', Wagner and Strauss as background to a continuous exploration of German literature and painting. With every unspent shilling, they bought records and books, and tickets to hear Fischer-Dieskau and Rubinstein at Wigmore Hall.

Neither wished to revisit the blood-soaked soil of Germany, so they did their hiking in the Welsh mountains. But these efforts to exercise, relax and discover new landscapes were ruined for Rainer by his encounters with what he regarded as inquisitional others. He could not abide being asked where he came from or what he did. The rift between his deepest self and his native place had been severed. He felt estranged.

The effort to survive had been too much for him. He had been ejected, he had not negotiated his exile. Everything had become *unheimlich*. He belonged nowhere, whereas Charlotte made friends among her clients and suppliers, and through them with others. Though hardly intimate with any one of them, she kept accepting and returning invitations. However, she had had to learn the extent of the English emotional compass – English women preferred to keep their sorrows to themselves – and Charlotte understood that it would be inappropriate to confide the fate of her parents or explain what it was like to be transplanted from one's cultural roots. The English were embarrassed by mention of concentration camps and uninterested in German culture, and so Charlotte kept to the exchange of recipes and knitting patterns.

———

Charlotte was aware of the Herr Doktor's comings and goings. Indeed, his movements had become her obsession. She observed that he left the house at ten in the morning and more often than not returned towards midnight. From time to time, however, he rushed back in the late afternoon to change before going out again. On those occasions, he would leave the house, turn left into Belsize Terrace, and after five or ten minutes stride back past the house in the direction of Swiss Cottage Tube station with a bottle of champagne under this arm. With whom, she wondered, would he be celebrating?

Caspar Anders was a couple of years younger than Charlotte, but that was not obvious. He was six foot tall with fine bones and unblemished skin, but his lips were thin and his eyes reflected a cold north sea. Had he allowed a smile to pass his lips and brighten his eyes, or some excitement to colour his cheeks, he might have been attractive, but he walked with the impression of having a bad smell under his nose.

'Herr Anders,' Charlotte wrote in German, 'it would give me great pleasure if you would take coffee with me on Sunday morning. Would eleven o'clock suit you? Perhaps you might care to try the Bechstein?' She left the note on the hall table where she stacked his post. It was Wednesday. He had time to consider her suggestion, and she had time to bake.

Anders rose later on Saturdays and Sundays than on weekdays, and dressed in tweeds, oversized sweaters and boots. Charlotte wondered whether he walked on the heath or took the tube to its terminus and explored the countryside. She was turning over these speculations when he knocked on her workroom door.

'I would be pleased to accept your invitation to coffee on Sunday,' he said in English, turned and left.

It was close to eleven o'clock. The coffee was brewing and Charlotte was dusting the chestnut cake with icing sugar. Just as she started to whip the cream, she heard Anders at the kitchen door.

'What a fine day!' he snapped, and it was, but behind his observation Charlotte heard the echo of clicking heels.

Anders extended his arms in a gesture of willingness to carry the tray. He placed it on the prepared table, pulled out a chair for himself and watched as Charlotte distributed plates, cup and forks, and sliced the cake. Then Charlotte sat down facing him. From the first acknowledgement of her, he avoided catching her eye. Instead, he examined the placements and then his spoon as he dipped into the whipped cream. While he ate, his eyes scanned the sitting room.

'Are you enjoying your stay in London?' Charlotte tried, in German.

'Very much,' he replied in English. Clearly, Anders was not to be enticed into conversation, whether in German or English. Charlotte was reminded of those religious men who avoid being photographed for fear of losing their souls. Or was he simply making himself mysterious, as hollow people do? She felt a mixture of embarrassment and anger. Her plan to engage with Anders on German culture was not to be. Why, she wondered, had he accepted this invitation to morning coffee? Did he regard it as the bare minimum of social nicety to which he could commit without too much irritation while he was staying under her roof?

He wiped his mouth on the linen napkin with excessive care before turning his attention to the piano.

'You are most welcome to play,' Charlotte said, and he rose and moved towards the piano. He wound the stool up and down before deciding just how he needed it to be, pushed up his sleeves, measured an octave and flexed his fingers. Turning to Charlotte, who had remained seated at table, he said, 'I prefer to be alone when I play.'

She loaded the tray with the cups and plates and took it into the kitchen. Then she returned to close the sitting room door, went into her work room and took up her drawing board, but felt too disturbed to work. Was Anders confusing her natural hospitality with something else? Did he imagine she had designs on him?

She had no designs on him. She did not desire him, but she did not expect to go unnoticed by him. There was a difference, she thought. His whole demeanour reflected the most inflated self-esteem. He was so confident of his superior worth that he felt absolutely no need to ingratiate himself. She had asked him if he would address her in German and allow her the opportunity to brush up her fluency. He had said neither yes nor no, but spoke in English on every occasion they came across one another and needed to speak of laundry or timetables and the location of bookshops. She had been foolish in her expectation. She had forgotten that as Goethe told Eckerman, a woman must first become an object of desire before she becomes an object of interest. Anders was not going to explore ideas with her. He was not going to revive in her an untarnished memory of German culture. It was to be irrecoverable. But this must not be allowed to discompose her. After the hell she had gone through with Rainer's death, it amounted to no more than disappointment, and with that she would cope as she had with other trivia put to rights by the plumber and the electrician.

And then the strains of Schubert emerged from the sitting room and Charlotte's heart leapt in pain. Oh my God, not that! The sonata was the last that Rainer had played to her, since when the Bechstein had stood silent.

When Anders stopped playing, Charlotte expected to hear him returning to the Garden Room. She waited for what seemed an eternity. What was he doing? She went back into the sitting room to find him with Vogel's framed drawing in his hands.

'What is this? Where did you get it?' he asked, as if he had found something of value stolen from his room.

'It is something I was given a long time ago.'

'By whom?'

'The artist.'

'And who was the artist?'

'I don't really know. He was mute and called himself Vogel.'

'Where were you when he gave you this?'

'I was in the Bregenwald.'

'And when was that?'

'In the spring of 1938.' Charlotte would have liked to bring this interrogation to a close, but Anders had found his voice and would not be silenced.

'I must have this for my exhibition!' he said. He was excited but vexed. Someone had got to Vogel before he had, and had something which he might never prise from this room. Ignited, he burst into his subject. He had discovered Vogel! At The Horn Inn in Breger, where he lodged when he went skiing in the Blauenberg, the dining-room had been hung with portraits of local tradesmen and farmers who had allowed a vagrant artist to paint their likenesses in return for food. Vogel's life and work were his property! It was because of this hitherto undiscovered artist that he had come to London to arrange an exhibition of his work. Smidt Holdern, in Cork Street, were showing interest, and he had a patron in Princess Michael of Kent. 'She is from a distinguished German background, you know.'

Charlotte found mounting distaste for Anders. It seemed that somehow he had come to assume he had sole right to the life and work of a casualty of war. No doubt this was something the German art world was questioning. Anders's discovery and prospective launch of the dead artist had to be made abroad and was in the service of his own reputation.

In German, Charlotte asked Anders to describe Vogel's work and, in English, Anders spoke of his method. For his paintings, Vogel had access only to the odd ends of house paint he found or was given. He gave this work a three-dimensional quality by throwing sand and straw and even shards of stone at the paint. For his drawings, similar to the one he had given Charlotte, he stuck to making marks like hieroglyphics. And he made sculpture: the pieces salvaged from his time in the forest were composed of grafted timber, roots, pine needles and cones, just discernible as animal forms. When the war was over and he came down into Breger to settle, his natural materials had given way to discarded parts from bicycles, prams and carts.

Anders had persuaded the owner of the shed to keep Vogel's work where it was. He gave him a little money and promised to come back with more, and have the work removed. The tradesman could see no value in stuff paid for in food and would have liked to throw it out, but having paid him to keep it, Anders was confident it would be there when he returned.

He had made exhaustive enquiries to discover Vogel's identity. He said he had trawled through missing-persons files and the records of art schools, but many of those had been destroyed in the 1930s. Charlotte listened carefully to his account of tireless search and speculation. At every place where he had questioned people for memory of the artist, he made the point that Vogel was dumb: they could not have forgotten, of that he was certain. Charlotte felt otherwise, but she was not going to reveal why. The chances were that Vogel

had been one of the 'degenerate artists'; his art had a sophistication that no amateur could have achieved. He might have
been Jewish, had no way to escape and had chosen to become
a non-person. His disguise was to assume mutism. He had
lived to go on working: it was his protest.

Charlotte asked Anders whether he had met Vogel. He
had not. Vogel had died shortly after the end of the war. And
Anders had not found himself at The Horn until the beginning of the 1950s.

'How did he die?' Charlotte asked.

'In his sleep, in his shed.'

'And so I am the only person, other than the good folk of
Breger, who had come into contact with him.'

'It would appear so.'

———

Herr Doktor Anders left precipitately during the first few
days of July and wrote a cheque to cover that month and the
next (unsolicited) because he had not given notice of his early
departure. There was no mention of a forthcoming exhibition
of Vogel's work, just a throwaway remark as to the lack of
imagination among British dealers and critics.

Charlotte consulted her feelings. They were many and
they were tangled, and she could make no sense of them. He
had taken his departure without warning. He always managed
to hold the cards in his two hands. No doubt he had come to
dislike her as much as she disliked him. Did she have man-
nerisms that set his teeth on edge, as his sniff irritated her?
Or was there something deeper than mere incompatibility?

Certainly his presence had managed to disturb her stability. But she was to blame. It was she who had connived at the violation of Rainer's study. How was she going to lay the ghost of her impropriety?

The Contract

'Do you know my Tatyana has rejected Onegin? I never expected it of her.'
Pushkin

'My mind is made up, Ivan. I am going to marry. I've had just about enough of the gossip, not to mention the threats. You know, I may not be able to rely for ever on the patience of his Excellency in the face of this scandal. He has already intimated that I am *persona non grata* at Osagin's investiture.'

'Marry? To whom?'

'That is a matter yet to be decided. I can't say definitely to whom, but I can say to whom I shall certainly not be proposing: those capricious belles of high society who, despite my age, my obesity and my reputation would readily accept me for my connections, my military honours and my wealth.'

Prince Andrei Nicolaevich turned back to the task in hand, that of knotting his cravat. Because his fingers were swollen and arthritic he was clearly having some difficulty. Ivan, his adjutant and friend, stepped forward: 'Allow me.' The cravat in place, nicely knotted, the Prince turned to the looking-glass. His eyes fastened on the large black pearl driven into the salt-white muslin of his neckpiece. He sighed.

'I would be a lot happier were tonight's ball masked.'

It was winter. Moscow was overflowing with young women up from their country estates to attend balls, wedding feasts, theatres and banquets. Any one of them offered the perfect opportunity to entice a socially and financially well-endowed man into matrimony. While determined mothers scavenged, daughters flocked to compare their assets – figures, faces and dowries – in a bridal fair to which it would be demeaning to have to return for a second season.

Prince Nicolaevich, a general in the Lifeguard Jagers much revered by the Tsar himself, was a career soldier. His father, dead for some years, had been a close friend of the Tsar's uncle. The Prince himself had fought bravely against the French at Borodino and been lavishly rewarded for his pains with grants of lands and serfs. He had the distinction of speaking German and Italian as fluently as French and was an authority on military history. He was a man's man. The only women he trusted were his mother and sister Sonya; his mother having enjoyed his utter devotion from his birth and his sister an affection combined with something more rare: understanding. Brother and sister refrained from all elaboration of an intimate nature and Sonya neither asked questions nor sought to advise. She knew that her brother preferred the company of men to that of women, and that although he enjoyed the presence of children he had no desire to sire them. He was fond of her son Dmitri and happy for him to inherit his estate when the time came.

But in recent times Andrei's unmarried status, long a matter of conjecture, had become one of intense speculation at court. Acting on a tip-off, the police raided Moscow's Club Dandy and took away the list of members on which the Prince's name featured. He was immediately brought before the commissariat where questions were put to him regarding the purpose of the Club and the nature of its members. On inspection of the building, the police had discovered rooms decorated with obscene images and furnished in decadent taste. They closed Club Dandy. Rumours spread like the mists of autumn over the Neva. There were many at court, and within the regiment itself, who had waited long for such an opportunity to undermine the Prince's seemingly impregnable position vis à vis the Tsar. Within days, the Prince heard that plans were afoot to dispatch him either to Siberia to supervise a penal settlement or to the Crimea to investigate the ravages wrought by a plague of locusts. It was too much for his sense of entitlement to bear. If he were exiled from social and intellectual life in Moscow and St Petersburg, the peace of his country estate in the Simbirsk region would be insupportable.

Observation of the marriages of his comrades had led the Prince to the view that it was rarely a continuously rewarding state of being. It might start well, but it was never long before it degenerated into boredom and dissatisfaction. He judged the cause of this to be that most marriages were founded on erroneous principles; the need of the woman for protection and the need of the man for an heir and for money to endow his estates. Such conditions would not apply in his case. He had enough money from his iron exports alone to keep half a dozen estates if he so wished, and he made his own arrangements to satisfy his sexual preference. But what woman would agree to his terms? An impecunious woman might be grateful that her lack of dowry could be overlooked, but would she insist upon children? And if he were to be obliged to spend the last quarter of his life shut up with her for months of the year in Samara and entertain with her in the city, his wife would need to be compatible, share with him his love of foreign travel, of collect-ing art and of reading foreign novels and listening to German music. Such a woman would not be easy to find in Russia.

That evening he was most enthusiastically received by the Italian ambassador and his wife. They appreciated his flu-ency in their language and his knowledge of their culture and introduced him to stylish women of their acquaintance. Italian women had something about them to which the Prince's taste responded. Each or any one of them would go well with his furnishing; he laughed inwardly. And they would conduct a din-ner party with the same authority he mustered in preparing for battle. However, they would almost certainly complain about all things Russian: the weather, the servants, the sheer lack of Italian vivacity. No, that would not work for him. It was while he was brooding over such thoughts that the ambassador's wife confided that she knew the precise whereabouts of his estate in the province of Samara: her father owned a fourteenth-century map on which the Volga port of Samara featured. No, this would not do for him: too intrusive, too competitive . . .

'Do you really imagine that at your age you will be able to adapt yourself to such a radical change in your circum-stances?' Ivan enquired.

'I shall take advice.'

'From your delightful sister?'

'From dear Sonya, yes. But I have in mind to consult the Elder at Optina Pustyn. Mme Elagin speaks of him with almost reverential respect and affection. He is renowned for his wisdom on the negotiations required in marriage.'

'But Andrei, there are marriages and marriages . . .'

'Leave it to me!'

———

Prince Nicolaevich was a frequent attendant at Mme Elagin's salon, where philosophers and writers felt free from the constraints that in other salons inhibited the expression of radical thought, and Mme was both civilised and intuitive and able to disregard a man's shabby appearance and unfashionable garments when they cloaked elegant ideas. Such people shared a genuine desire to bring about a reconciliation between the intelligentsia and the common Russian people. Furthermore, Mme Elagin had met the Elder, Father Nabolkin, at the monastery of Optina Pustyn, and felt qualified to assess his wisdom. She found the atmosphere of the monastery and the blessing of a good monk soul-soothing, and at one of her select salons she expanded on the virtues of contact with piety, learning and solitude, and recommended to her friends the experience of retreat. The problem, as she saw it, with Russian life in the country, was that most men and women found it unbearably boring. All they found to do was eat, drink and smoke and, in the case of the men, vent their dissatisfactions on unfortunate boar, hare and game birds. Whereas in retreat, one learnt how

to *expand* in solitude. Mme Elagin spoke of the Elder's reputation for clear-sightedness regarding marriage. He, too, saw
boredom as the prime reason why those in society were led
into licentiousness and debauchery, appetites more harmful
than those of gluttony. It was the women who suffered most
and some had even risked the treacherous road, with its deep
flooded potholes, ditches and storm-tossed trees, to Optina
Pustyn. On their return they reported how, armed with the
wisdom of the Elder, they had been successful in salvaging an
unsatisfactory marriage. In hushed tones, and with consider-
able embarrassment, some confided that the manners of the
Elder were not in line with those to which they were accustomed. But none elaborated.

Prince Nicolaevich ordered up his carriage and told his
servant Boris to prepare horses for the fifty-mile journey to
Kaluga. For the first few miles the Prince felt well, but suddenly his stomach revolted, unable to withstand the jolting
of the carriage. He shouted to his servant to stop, not much
further than ten miles into the journey, at a staging post, where
he ordered up a rested horse and rode on alone.

Seemingly endless forests of birch rose right, left, behind
and before, and sealed the Prince from the world. He was
making a pilgrimage, hoping to find a way in which to combine his personal appetite with social acceptance, but at no
cost to the dignity and emotional well-being of another. Was
this a proposition that would sit easily with the spiritual direction in which the Elder would undoubtedly point him?

His horse picked its way delicately. The birch trees were thin-
ning out a little. To his left and far ahead there was evidence of
heathland, to his right a rough signpost that indicated the track

to Optina Pustyn through dense plantations of pine trees. The horse rose on its back legs and whinnied. The way did indeed seem haunted, filled with dread. The Prince spoke gently to the animal and leant forward to pat his head and fondle his ears.

Sparks of light flickered within the dense dark of the pines, and with their appearance Andrei's fatigue lifted. Presently the lights revealed themselves to come from domes, pinnacles and elaborate weathercocks as unreal as if landed from the heavens. As he approached, he found a complex of pure white buildings rising from a clearing in perfect equilibrium, an harmonious enclosure enfolded in thick silence, a place in which antimonies might be resolved. At the back, a walled garden could be seen with neat rows of vegetables and behind that, an orchard and beehives. A post pointed to The Hermitage. The Prince dismounted, tethered his horse and continued on foot along the banks of the Zhidra.

Andrei Nicolaevich regarded himself as lover of wisdom, a man of the world, whose military life and taste for a particular chase in society had diverted him from the path that might otherwise have fulfilled his destiny. Indeed, at his country estate he had experienced a harmony whose allure positively frightened him: one of solitude without loneliness, in which the music of the mill race, the breeze that 'raked upon the strings of the Aeolian lute' and the noble, unflinching reserve of the trees contained all the messages his soul required for its satisfaction. If only he might learn from the spiritual direction of the Elder at Optina Pustyn to avoid the material and worldly temptations to which he was irresistibly drawn. Licentiousness! Such ecstasy! Would he be obliged to forgo the descent into perversity which alone satisfied his carnality?

And what of his vanity? How to rid himself of that? And his love of wealth and display?

The sheer weight of his corruption overtook him. He could not proceed. He dropped down to the water's edge and watched the unstoppable current.

The recent torrent of events that had threatened his reputation must be staunched. He must find a floodgate. But were there other options open to him apart from marriage? Should he simply abdicate his professional roles and life in Russian society and retire to Italy? Was it in him to reform? Or should he just learn to perfect his life of deception?

Andrei got to his feet. He felt dazed and did not hear the footsteps behind him. He was surprised to be overtaken by a young monk who introduced himself as Brother Maxim, assigned to him as confessor during the weeks of his retreat. Maxim pointed him back in the direction of the monastery and library that stood adjacent to the church, with its brightly enamelled domes and cupolas. Lying low amidst the opulence crouched a noticeably more humble, one-storey building of cells reserved for pilgrims.

Brother Maxim ushered the Prince into a pinched interior with space for a narrow bunk and a small pine table and chair. Fixed to one wall was a shelf of religious books, and on the facing wall, a painted icon. Brother Maxim indicated a handbell on the table. A serf was available to bring water and to empty slops. The Prince would take his meals three times a day, in silence, in the refectory reserved for pilgrims. The church was open day and night for prayer and pilgrims were welcome to attend sung services. It would depend on Brother Maxim whether to recommend the Prince to the Elder who, for the time being, was in retreat at The Hermitage. Then it would depend upon the Elder's mood, and whether he felt himself at peace to take on the problems of a pilgrim. Brother Maxim's tone indicated that the Elder could be capricious in his decision-making, particularly during those times when he himself was in spiritual chaos. Maxim left the Prince in his cell and closed the door.

Andrei was shocked. He had never imagined he would find himself confined to such a cold, damp space. His horses had more room in their stables! His dogs would grow fevered, restricted like this. He stood, with his arms outstretched, one hand on the Bible, the other on the icon.

Prince Andrei Nicolaevich drew his bearskins closely about him. The little chair provided creaked under his weight and girth. He had never felt so alone, so perturbed. He had envisaged an altogether different welcome, one in which he would be taken immediately into the presence of Vassily Nabolkin. It had not crossed his mind that he might be expected to prepare himself spiritually and intellectually for such a meeting. Time was not the problem; he could sit this out for as long as was required. It was the discomfort, the solitude, both physical and mental, that unmanned him. He was not used to accepting cold and damp. Nor was he accustomed to working things out alone. Military strategy was planned in conjunction with his officers, his waking and sleeping supervised by servants and every occasion between the two accompanied. Even his collecting was the result of intense discussions with fellow enthusiasts. He lay down on the narrow bunk and for the first time in his life considered what it was to be completely alone.

The Prince found the rigorous routine set by Brother Maxim difficult to adhere to. Brother Maxim would not allow him to walk about the grounds, explaining that the Prince's mind would be bound to wander to thoughts of architecture, the rotation of crops, the produce of the hives. He would be tempted to talk to the garden serfs and survey the coming and going of the brothers. No, to settle his mind, to control his thoughts, to discover something in the peace of tranquillity, the Prince must first learn how to empty his mind of chatter, and gain control. Then, when he was in firm governance, Brother Maxim would set him free.

Prince Andrei fell into something of the rhythm soldiers achieve marching, but his rhythm was measured by prayer, the reading of sacred texts, contemplation and physical chores. He scrubbed his cell, whitewashed its walls, bleached the floorboards, mended his shoes and groomed his horse, occupations for which he had had no preparation and which he had been raised to believe were for others to undertake. He achieved this with no feelings of humiliation, but with the determination not to return to them. When, finally, he was permitted to wander, his eyes were opened to the natural world in a manner totally different from that of the past. He saw a world with its own reason for being, one that existed independently. From a distance he watched, drifting across the landscape, monks enfolded in a world of silence, whose way of life was in no way akin to his own.

No one had alerted the Prince. Brother Maxim had mentioned that it was not possible to forecast when the Elder would be ready to see him, but not why that was so. Evidently Father Nabolkin switched spontaneously from Holy Fool to Holy Sage, acting out both roles in the service of God. His role as Fool was to disorientate, that of Sage to orientate anew. As Holy Fool he appeared mad but 'chosen'; stupid, but endowed with miraculous, unmediated forces to shock and shake a pilgrim out of his habitual self, his self-satisfaction, and open his way to pure thought and morality. As Sage he spoke rationally, with biblical authority.

———

'You must come nearer, my man, to know how I stink. Come! Come! Give me your hand. Let us see what is written on your palm. Trouble, indeed! You are disgustingly fat. You are a glutton, a drunkard, too. Fornicator! Blasphemer! Thief! I see it all.'

The wizened little man turned on his heels and executed something of a dance which involved twirling in circles, singing 'tra la la' in time to bells attached to his ankles. 'Who would want to marry you? I see vanity positively pouring from you.' From the floor he took a handful of straw thick with droppings, and ate from it.

'I am told you are indecently rich.' The old man spat his words at the Prince, whose astonishment and sense of affront left him speechless. Was this the wise man for whom he had prepared himself spiritually and mentally, of whom Mme Elagin had spoken so admiringly? Had he received her half-, and now fully naked, to expose a mass of suppurating sores where lice had burrowed?

All the senses he had sharpened during his time of preparation were being violated. The little man hated him, the little man was foolish and contemptuous and impure himself. He now insisted Andrei enter the windowless hut where he sat boiling herbs in a cauldron. From time to time he dropped a beaker into the brew and made Andrei drink from it.

Prince Nicolaevich could no longer smell the scent of pine or luxuriate in the qualities of tranquillity. He felt unable to rise from the upturned box on which he sat, unable to challenge the accusations being launched against him, unable to take his leave: the Fool was hypnotic. One humiliation after another was being brought down on Andrei's head.

'You are right,' he heard himself mutter. 'I am a man without wisdom, without compassion, without virtue. And my taste is honed purely in the service of my vanity. I know it! I know it!'

When, after a further month of retreat and contemplation, Prince Nicolaevich was called to an audience with the Elder, Father Nabolkin was unrecognisable: clean-shaven, smelling of incense and dressed in immaculate vestments. He spoke mellifluously and foreswore all the infelicities of speech which had punctuated his fractured language as Fool.

The Prince outlined his predicament and the Elder, far from advising Andrei how to proceed, drew from him the decisions to which he had come by himself in the quietude of his cell. Above all, he could only achieve what his appetites permitted, but this must be in conformity with consideration and kindness. And in truthfulness, it was not in Andrei to be selfless, but at all times he must be conscious of his actions, for it was his consciousness, ultimately, that was all he might properly possess. We are all two persons.

———

Meanwhile, much further south of Moscow, in a somewhat remote province, a mother and daughter were pursuing their lifelong differences.

'Tatiana, my child, you vex me!'

'I am sorry, Mama; I do not mean to.'

'It's all this reading that has made you melancholy!' Mme Larin threw open the windows as if to encourage the heavy presence of melancholia to take flight. 'And it cannot be good for your eyes,' she added. 'I shall send for Dr Steinberg.' Dr Steinberg had treated the disease and officiated at the demise of M. Larin some years ago. The doctor was a kindly man, referred to nonetheless by M. Larin as 'that German quack', but consulted on the grounds of his proximity and that, being German, he had to be better than any Russian doctor who would rely on dog-Latin of leeches.

Tatiana knew it useless to argue with her mother who, despite feeling it her duty to consult a medical man, was of the opinion that 'falling in love' was nothing but the symptom of an overheated brain, for which the cure was marriage. It was not the man who mattered but the institution, a given way of life. Tatiana had been besieged with offers, but to her mother's despair, had turned down each and every one of them. She said she wanted to leave her life open to unplanned possibilities, if you please.

Mme Larin exclaimed and continued to make every effort to persuade her daughter down the rocky path on which she herself had fallen and fractured her hopes.

Always in the clutches of the benign moon, bewitched by its celestial lamp, reassured by its serenity, suddenly and without warning Tatiana had fallen prey to an act of violence and ugliness, another aspect of its influence; that of mendacity. The moon had diverted the course of her life, taken her on a blood-soaked journey from childhood to womanhood. What betrayal! She felt herself violated. Henceforth, she would never know innocence. Overwhelmed by lightning spasms of the flesh, her feelings lay like open wounds at the mercy of the passing wings of a butterfly.

Tatiana rose and left her mother in the parlour and wandered into the garden. It was Dr Steinberg's view that she had suffered a delirium on becoming a woman, and it was his potions she needed. Tatiana knew better. She would gather mouse-ear, the moon's own herb, and suck out its soothing white milk. She must not blame the moon, who had her reasons and who, too, suffered painful changes.

It had been three years since her first 'strange and fateful interview' with Eugene Onegin. Throughout her childhood years, while others of her generation played games preparing them for marriage and motherhood, Tatiana had been devouring romantic fiction, preparing herself for passion. Thus it was that she was ripe to fall in love with Onegin from the first moment. Scarce had he entered, instantly she knew him: he was the man for whom she had been placed on earth! Onegin was a soulmate, someone to inspire her emotionally and creatively. She felt urgent excitement, tinged with anxiety: would he be guardian angel or treacherous tempter? Whatever the case, she was ready to surrender. He was older than she and had a life in society she had never known. She was a child of Nature, Russian to the core. Onegin was worldly. Tatiana agonised over their differences but sensed something deep in him that united them. There was an authenticity! He might dress as a dandy, pose as indifferent, reject the unadorned, be constantly on the move, but for what was he searching? From what was he fleeing?

He had arrived uninvited, brought along by his friend, the poet Vladimir Lensky, who was betrothed to Tatiana's sister, Olga. He was made welcome, very welcome indeed, for he had inherited an estate nearby and was known to be rich and fashionable. What was not yet known was that he was bored and dissolute and lacking in manners. Onegin found the provincial atmosphere at the Larins quite suffocating and could not escape quickly enough from their conversations, revolving as they did around rainfall, cattle and flax. In response to Lensky's enquiry, he admitted he had noticed Tatiana fleetingly, sitting by the window, 'sad and silent'.

Onegin had left without addressing a word to her. She confided her nervous state to her beloved nurse Filipyevna who, in concert with Mme Larin, regarded Tatiana's emotional convulsions as symptoms of an indisposition best relieved by prayer and a sprinkling of holy water, but who nevertheless was always at her charge's command.

'My dearest, sweetest child! This is a sign. You are ready for motherhood!' She took Tatiana into her wide embrace, where Tatiana felt safest.

But Tatiana had never yearned for marriage and motherhood as exemplified either by her parents' experience or that of Filipyevna, married at thirteen in tears. She had learnt from them that marriage and love are incompatible moral values destroyed by religious and social codes. Tatiana's dream was to be continuously in love. She had entered the world a free spirit and wished to remain so, never to be suffocated by the fumes of convention.

Defying every particular in the code that governs relations between a young girl and a possible suitor, Tatiana gathered pen and paper and wrote to Onegin. She was in a state of tense excitement, her heart was beating furiously and her cheeks stung with blushes. She knew what she was doing was improper. Only fictional heroines declared the contents of their heart

However, her commitment to Onegin, her soulmate, overcame all feigning. She wrote that in him she recognised the hero of her longing. He was an inspiration, a cloudburst refreshing her barren existence. Fate had brought him to her and she begged him not to allow any negative agency to lead to her abandonment.

Far from flirting, Tatiana sought passionate friendship. She invited Onegin to a weekly rendezvous with time between to ponder over what they had conveyed to each other, and to prepare for the next time they met.

Reading Tatiana's letter, Onegin felt the echo of feelings buried deep in his past, when he was innocent and unworldly. It was this faint arousal that decided him to go at once to Tatiana and acknowledge her confession with his own. But in her presence it was the dandy, the epicurean, the dissolute who spoke. He was not the marrying sort, he was not going to subject himself to the limitations of domestic bliss, it would all end in tears. He ignored the fact that Tatiana had expressed no wish for marriage but the establishment of a pure and noble friendship. She would not want to yield to Onegin for fear of breaking the spell.

Tatiana was plunged into despair. She grew pale from lack of sleep and nourishment, withdrew into herself. Occasionally, she overheard gossip relating to Onegin. He was living like a hermit, he was tired of philandering, he was starting to behave like any other rich, provincial landowner, managing his estate and consuming inordinate amounts of food and wine. She wrestled with the discrepancy between her image of Onegin and the one the neighbours provided.

———

It was Tatiana's nameday, and Mme Larin had been enthusiastically preparing for it for weeks. She had organised a party appropriate to such an occasion. First she instructed cooks on the chain meals to be served from the twenty-foot refectory table: hors d'oeuvres, soups, pies, poultry, roasts, fruit and sweets available from mid-morning to midnight. Then she ordered the estate manager to gather a band to play in the hall throughout the celebration. The house servants must wash the lustre chandeliers in the ballroom and see to it that a plentiful supply of candles was available.

The corners of each room were to be kept dimly lit; those whose pleasures were taken sitting to gossip must also be catered for; assignations were likely to be made, notes passed, business discussed. Accommodation must be made for life's little secrets, so blazing fires were to be kept alight all over the house.

Mme Larin looked forward to this celebration. She had expectations. In the event, everything she had arranged went to plan with the exception of Tatiana's dress. Mme Larin had wanted pink silk with ballooned sleeves and fringes on the wide ribbons at the waist. Tatiana dispensed with pink and fringe and chose close-fitting sleeves.

'But my child, I know what is fashionable so much better than you!'

'Mama, do allow me to choose what I am to wear on my nameday!'

'You will look so pale and so countrified.'

On arrival at the Larins', Onegin pushed himself through the crowd under the broad portico, leaving Lensky to his own devices. Lensky, ardent and pure, wasted no time in finding Olga. Onegin stood to nod in all directions, expecting to be recognised and welcomed. But the local squires and their wives were not to be seduced by a neighbour known to be above himself, and Onegin pushed past, 'unfit ... to herd with man', abrasive and chilly.

At the end of the vestibule, where it met the wide stairs, he caught sight of Tatiana gracefully accepting congratulations, dressed in white muslin, strands of moonstones at her throat descending to her bosom. Her hair had been dressed away from her face, with a few dark curls left to soften her brow. Her well-wishers were moving towards the parlour and Tatiana was left standing alone, still as marble, yet so fragile that a sharp-edged word might fell her.

She became conscious of Onegin staring and she returned his gaze. Behind his regard she detected a spark of tenderness. She felt her cheeks warm and a little spasm of excitement rise within her. But the spark did not catch fire. It was not with Tatiana that Onegin chose to dance but with Olga. Unlike other guests, Onegin did not stay to take supper and enjoy midnight entertainments, but rode home without so much as taking his leave.

Young women guests invited to share Tatiana's bedroom for the night chattered irrepressibly about their latest conquests, their clothes and their expectations for a gilded marriage. Tatiana found nothing to contribute, nor could she sleep. She sat at the window gazing at the moon. Her heart had been torn from its roots. She knew she was never going to find happiness with Onegin. And yet she would rather live in a continuous state of desire than one of indifference.

Tatiana did not know that Onegin's presumptuous flirtation with Olga had led Lensky to challenge him to a duel. Had she known, she would have stopped its taking place. In the event, Onegin's first shot killed the trusting poet. Olga was left desolate and despondent but, as Onegin remarked to Tatiana in a cynical attempt to console her of her unrequited love for him, 'a youthful maiden . . . no more grieves than when a sapling sheds its leaves'. Within months of Lensky's death, Onegin's prophecy was fulfilled: Olga allowed herself to be wooed and married by a handsome Lancer.

Olga and her Lancer moved away from the province; Onegin, shattered but unhurt, escaped abroad. Tatiana was left at home to suffer a sister's grief for the death of a romantic poet and, on her own account, despair. She feared she might never see Onegin again. The earth had been ravaged, its foundations shattered. Onegin was a killer; Onegin was gone. He was her inspiration; he was her disillusion. He had abandoned her. She felt his absence as a death.

The four walls of the parlour pressed in on her. Where once she sat absorbed, reading and sewing and listening to Mama at the piano, she was now entombed in a reliquary of her griefs. Her books had nothing to offer, nor the daydreams stitched into her embroideries. All that made up her existence, where she recreated life in her imagination with the help of what she read and what Filipyevna told her of the unseen world outside, was ensilaged.

Tatiana gathered up a shawl and exchanged silk pumps for boots. She would breathe better in the open. But Nature was not eager to lift her sense of desolation. Not now! The lovely lake shaded by willows, abundant with fat pike in pellucid waters, turned in her nightmare to a fetid pond. The land, once husbanded with loving care, was strewn with rotting, felled trees and dead animals.

She walked on, her eyes averted, frightened now by the malign spirits of the forest that stirred the barking of the dogs. She did not care where her legs were taking her and found herself ankle-deep in water-logged moss fed by the run-off from the hills separating the Larin estate from Onegin's.

She took the stony track that wound along the edge of the hill, rose for a fine view and descended to a small village where the large, moated manor house stood. In her childhood she used to collect bilberries on this hill. She noticed that the little hut in which the bee-man lived had been swept away, and she was pleased he was no longer about, for he used to lay traps for the hares in their forms, something she would want to put a stop to now that she knew the hare as a child of the moon.

Dark quickened; Tatiana hastened. Wary dogs tethered by a crowd of serf-boys alerted Onegin's housekeeper that a stranger was about and brought Anisya to the door. Tatiana was made welcome and once her identity was confirmed, Anisya took her round the house and gave her an account of how her master spent his days: mostly alone, killing time. Although pleased to have a picture of his treasures and his routine etched on her mind, Tatiana felt herself a thief. From each object in Onegin's house, from every detail of his days, she stole knowledge of him he had not himself offered her.

Night was falling, and for safety's sake Tatiana would need to follow the long route home. Anisya suggested she return early another day to read from Onegin's library.

That night Tatiana lay awake looking out on the immense blackness, praying to the moon to purify her soul. She could see in the distance a stooped figure, possibly a witch gathering herbs. That was a bad omen. She feared portents.

At dawn, she rode her horse across the dew-soaked meadows. On the drive of Onegin's house, a liveried groom greeted her, tethered her horse, and said he would feed and water it. Anisya threw open the door. The samovar was ever-ready. Despite the friendly welcome from both servants, Tatiana felt uneasy. She was allowing herself an intimacy with Onegin's life that he had not sanctioned, was not rightfully hers.

The library was spacious, with two book-lined walls and a double door onto the parterre. Brass lamps overlooked two large English winged chairs, and Turkish rugs lay scattered on the wood floor. A fire blazed warmly in the grate, the air smelled of cigars and sandalwood. Tatiana's father's library was a rather shabby room, yet somehow more Russian. Onegin belonged elsewhere, to the great foreign cities in Germany, Italy and France, where more emphasis was placed on style. She turned to his books. There were a few Russian items occupying a shelf of their own. They were not as well bound as the English and French Romantic novels she knew so well. There were fine editions of German philosophy, Italian poetry and the Greek and Roman classics.

It was in Onegin's choice of reading, and particularly the abundant annotations he had made in the margins of his books, that Tatiana discovered that he was nothing but a shadow of his literary heroes. He was a poseur, modelled on Byron and Napoleon but, neither poet nor man of action, he had appropriated their qualities in name only. In him all was outward show.

Anisya brought Tatiana sorrel soup, game pie and almond pastries hot from the stove. The warm waft of wormwood and the honeyscent of buckwheat hung in the air. Unusually for Tatiana, she ate with pleasure and being replete and warm, became drowsy. But she was determined to make one further search among the markers he had placed in the books that had provided her with the most illuminating accounts of him. She copied two starred but unannotated lines from Byron's 'Childe Harold': 'Soft remembrances, and sweet trust/ in one fond breast, to which his own would melt.' Byron had had Augusta, his daughter, in mind when he composed these lines, but of whom was Onegin thinking when he stopped to underline them?

At first Tatiana was puzzled. Why would Onegin wish to put on the mask of vanity, selfishness and depravity? Why, given this beautiful world, assume boredom and develop a wit only to sting with it? If he did not love the Russian world, why did he expect it to love him? What was it that made him identify with the 'poisoned springs' of life, and 'carnal companie'? What turned his hopes to dust, made him so restless, unable to be 'stirred by wonder', and eschew 'domestic peace'? Her beloved Onegin clearly occupied a spiritual winter, and hopelessness had crushed his soul. It made Tatiana weep; she did so love the truth and here, in his library, where his books were taking their revenge, she found Onegin in error. How was she to hold in her heart what her mind rejected?

In her despair, Tatiana was shocked by time's indifference to the sufferings of the individual. Man is victim to forces he cannot control; crops fail, cattle sicken, disease attacks, and it is left to his wit to find both initiative and compassion to deal with each catastrophe. And so it is with the stricken heart. What was the point of going on? In her desolation she recalled the tale of the old peasant with a load on his mind and another on his back who calls on Death to take him, but on seeing Death's towering form simply asks Death to put back the load of faggots he has thrown on the ground.

———

It was winter. Tatiana became more serene when the air was hard as glass, snow concealed, the sky slumped grey-brown over the roofs and voices lowered. In solitude she gave birth to something new in herself. She had learnt to surrender to dreaming where a dissolution between her Onegin and herself gave way to a feeling of wholeness. She played the clavichord, read the chapbooks of Lazarevich and Kovolovich, translated Pary's 'Eleanore' into Russian and wrote up her diary, interspersing a record of what she was doing with a record of how she was feeling.

Her love and reverence for the moon persisted. In the biting cold of night she stole out into the kitchen yard and peered deep into the well for the moon's reflection. She took the metal cup on its chain and lowered it into the face of the moon. But should she drink? Such a potion could bring her a moon-calf; the peasants attested to this. Or might it act as a restorative, heal her agony and interpret her dreams of

Onegin? Uncertain, she left, her thirst unquenched. She could not sleep but waited for dawn, when she would walk out into the meadows and wash in the dew. Moonwater was infallible; its sweet texture both cleansed and purged. She came away from her rituals with the moon's blessing: her earthly companion was 'other' as she herself was 'other'. The harshness of reality, Onegin's apparent indifference towards her, his absence and his meretricious character only intensified her determination to restore him. Friendship was without profit, and truth triumphed over error.

Onegin did not write. Rumour had it that he was in Greece, Turkey, Italy, but no one knew for certain, and if Anisya was *au fait* she was not saying. Whether Onegin was going to return or not, Tatiana would nevertheless nurture her desire to consummate her life with an inspirational friendship, rather than a marriage. Moral codes were destroyed by social codes. The stability she wanted was that of obedience to herself.

———

'Child, you have been courted by Buyanov and Peushkov, you have been pursued with gifts from Pykhtin. There has been a continuous stream of *billets doux* arriving at this house over the past years from the most eligible of men. I simply cannot afford your behaviour any longer. Your dowry is exiguous, which is not my fault. Your father was never any good at making provisions. You are no beauty. Compare yourself with Olga! She made herself agreeable to men and only months following her sad loss found a husband. Why are you doing this to me?'

'Mama, I am not doing this to you. It is my life I am considering.'

'If you carry on the way you are, you will have no life.'

'But I don't love any of those men!'

'Love! And what has love to do with marriage?'

Why did her mother so wish to push her into marriage?

Mama had been disappointed in her own, which had not provided the life she had wanted. Why condemn her daughter to the same misery? Mme Larin had hoped for a more lavish table and the opportunity to be the toast of the local gentry. She planned for a passionate husband, jealous of all the attentions she would receive from army officers and civil servants. Her desires had not been met, since when she had done with loving and had no patience for it. *Is this really what she wants for me,* Tatiana asked herself?

Mme Larin had, however, had made up her mind. She would take Tatiana to the bridal fair in Moscow.

Tatiana had long feared this might happen, for it was the way with many of her neighbours' daughters who had turned down the farmers, professional estate managers and elderly civil servants at hand. The choice was more extensive in Moscow. She was appalled by the prospect of having her freedom torn from her.

In an effort to fill her mind with fond images, she spent the following weeks on her dog-drawn sleigh visiting every far-flung corner of her world. She skated on the silver snake of the river Laranskia that coiled around the estate, visited the old men and women who might not survive the winter to be there in the spring, when surely she would be back. She consulted a palmist: 'You are going on a journey. You will find what it is you are looking for.' But she was not looking for anything. She had all she needed there.

Tatiana knew that her mother's plans were immutable. Coffers had been filled; there was no turning back. She was destined for Moscow. The journey would take seven days and seven nights. Mme Larin had had the old family coach restored, eighteen horses made ready and a whole household of kitchen battery, linen, china and glass put to one side to accompany mother, daughter and countless servants on their dangerous, uncomfortable drive on broken roads to dirty, bug-infested lodgings and filthy food en route. And matters would not improve on arrival. Tatiana would be subjected to fittings for clothes suitable for wear at banquets, balls and wedding feasts, each of which would be more lavish and sophisticated than any held in the provinces. She would be shown a variety of styles, dictated by Paris, in which to dress her hair, and advised with what and when to apply colour to her cheeks. She would require beaver-lined coats and hats for skating on the Moskava, shopping in the market and being amused at the fair. There was nothing in Mama's arrangements to appease Tatiana and there would be nothing to pacify Mama if Tatiana were not to prove a success with the men she would meet.

This trip was an investment.

Tatiana submitted quietly and politely, if without enthusiasm, to Mama's timetable and, in the course of fittings and the inspection of jewellery to be loaned by her aunt and married cousins, was surprised to see herself emerge differently from what she had expected. The Empire line which this season focused all attention at its hem suited her small slender frame. Silver and gold at her throat and in her hair embellished rather than embarrassed her. Heavy satins with silver and gold thread, light muslins sprinkled with pearls, sable sleeves on heavy woollen cloth and deep velvet berets in sapphire, ruby and topaz were all becoming. Once again, Tatiana's appearing other than she really was pleased Mama.

Elderly aristocrats held tea-parties for the debutantes seeking invitations to the most prestigious balls and banquets. Their role was to separate the chaff from the grain. It was at one such gathering that Tatiana was introduced to Sonya Nicolaevich, whose accident of birth was regarded as especially appropriate for the task. Suitable wives for the higher echelons of the army and civil service needed to be beautiful, respectable, but not necessarily serious-minded. Tatiana watched and listened to the flock of young women taking tea and twittering like bluetits about dress and conquests. They speculated without restraint on their suitors, atomised their appearance, their fortunes and their social status. And because Tatiana shunned such topics, they regarded her as a prig. Not so Sonya Nicolaevich, who found her reserve charming and such observations as she advanced interesting.

The two newly formed friends confided that they waited on Nature, their tutelary genius, where the Russian soul was embedded, and took their soundings from the peasants who husbanded the land. Somewhat shyly, Tatiana admitted that she perceived in Nature a spiritual essence, something with which her old nurse, Filipyevna, seemed intimate.

'But my mother scorns this in me. When once I told her how I had seen demons, all she said was that I was clearly overexcited and should take some of Dr Steinberg's potion. I told her I had called upon the moon to rout my tormentors and sought the assistance of a shower of falling stars!' The friends laughed together and then they exchanged descriptions of their family estates, and in the telling found themselves taken away in spirit from their present highly confected surroundings and returned to the remembrance of what they both valued.

Sonya had witnessed peasant sorcery on her estate. A very old female peasant, thought to be in her eighties, was pulled from her bed and yoked to the plough and set to describe a vast circle round a diseased meadow while half-naked villagers chanted throughout the night. It had worked! Within the bounds of that hard-earned circle, the land quickly restored itself to health and the once sick cattle that had fallen lame were made well.

Mme Larin was not entirely satisfied with the reception she herself received in the Moscow salons, balls and banquets. Had she been accompanied by her husband, always a disappointment to her and now a downright hindrance, being dead, she would have fared better. She should never have settled for habit rather than happiness; now there was neither. However, Tatiana was looking surprisingly well in her new outfits and was being invited all over Moscow.

There had been a lot of skating on the frozen river and visits to the fairs with groups of young people. Tatiana sounded quite enthusiastic about all that, in addition to which she had made a very aristocratic friend named Sonya Nicolaevich. That might lead to something!

'Now, my dear, you must always bear in mind that you are in competition here. There are plenty of young women

better looking, with larger dowries, more illustrious connections abroad and at home. You are at a disadvantage . . .'
Mme Larin trailed off as if Tatiana's route to marriage were
all but impassable. Her charm would have to be that of the
mind, although given her eccentricities, that was not likely
to appeal in society. 'What do you speak of to the young
men?'

'The weather, last night's ball, the theatre tomorrow.'

'Good! Good! Yes, that's the right way.'

And then a silence lengthened uncomfortably.

At a dinner given by the Princess Noranov for a visiting German baritone, Tatiana found herself seated next to
an older man to her right and a young Hussar to her left.
Her gaze fastened upon the Sèvres plates, the ivory-handled
cutlery and the gorgeous crystal. The food was rich and
plentiful and the wines from the finest vintages. There were,
perhaps, fifty guests at her table, reflected into infinity by
the floor to ceiling mirrors. The dazzle from hundreds of
flickering candles and the blazing colours from oriental silks
and jewels made her feel slightly giddy. The young Hussar
introduced himself and enquired of her from which province she came.

'Fine hunting there!' he pronounced, and showed no further interest in her once she had said that she did not hunt
or like to eat small song-birds. The older man to her right,
however, asked not about her family but herself, and appeared
to find her tastes similar to his own. Mme Larin, peering from
a table set in an alcove where other chaperones, ferocious
dames, were seated, noticed that her daughter was rapt in conversation. She was not reassured.

Elisabeth Russell Taylor

'Tatiana, how was it that you spent your entire evening entertaining a man old enough to be your father? Plain, at that?'

'I found him interesting, Mama.'

'You are not here to be interested, child!'

'He is Sonya's brother, Prince Nicolaevich.'

'Oh, is that so? Surely then he must be married? And if not, why not?' But Mme Larin did not pose that question out loud.

In fact, Tatiana and the Prince had spoken of Krasov's cantatas, daring in each other's company to deconstruct them, bar by bar, to satisfy their judgment that although less appreciated in society than his contemporary Braun, he was the finer musician. And then they had turned their attention to Rousseau and his identification with Nature, and Tatiana found herself able to speak of her love of Nature and books. They agreed, too, on the icons in the great basilica of St Xavier, which Tatiana had seen for the first time, overawed by the experience. The Prince was touched by Tatiana's modesty and she by his apparent pleasure in talking with her. There was no flirting, for which both were grateful.

On the way home Mme Larin hardly knew how to contain her pain and fury. All that money donated so generously by her friend for the purpose of marrying off her recalcitrant daughter, and with what result? Two dangerous, uncomfortable journeys, humiliation in society and no prospect of anything better on the horizon. A desert of unpunctuated time lay before her. She had hung about indecently until the very tail end of the season, pretending that she had to wait for the roads to clear but in fact in the hope that her investment might still pay a dividend.

Tatiana, on the other hand, was delighted to have escaped back home. Throughout her time in Moscow she had never chosen the company she kept and never spent a moment alone. She felt shattered. Only Nature could mend her.

———

Spring, and the pale sky was washed clean, the kingcups were sprouting on the banks of the pond and tight moist buds would shortly burst into leaf on the trees. Soon the beasts would lumber and groan under the weight of new life to be dropped where they roamed. An air of unstoppable rebirth and regeneration surrounded Tatiana and gave her moments of joy.

And then Sonya came to stay. At last Tatiana had found another sister! They walked the Larin land, gathered wild strawberries by day and mushrooms at dawn. They rejoiced in a shared delight in 'Old Russia'. Sonya disclosed something of her brother's character, something of his social situation and a suggestion of his predicament. Tatiana spoke about her inextricable bond with Onegin. This friendship gave her something incalculable, allowing her the give and take of deep affection. Like Tatiana, Sonya had to keep some of her more Russian interests to herself, for she belonged to high society where tastes were more cosmopolitan than Tatiana's. She, too, had learnt to be one thing while harbouring elements of the other. When it came time for Sonya to say goodbye to Mme Larin and Tatiana, she said that whilst separation from her husband, who had to be abroad for three months given the scope of his work as a surveyor, was something she must accept, separation from her son Dmitri, whose grandmother had laid claim to him for the summer, had been painful. But time spent on the Larin estate with her dear, new friend made up for it all. It had been an experience of rare happiness.

Some weeks following Sonya's departure, Mme Larin, with a sheet of paper firmly clutched in one hand and dropping all she had been carrying from the other, burst into the parlour where Tatiana sat reading and announced that Prince Andrei Nicolaevich was asking her permission to embark on a formal courtship of her daughter. Mme Larin fell onto the chaise and fanned herself strenuously.

'A Prince! A friend of the Tsar! Money! Land! Tatiana, what in the name of heaven does he see in you?'

She took up her pen and wrote at once to her cousin Alina in Moscow. Then she rang for a servant to take a letter round to her wealthy, generous friend nearby asking for a meeting within forty-eight hours. She needed advice on the form and content of the letter she must write in reply to the Prince. How to express contentment without relief?

Between summer and the snows a correspondence ensued between Tatiana and the Prince in which they elaborated what they had confided in Moscow. They laid out the terms on which they would be able to agree to marriage, but Tatiana was positively overjoyed that it came with a sister-in-law whose estate was adjacent to that of her brother.

Mme Larin's relationship with her daughter did not alter. She was satisfied with the alliance but she could not restrain her hostility towards Tatiana. Such an unlikely marriage for a young woman steeped in Romantic literature, in love with someone else!

'I know you do not love the Prince,' she said.
'Enough, Mama,' Tatiana answered.

———

St Petersburg,
December, 1825

My dear Tatiana,

I am delighted that we have been able to agree conditions. I feel privileged to have encountered in you such seriousness and dedication and such tolerant understanding of my position.

I fell to thinking about when we first met last season at the Noronovs'. I could see your unease in that company and the way you managed to put it aside with dignity. I was aware from the first that behind your modest demeanour you safeguard an inborn understanding of life, and tolerance for those who have not signed up to all of society's codes of behaviour. Not that we discussed such matters in any detail at that time. But I believe you had already gathered something of my situation from Sonya? You inspired in me such respect and esteem for your indifference to rank, fortune and nobility – whilst at the same time I noticed how you refused to judge those priorities in others. Seldom, if ever, had I experienced such an easy and rewarding encounter with a young woman.

It has been wise, I believe, to take a year to consider our contract, for it must be a decisive one. You understand that whereas neither of us can change his nature, we can adjust our behaviour in an effort to protect one another. In addition, we agree that the conditions of our contract and the manner in which we are to observe its clauses must accommodate the reasons for its design and remain utterly private.

As you know, my interests have taken me around the world, my military successes have assured the place I already held in society. I relish my position and wish to maintain it at all costs. We have become one another's support and alibi. But above all, we are two individuals wanting to be true to our innermost beliefs. This will, I hold, bind us indissolubly and ensure our tranquillity. Lifelong companionship that makes room for extended absences will provide each of us with the concerned support and intellectual stimulus to live within the confines of our individual predicaments: you, deeply desiring a man you are committed never to marry, I, committed to a perversity I neither can nor wish to control.

Like you, I believe that friendship is the noblest of bonds. Unlike marriage, a bargain made for other ends, friendship exists for itself. We are to be yoked as inextricably as links in the Greek key pattern. It is the determination to be true to oneself in a friendship that supports our particular truths that makes our contract free from egotism.

I am older than you and have no wish to sire descendants. Dmitri will inherit my estate, but only after you have died. It has to be faced: I am more likely to die before you.

There are demands I am going to have to make on you and to which you have consented. First, I shall want you to travel with me to Italy and Germany and play your part in the selection of pictures and ceramics for my collections. And then to France for bronzes. You will no doubt derive particular pleasure from my book collection, for literature is your keenest enjoyment. But I have an ulterior motive in taking you to France: it is there in Paris that I want to order your clothes. I hope you will agree to embellishing your gowns with my late mother's jewels, left to me in her expectation of a wife I never imagined I would take. I know that so far in your life these vanities have not been of concern to you, yet they are to me. Not only do I need to feast my eyes on all that is beautiful; you and I need to make an impression in society, one of a passionate alliance. But always bear in mind, dear Tatiana, you will be far more than an ornament to me.

The Contract

Life in society is more devious than you may imagine. Adultery is the norm. Men decorate their wives to display their wealth and to make them desirable to other men. For my sake, I want you to look beyond compare but at the same time I want you to avoid the glances, the billets doux *and declarations from the numberless men who will be hellbent on possessing you and dishonouring me. Most husbands put up with these attentions, even encourage them, because on the one hand it flatters them and on the other it excites them to think of their wives in other men's arms. I do not share in this complex, of course. But since it is going to appear strange that such a lovely, innocent young woman as you has married such an unsightly old man as me, it is necessary that no evidence of our arrangement be remarked. I do not want it to be said that you have mistaken for an eel a snake.*

You have asked me to make it possible for you to live largely in the country rather than the city. I understand how much you will miss your family estate. Of course, you must return to it as you so wish. However, I hope and believe that eventually you will come to regard Samara with something approaching my own devotion, and that your presence there will both sanctify it and be sanctified by it. During the season, a steady flow of entertaining will be offered and accepted in both St Petersburg and Moscow. I hope that this will become less onerous for you, and perhaps even agreeable as time goes by.

You have committed yourself to a particular relationship residing in your heart that can be neither fulfilled nor dissolved. You are right in thinking that in some situations, no satisfaction endures and renunciation is the answer. I respect your determination to honour this commitment and to keep your emotional independence. Should you at anytime wish to entertain Onegin, I shall not stand in your way. He is my kinsman, even if by several removes. Of course, you could not marry a man who shot your sister's fiancé, but I understand that the action for which he was responsible and that which provoked the duel is not a matter that alters

75

human love. I respect your love and your pain and I shall do what I can to show you understanding. Our friendship will reach beyond jealousy and selfishness. We shall sustain one another in all our difficulties. We have found a way to accommodate the apparently intractable . . .

Andrei Nicolaevich's letter continued for many more pages. He turned to practical matters, describing his domestic arrangements in each of his three houses in Moscow, St Petersburg and Samara. It would not be Tatiana's responsibility to determine the running of these well-oiled machines. However, if there were alterations she would like to make, she would consult with her husband and together they would make room for such.

Tatiana was overwhelmed by the length of the letter and its detail. Life might be difficult; she had never considered submitting her actions to the consent of another in perpetuity. True, she would be freed from many constraints: she would not need to pretend to be other than she was. Andrei knew all and accepted all. And her role in society was a role to which she was going to accede. It might even be enjoyable.

From the moment of her marriage Tatiana committed herself diligently to the three Nicolaevich estates. Her love for Russia and her preference for speaking Russian over French won her favour with all who worked for her – housekeepers, grooms, valets, ladies' maids – only the French chefs demurred. She travelled with Andrei, submitted to closer attention to her appearance than she liked, and started her own collection of manuscripts. Under Andrei's guidance, she became one of the most celebrated society hostesses, and Andrei's position in the military and at court was restored.

The couple grew close.

———

Onegin was wandering aimlessly through the countries of the southern Mediterranean, drawn by his reading of Byron with his 'more beloved existence', who knew himself to be the most unfit of men 'to herd with Man, with whom he had little in common'. And so he stayed away from these provincial neighbours and empty-headed society dames. There was money enough to ease his path and women to assuage his thirst.

Onegin as a child had been sensitive. Often vain, selfish and unkind but, despite his flaws of character, not irredeemable, he had experienced emotions too tender to endure, and had later put on cynicism to protect a soul more susceptible than his chosen life of debauchery could bear.

He returned to St Petersburg as he had left it, without work or purpose but 'like Chatsky, leaving boat for ball', and set out at once to be seen. He made for his kinsman's palace. While a servant lifted his coat from his shoulders, Onegin extracted his lorgnette from under his jacket and peered across the crowd. His eye roved until he caught sight of a ravishing woman who not only excited him but stirred something unsettling within him, something of the past, something reprehensible. Could it be she?

Onegin turned to the Prince. Did he know that woman in the 'crimson beret', a confection of tulle studied with rubies? 'Who is she?' he asked.

'My wife, dear friend,' and he guided Onegin to Tatiana's side.

Tatiana's transformation so confused Onegin that he could not speak. Married to his kinsman! Become a Princess!

It was inconceivable. But her wealth and status had given her simple prettiness a quality of unapproachable remoteness, so alien to the young girl who had allowed her feelings spontaneous expression. He stood before her. On her face lay cool indifference. Could this really be the woman he had lectured so unfeelingly, even abusively, and then ignored? She looked through him and showed no emotion.

Onegin wondered whether she had really recognised him as she glided away on her husband's arm. He was baffled by how such a character change could have taken place, and disturbed by feelings for which he could not account, or could not put away. Was he sorry, now, to have rejected Tatiana when she was simple, poor and accessible? Was he threatened by her sophistication, self-possession and disdain? Was his behaviour in the past snobbery, or a refusal to be led by the heart? Questions such as these were not ones Onegin was in the habit of asking of himself.

But he had fallen instantly in love with this new Tatiana. His passion reflected all the elements of the selfishness that had led him to reject her, his emotions supplanted the flawed priorities he had then valued. His life stood still. He was speechless in her presence, his stomach churned, his nerves frayed, his heart tripped. His mind was so engorged by emotion as to restrict all thought of anything but her. Her detachment was unassailable; she gave no sign of what she was feeling. The tables had been turned.

To be ignored was something new for Onegin, unpalatable. He felt ill, looked pale and frail and feared he was dying. He had to find some outlet for his derangement, and he did as once Tatiana had done. He wrote her long letters. He acknowledged that in the past he had prized freedom above her and believed that 'liberty and peace' could take the place of happiness. He had been wrong.

Tatiana ignored his letters and his visits. If an ocean of saltwater swelled within her, it was never to flood the shore. She would rather drown in it. Onegin detected anger in her face. He retreated to the country.

———

Throughout the cold, dark days of the Russian winter, Onegin shut himself in his library but could not read. His mind wandered, perpetually disturbed by his desire for Tatiana. Gone was his yearning to travel the world, to be entertained in high society or in lust. Life had lost its tonic quality. Clearly, he had no chance of making a life with Tatiana; his kinsman must be confident of that or he would not be so generous with his invitations. Was Andrei testing his wife's fidelity? Was he intercepting his letters? Tatiana espoused Russianness, at the heart of which was a respect for obedience. Was her avoidance of him her commitment to that ideal?

There was still enough of the arrogance of the younger man in him to wonder how it was that he was being spurned.

Spring was transforming the land again. The snows were melting in torrents, the dykes flooding, rivers breaking their banks and washing away the paths. Fish found themselves swimming in the meadows and geese flying distractedly low, uncertain where to set down. All old demarcations were obliterated.

Onegin noticed paths emerging and trees putting on growth. He would confront Tatiana. She had scorned the letters in which he had debased himself and begged her forgiveness for his past behaviour. It had been contemptuous. Now it was he who implored conversation with her.

He arrived at the Nicolaevich palace to find the vestibule unmanned. It was early afternoon, the servants had completed their chores in the reception rooms and had retreated behind the green baize doors. There was an eerie quiet about the place. He walked into the drawing room and noticed that the door to the small reading room was ajar, and the shadow of a becalmed form spilled across the floor.

Tatiana, simply dressed, unadorned and with her hair fallen about her shoulders, was sitting with Onegin's letters in her lap. Holding her head in her hands, she wept silently. Onegin approached slowly and dropped to one knee before her. She let her hands fall to her lap and raised her eyes to look into his face. Before her was a broken man, mute and humble. She allowed him to grasp her hand in his and to kiss it. For a moment she was returned to the past, but only for a moment. She heard herself telling him somewhat sharply to rise and listen to what she had to say.

She reminded him that when first he crossed her path she was very young, artless and unaffected. He had responded to her spontaneity with a cold and patronising manner. Why was it that he was pursuing her now? Was it because of her new wealth and social status? Were those considerations of more worth to him than her simplicity? Would it enhance his position in society if she were to submit to his advances?

Tatiana allowed time for her questions to take hold before revealing her deeper feelings. She admitted that she would willingly forego all that she had acquired in terms of social status and wealth if she could return to the Eden of her youth. She brought to mind her parents' estate, her library, her whole way of life. And Onegin's brief appearances and the rapture she had felt on first seeing his face, even though he was so unyielding and could not be bothered with her, and read her a homily on propriety.

Onegin realized that Tatiana was beyond his reach, but not why this should be so. He knew that in the past he had behaved heartlessly, that his foolish flirtatiousness had led to Lensky's death. And yet he felt that it was not for all this that Tatiana was rejecting him. Her marriage to Andrei was unfathomable; it would appear to have brought Tatiana all she had once despised. And why, after years of eschewing marriage, had his kinsman changed his mind? Tatiana looked straight into his eyes. He thought she was about to say something, but the seconds ticked by without a word.

And then suddenly she said unflinchingly, 'I love you. Why should I disguise it? But I am someone else's wife. To him I shall be true for life.'

Tatiana's words echoed in Onegin's mind but made no sense. If she loved him, why was she for ever another's? Did this mean he and she were never to be together? His mind curdled: reason clotted, sentiment turned to whey. Rooted to the spot, he felt his stomach muscles loosen and his throat tighten in spasm. For months his inner life had been absorbed by his passion for Tatiana. It had become his occupation. What was there to live for now?

He watched Tatiana silently return to the library. In the distance, he heard the clink of spurs.

Andrei Nicolaevich was returning home.

Passed Over in Silence

The announcement of the forthcoming marriage of Melanie Lloyd to Miles Cardew was welcomed by all who knew the couple. Both Lloyd and Cardew families were more than satisfied with the choice their offspring had made. Not only were the participants themselves charming but the families so suited to one another, delightful additions to their respective circles. And Melanie was beautiful and Miles was handsome and had wonderful prospects. Melanie's father had forked out for a house in Chelsea for the couple. Miles's father, having first arranged for his son to acquire stockbroking skills in a large City firm, now took him into his own and made him a partner. The couple was set fair for a more than comfortable life.

Until she was four months pregnant with her first child, Melanie continued working on the fashion magazine she had joined after graduating with an inconspicuous degree. From then on, through the births of a further two children, she would occupy herself exclusively with the home and the needs of the little ones – and those of her husband.

But not all of Miles's needs. The couple had married young. Melanie was twenty-three and Miles twenty-five. The children arrived in quick succession and by the time Melanie was in her mid-thirties her hormones had let her down. Despite her genuine and exclusive affection for Miles, the mere thought of that aspect of expression was anathema to her. She recognised she had a problem, but not where she might take it. Certainly not to her G.P. It was not as if she were ill. Miles was understanding – that was to be expected – but he was quite wrong in his judgment as to the cause of his wife's frigidity. He thought it was her fear of more pregnancies, and despite his initial prejudice against the pill for the possible risks it threatened, he suggested to Melanie that she might take it for a while.

'See how you feel!'

Melanie felt nothing but distaste and mounting guilt.

Miles was working long hours and making much more money than the couple needed. He was generous to his wife, imaginative with the children, responsible as regards provision for all their futures. He bought a house on an estuary in Hampshire, a holiday home from which they could sail. Whenever Melanie considered the lack of physical intimacy between herself and her husband, her thoughts entangled themselves and she could make no sense of them. Miles was the perfect husband. She was utterly to blame for something over which she seemed to have no control. While some of her women friends complained about their husbands' excessive drinking, meannesses, squalid personal habits or lack of consideration, Melanie could only produce a picture of Miles as the perfect companion.

She kept her problem and the guilt it engendered in her to herself. However, she fancied it must have something to do with the fact that she and Miles were spending less and less time together. Miles was always exhausted when he got home from the City, with barely the energy to say goodnight to Rosa, Hugo and Tertius, or gurgle over the baby and pour himself a drink, let alone indulge in conversation with his wife. His silence was not, however, hostile, Melanie thought; he had been talking all day. It was natural that he should want to stop when he got home. That was probably why he seemed so indifferent to their entertaining old friends at home. Nowadays, there always had to be an *occasion* to celebrate, an anniversary of some sort – or Christmas. Miles was entertaining clients at restaurants – sometimes as often as three times a week. 'Do you prefer to entertain clients this way?' Melanie asked him. 'Indeed I do!' Miles assured her. 'I don't want clients invading my privacy.'

Melanie continued trying to work out why she felt numb. What were the reasons? But as soon as she started to think, her thoughts scattered. She was not analytical by nature. Her expectation of marriage was born out of her observation of her parents' experience. Like Miles, her father had been out of the house all day and was either exhausted in the evening or out entertaining clients (although her mother had more often than not accompanied him). At weekends he had played golf, walked the dog and read the papers. She could not remember her parents talking much. Unlike Miles, who did take an interest in Rosa, Hugo and Tertius, her father had never done much with her or her sister. And Miles's interest in her appearance was quite unlike the apparent indifference her father showed to her mother, or his tight purse strings when it came to her clothes. Miles would always comment on what she wore and never on the sums she spent on her couture wardrobe. All in all, he really was the most excellent, if not the most desirable, of husbands.

By the time Melanie had reached her mid-thirties, she had to face the fact that Miles hardly ever spoke to her. It was not that he ignored her, it was that he never initiated a conversation with her. And of course, he was frequently away. It had become a habit to spend one Sunday a month in Winchester with Miles's family and one in Selbourne with her family. But even these pleasant obligations were being eroded. The house on the estuary was seldom used at weekends; Melanie used it for the children's school holidays. When Miles managed to get down, he sailed with the children by day and in the evenings went off to the club, while Melanie played board games with her brood, or read.

It was following one such long summer holiday that Melanie noticed a dramatic change in her husband's mood. He had come down for one of the six weeks Melanie was staying. He was positively talkative, even jaunty – not a word with which Melane would have thought to describe him in the past. Nothing seemed to have changed in the routine of their life, nothing she could identify. When they returned to London, he was out in the evenings as often as before, and well into the night. 'Just dining a client. I'll be late: he's a talker!' And Melanie registered it would not be necessary to have the table laid in the dining-room and three courses prepared. She would ring a friend and suggest they eat something together round the fire, or go to a cinema. 'Where's Miles?' 'He is entertaining a client.' One rather flighty divorcee did wonder aloud whether the client was male or female. The subject had never crossed Melanie's mind. 'All Miles's clients are male. What women do you know who manage their own portfolios?'

Melanie and Miles never referred to their problem, believing that 'What we cannot speak of we must pass over in silence', but certainly not knowing who first had made the point and à propos of what. Nor did Melanie discuss her private life with old friends or the elegant acquaintances she made through her children, first at prep school and then at Westminster. She was seen by her contemporaries as devastatingly attractive, rather withdrawn (was she vain?), and the women tended to be envious of her perfect marriage. Even her children appeared unusually well behaved and well balanced. As much as Melanie held others at bay, so the women took their cue and kept their distance. As for the men, with the instinct of animals, they sensed they did not stand a chance with her.

———

Melanie's birthday loomed. She was to be fifty. Miles came into the dining-room where breakfast was laid and told his wife to pack a weekend bag for them both. The chauffeur would pick her up at three that afternoon, then collect him from the City office. No, he would not say where they were going. It was to be a surprise.

The Cipriani was an unusual choice for Miles to have made, Melanie thought. She would have preferred the Gritti . . . But she was certainly not going to say so. It was so unexpected of Miles to have planned all this. And the brooch he gave her over dinner was stunningly beautiful. Melanie knew from the glances she received that in her glorious Versace silk, with her jet-black hair – not a single grey transgressor in its midst – her size-twelve body and size four feet shod in M. Clergerie's best, she was looking as good as she was able. Miles was wearing a linen suit she had not seen him in before – 'Armani,' he told her – and a shirt with a cossack neck and no tie. How youthful he looked! Melanie felt elated. She knew they would talk that weekend.

After dinner they took the private launch over the lagoon to seek out a little bar they had visited years ago, and sat drinking. Miles was full of what it was they were going to see over the next three days: the Carpaccios in that dimly lighted, tiny church; the Giorgiones, the Titians . . . They would explore the labyrinth of alleys in this altogether enchanted city and rise at dawn to watch the first rays of dazzling sunlight on the Campanile. Miles had tickets to the Bellini at the Fenice. And all this was just to whet their appetite for a longer visit in the future. 'We've been doing too little together, alone,' Miles said.

'Yes,' Melanie murmured, more to herself than her husband.

Lying in the dark in bed, not touching, like two marble effigies on sanctified ground, Miles asked Melanie how she would feel if he were to move out of the house. She thought the question was hypothetical and answered that she would feel dreadful. But Miles continued in the same vein, pointing out that they never saw one another during the day and he did so much entertaining in the evenings, they hardly spent more than two or three together each week. Melanie said she would still feel dreadful, but recognising that this matter was more urgent than she had at first registered, she asked Miles where he would go.

'To Frances, my mistress!'

Melanie was too stunned to speak.

'You must have realised there was someone else. Surely, you knew I would *have* to have someone?'

But Melanie had never realised that.

'I was sure you knew and were just too well mannered to say anything. All those dinners with clients, those weekends golfing, those telephone calls late at night . . . Didn't you see through it all?'

No, she hadn't. Not only was she inadequate as a wife, she was stupid. She was going to have to pay for both. She felt undone.

Miles told his wife that many years ago, he had promised his mistress that when her elderly husband died – so long as his three children had left home – he would marry her. 'I promised. I always felt I was using her. Now the time has come for me to absolve myself from my guilt by honouring my promise,' he continued, assuring Melanie that if she were to agree to the future he had mapped out for them they would be together just as often, if not more, than in the past. 'We would spend two or three evenings a week together, either at some form of entertainment and then a restaurant, or at the house, whichever you preferred. I'd come down to the estuary once a month for the weekend. We'd go to your family and to mine once a month on Sundays, as we have always done; and instead of my being *absent* abroad, you and I would be taking those trips together. I really do believe we'd be seeing more, rather than less, of one another.'

Despite Melanie's lack of imagination regarding her husband's needs and their fulfilment, despite Miles's misplaced reading of his wife's imagination, their understanding of one another's behaviour patterns was reliable. Neither made scenes. Whatever the situation, they behaved with courtesy to one another.

What neither foresaw was how turning Melanie into a mistress would alter their relationship dramatically. Six months of being wined and dined, entertained at the theatre, the opera and the concert hall and being whisked off to Paris, Vienna and Rome for the weekend had the most stimulating effect on Melanie's hormones. Miles telephoned her at least twice a day. They talked at length. Miles bought his wife lingerie from Janet Reger and had exotic cut flowers and pot plants delivered to the house each week. Melanie had always been well dressed and well groomed, but only now did she start to pay attention to her diet, attend the gym regularly and have massage. Once every three months she spent five days at a health spa.

Miles had become a skilled lover. Quite different from the old days. Melanie wondered about Frances: was it to her that she owed Miles's proficiency? She was too courteous to enquire.

All might have proceeded seamlessly had it not been that Frances was a woman of few perceptions and a conformist's view of marriage. She believed she had a right to know where and with whom her husband spent every minute of his time, his time being hers as well. Miles's refusal to play the game according to her rules exasperated his second wife. And when Frances smelt Joy on his clothes, she exploded and lashed out with her fists and gave Miles a black eye. She wasn't going to be treated like his first wife! No way!

The subterfuge involved in Miles and Melanie keeping their arrangement from family and friends added spice to their situation. They laughed and joked together, imagining what people would think if they knew. It came as a revelation to Melanie that the role of mistress suited her so much better than that of wife. It came as a revelation to Miles that what aroused and interested him in Melanie were qualities for which he had not married her.

Belated

My husband Daniel Stein subscribed to art journals I rarely read, and so it was pure chance that led me to pick up a copy of the *Revue Zahler* one day in 1998 and find in it an obituary of Guy la Roche, the French painter with whom I had shared my life during the nineteen-fifties. The elegance of the piece struck me, its balance between intimacy and objectivity. I had not heard of Sasha Mèndès, the critic and Guy's would-be biographer. Evidently Mèndès had followed Guy's work since his marriage to Sylvie, a scion of the French Pretender with whom he lived *à la Germantes*, and got to know him personally only during the four years between Sylvie's death and Guy's own.

I wrote to Mèndès. 'If you want to understand Guy la Roche, you will need to know about him when he was derelict but authentic. He and I lived together in Paris fifty years ago. I have his early work on my walls.' So in January 2002, Mèndès journeyed from his home in Biarritz to interview me in London.

I arrived at the restaurant in advance to welcome a stranger, and sat reading until I felt the hairs on the back of my neck rise uncomfortably. I was aware of someone standing unnaturally still, staring at me adhesively. I raised my eyes, the word *éblouissant* in my mind. I remember how we sat, where we sat and every detail of the ambience that enfolded us. It was as if the whole episode had been professionally lit, like a still from a drama.

I rehearsed the tragedies of Guy's early life, the love and war in which we engaged, and the final truce. At first, Guy was our loadstone but the dense pool into which we plunged to dislodge the past emptied its shoal of dead fish quickly and this became 'a strange and fateful interview', mixing memory with desire.

It was in recalling the desire that had led Guy and me to share life together that I became aware of the desire I was feeling for Sasha. Such desire as he felt was to discover more about a man whose work he admired, and with whom he had enjoyed warm friendship. But the sheer force of desire dissolved distance between us, and a vivid understanding consumed us, an enhanced awareness of the *autre*.

A quoi bon? Neither of us suggested a further meeting: if matters requiring clarification arose we would attend to them by post. We took leave formally. I left Sasha Mèndès standing transfixed at the windows of the restaurant of the National Portrait Gallery, looking over London. I wandered up the Charing Cross Road feeling flayed: emotional detumescence cut me adrift, empty and depressed.

Six months later, I was surprised to receive a summary of that meeting. Sasha wrote: '*Notre premier regard ne fut pas véritablement un coup de foudre mais, malgré notre différence d'age, une immense tendresse nous lie ...*' At the time, I had not registered the difference.

I was surprised by the drift of this summary and impressed by the exquisite propriety it achieved while it spoke of and to the human condition in an unusually frank manner. I made no reply, but when I came across letters, photos and catalogues relating to Guy, I posted them to Sasha Mèndès. It was evident that my input would be a godsend since I was the sole surviving witness to Guy's early days. Furthermore, I had kept in tenuous contact with him during his marriage and after Sylvie's death. Mèndès was going to have to rely largely upon gallery and museum archives for his biography, for Guy had not sustained friendships. My personal testimony would salt the dark.

I was myself plunged into darkness at the time, absorbed caring for my husband Dan, who was chronically ill and disabled. We had been together for forty passionate, creative and intellectually stimulating years. The threats that loomed increased our closeness. Even though I seemed to have no time to think and certainly no time to work, I felt privileged in my role. I stowed a half-written novel on an inaccessible shelf, and when Dan died I was consumed by shock and grief. I wanted no more of life and actively sought ways to dispense with it. I was overcome with lassitude. Grief clogged my system in stasis; I did not brush my teeth, comb my hair, make telephone calls, eat or sleep. I moved in and out of dissociative states, suspended in unreality. I saw myself as detritus, for I no longer had a role. I'd been whipped into submission, and the world without was no less superfluous. Dan took with him all we enjoyed together.

I started to try and live as he would have wished me to. But how could I, when the fine thread that attached us mind and body was snapped? I dared not visit Kimble Wood or open the studio and sort his work. I dared not look at his photograph. Inside my head, a mad woman shrieked continuously, 'Come back!' echoed by 'He is dead!' I felt defenceless without him.

And then I came across a note in his hand. It was not the contents that moved me so much as his hand, which had skimmed the page in a movement as graceful as that of a dancer's foot on the boards. I opened his cupboard door. A trace of his scent lingered. I went to his work table and took stock of the familiar chaos. After months of insomnia, I fell into a deep sleep and dreamed of him: young, lovely and ready.

Whatever the changes taking place in me, I did not feel enriched by pain. The scab was superficial and the wound bled intermittently, allowing the infection to spread. Time does not heal grief; it prolongs it in new embodiments. My soul-death morphed into half-life, and I could not cope with the abandonment.

I had first learnt the pain of abandon when, as a very young child, I watched my mother leave the nursery and close the door behind her emphatically. I knew – and I was subsequently to be proved correct – that in that moment and in that gesture she had left me emotionally for all time. A pattern of loss pursued me, submerged episodes resurfaced unpredictably and transmogrified to become abandon throughout my life. I understood the import of that syndrome, but my cognitive understanding had never withstood the force of my emotional reaction. In Dan's death, I experienced the maw and meaning of every abandonment that preceded it.

Dan had been dead for thirty-two months when to my astonishment Sasha Mèndes rang. He would be in London the following week and it would give him *grand plaisir* if I would lunch with him. I was not anxious to do so. I was not yet in a mood to socialize. I tried various excuses, but Sasha was persuasive. In the event, I was ineluctably drawn to his voice.

It was exactly ten years from our first that our second 'strange and fateful interview' took place. Like a sorcerer, Sasha handed me a mirror that reflected time: our eyes met, our smiles converged, and something beyond our control gripped us. Our affinity had lost nothing of its intensity. The knot of *tendresse* had held fast. But what did that imply? Surely, it could not mean for him what it meant for me? I was subsumed in widowhood, a stray left over from another age. I had been made to feel invisible, withered, even nullified for years. My body had entertained more surgeons than lovers, and aged me in advance of my feelings. Sasha, ever *éblouissant*, bronzed and toned, would not be drawn physically to a woman of my age.

I localised in his appearance all the potentialities of his life. He would do likewise of me. The fact that he might discern that I had led an interesting, creative life around the world, had been part of contemporary events and thoughtful about them, was not going to lead us to the same destination, chemistry and wizardry notwithstanding. And that was that!

But not altogether. We met four times over long lunches. Seated facing one another – and here was someone actually looking into me – I found his gaze peculiarly affecting. If it did not convey love *tout court*, it was of feeling, but one that shies from being inappropriate, for there are natural constraints between young and old. These were not meetings between young lovers, but between a man and a woman who remembered what it was to have been young lovers, *'heureux ... ivres de jeunesse et de liberté'*, as Sasha had observed in photos of Guy with me. He searched in my face and my gestures for Guy's lover of fifty years past and simultaneously responded to that person in the present. He did not explain. He entrusted his thought to his eyes. However, vivid imagination was producing unintended consequences. He dedicated a book he had written *'Pour Olivia, avec toute mon affection et ma complicité,'* confirming that he, too, was participating in an unusual emotional experience, beyond the reach of explanation.

He spoke intimately, perhaps more intimately than he had intended. His personal life was unsatisfactory. He had to undertake menial work to earn a living, he had almost no time to write. He compared this routine to what he had experienced during the month in London, where he had met congenial people and had had time to do his own work. He constantly repeated, *'Je suis si heureux!'* There can be nothing more delightful than someone in one's company feeling that, even if one's own contribution is exiguous. But I grieved the passage of each meeting even as I was experiencing it.

I knew I must avoid responding to confidences with anything that approximated to advice. I simply murmured to acknowledge that I was listening and hearing. In any case, desire would prevent what I said from having much relation to what was in my mind. Maternal and erotic feeling so intertwined as to have produced new order in my life, and without my censor working at full throttle, I would have cried out, 'Drop everything! Come and live under my roof!'

Sasha said he had come to London to find me and himself. He did not add, though it was clearly the case, that he had come first and foremost to gather more information for his biography of Guy. To find himself was more complex. In retrospect, I see that he was heading for collapse and needed to distance himself from what was suffocating him in Biarritz. His eyes would fill with tears when suddenly it occurred to him that the lovely times might be slipping by, irrevocably, before he had laid down imperishable foundations for a more fulfilling personal and working life.

We seemed to become ourselves in the presence of the other, like colours that profit from being placed in opposition, but our objectives were different. Sasha wanted to become himself; I wanted to be obliterated by him. He would need to be alone and I would need to be with him in order to stop obsessing about him. Yet if our objectives were different, our needs were comparable: both of us craved permanent revival, to exchange barren ground, on which each had been starving, for something fertile.

From time to time I managed to feel that Sasha's very existence could reignite my will to live, for he embodied the qualities inherent in the articulate, inspirational relationship I had lost and for which I longed. I retrieved my novel from its inaccessible shelf. But my more positive thinking was short-lived: he did not live in this country. How often would he visit? Would I not require frequent top-ups of his company? He was a bird of passage, en route, nesting elsewhere and with others. In some ways I exulted in my passion, but it left me thoroughly confused; there was such a disjunction between who and what I was and how I felt. Whereas Sasha displayed a wholly apt response to me – affectionate and courteous – I was driven by the force of emotional impertinence that wanted more, and continually. Part of me railed against myself for having no control over my feelings. But who has? And my behaviour had not been unrestrained. Of this time he later wrote: *'Comment te dire, chère Olivia, comme ces jours passés à Londres ont été beaux, hors du temps, hors du monde que je croyais connaître? Je les savais heureux, les avais intensément vécus comme tels, mais, desormais, coincés . . . ils me semblent plus merveilleux encore. Pas une minute depuis mon retour sans que je les compare avec celles passées à Londres durant un mois. Je ne m'étais pas senti aussi vivant depuis très, très longtemps.'*

I had been a component of his sense of revival, but only a component.

When he came to my flat to say goodbye, he repeated that his visit to London had been made expressly to re-engage with me; he might otherwise have gone to Tokyo or New York where he could equally well have worked. His expression was demolishingly tender. He took my hand across the oak table laid for afternoon tea and held it in his, silently consummating our friendship: *'le lien humain le plus noble'*. And then he left, faster than the soul leaves the body.

Those ninety minutes, months past, hang in my mind and twist the fibres of my heart. I see in a Vuillard setting two irreconcilable figures out of Ensor face one another from a distance. The deranged dislocation of this image embodies two unbridgeable realities: one thousand miles and thirty-three years.

The pain of parting from Sasha was different from leaving Dan's lifeless body to a dirty cell in a hospital, but no less lacerating. I felt the madness returning. So profoundly did I refuse to suffer the pain, I must unconsciously have connived with my body to detach itself from my mind. An infinity of successive losses presented itself and gave the illusion of unity.

A letter from Sasha arrived this morning. I picked up the post, threw the unsolicited items into the wastepaper basket and left Sasha's extended hand to lie alone, unopened.

The Meaning

My God, I'm bored! Maurice Levine dawdled along Hempstead Gardens towards home, a journey he had been making every day for over fifty-five years, ever since his marriage to Gina Jacobs. The appearance of number 16, identical to every other house in Hempstead Gardens, was the one sight he could rely upon to arouse in him instantaneous feelings of boredom, loneliness and entrapment.

'Gina! I'm home.'

'How's it been?' she asked, backing into the kitchen to pour boiling water over the tea bag. Maurice lifted his right arm to hang his coat on the stand and with his left hand removed the *Standard* from the pocket. He mooched into the lounge, crossing to the bay window, where he fingered the claret velour curtain while he stared out on to thirty feet of grass bordered by identical beds of flowers whose names he neither knew nor cared to know.

Gina placed the glass of lemon tea on a plastic mat with a picture of the Knesset on one side and the Mount of Olives on the other.

'Take care!' she said, as she always did. 'Hungry?' she asked, as always, and not waiting for an answer added, 'I've got a nice fowl in lemon sauce.'

Maurice had no reason to attend to details of the menu: he knew it by heart, oh yes! Instead, he turned from the window and stationed himself in front of the glass-fronted bookcase with its single, undisturbed row of books: English classics of even size, bound in navy Morocco. The set had been a Bar Mitzvah present to his son Aubrey.

Maurice remembered that day. It had cost him a bomb. Gina had insisted on a four-course menu and French wines . . . and she would not have the reception in the synagogue hall. She insisted on somewhere 'up west'. 'It's more convenient for the people,' she said. It hadn't been.

He would have liked Aubrey to be a doctor or a lawyer. A property developer in Westchester County was one up on estate agenting in north London, but it did not impress Maurice as much as he pretended to his friend Solly.

'He's a lot better off than he would have been staying here. He's got a fine place with a tennis court . . .' But the boy had never studied. It was the same with Linda. She'd been a good girl to her mother and she was a respected fundraiser, but what's a secretary, tell me that? He hadn't liked to ask. Once or twice when the conversation veered towards the subject, Gina turned away and took a *shtum* powder.

No one's so much as touched those books, let alone leafed through their pages, Maurice thought while he gulped his tea noisily. *The whole of England may be summed up there and I'll never know.*

'Gina!' Gina! Come here a moment. Tell me, how many books have you read in your life?'

'What a question! Don't bother me now with your questions. I've got the matzos *kleis* on the simmer.'

It's certainly all in books, Maurice mused. *I never had the chance to find out for myself . . . I never got the time. The button and braid business keeps you on the go fifty weeks a year – fifty-two, if the workers hadn't insisted . . .* And he thought back to his own holidays. As soon as he had been able to afford it – it had meant foregoing a Rover and keeping the old Vauxhall far too long – he had taken his two weeks in the south of France. Every year they had gone to the same comfortable hotel in Cannes, with Solly and Ruth. He remembered sitting on the terrace of the hotel in the sun watching the lovely young, slim, scantily dressed ladies go by. *Better than reading any day,* he had thought at the time. And what other time had he had? Once Aubrey had married and left for the States they had gone there for the Easter break. *Where's the time gone? Monday to Friday, eight to eight, driving to and from the city, stuck in traffic, synagogue on Saturday mornings. Linda and that husband of hers for lunch. I wish she'd married one of the other boys.* A show with Solly and Ruth or Becky and Gordon in the evening. And then on Sunday, the papers, a nice sleep in the afternoon in front of the TV and before you knew it, it was Monday again. *When could I have read books?* The trouble is – and of this he was quite sure – it was all there in books: the Meaning. *It's the Meaning that's escaped me,* he lamented.

'Gina!' he called out. 'Gina, does Linda read books?'

'Such questions. How should I know? Why don't you ask her yourself?'

Maurice sighed. 'I should never have retired. I was better off working.'

'You may have been better off,' his wife allowed, 'but you would have been dead better off.' She was standing at his side, duster in hand, waiting to mop up the tea he was bound to spill. 'You know what Dr Foreman said, he said "rest". He said your heart wouldn't stand the pace you set it.'

'I'm bored, Gina. The other men play golf all day and bridge all night. They don't want me around. I've got no interests. I worked all my life since I was fifteen. I've not had the time. It's different for you: you've got the house and the garden and Linda . . .'

And much too much else to sit and listen to your kvetching, his wife thought.

Maurice did not know how to fill the lines of time between the stops for meals. He was like a dog, wandering aimlessly, unable to settle for long in one place but not liking any of the alternatives better. 'Maybe I should buy a dog to take me walkies.'

Gina expressed her disapproval by ignoring this reflection.

It was warm and soft in bed. Maurice put his arms round his wife. The flesh of his stomach met that of her buttocks. Now he felt at peace.

'D'you mind, Gina?'

'Go ahead!' And he did. In silence. His mind drifted in the exquisite pleasure that was his own. This was what he had to live for. Filled with the matchless delight this experience occasioned in him, he ceased thinking, consumed by a single sensation. Unaware of its primacy, however, he made no attempt to prolong it. This he regretted when, spent, he rolled on to his back and faced the terrifying fact that this was his sole pleasure in life. *I could have kept it up a bit longer,* he mused. *I'll try next time.*

But when Maurice woke at 6.30 next morning, Gina was up. After fifty-five years of preparing his breakfast for 7.30, she had not accustomed herself to the new circumstance.

Oh my God! he thought. *Another dull, brown day.*

'There's a couple of rollmops to finish and some soured cream in the fridge. Save the tinfoil . . . And there's some fruit wanting finishing in the Pyrex bowl. I'm going up to Brent Cross with Linda to look at microwave ovens.'

Maurice did not feel inclined to picnic at the corner of the kitchen table. He felt the edges of the abyss crumbling. He needed to get out before they fell in on him.

He wandered into Golders Green Road and looked aimlessly into shop windows. He could not help noticing the new Rover in the showroom. He had always wanted a Rover. He wondered whether, if he knocked on Mr Klein's door, the dentist might fit him in? He'd been meaning to do something about that broken back tooth. He'd call in at the bank and see how much he had in his current account. Then, passing the salt beef bar, the idea of a sandwich occurred to him.

He drew himself onto a bar stool at the counter. The man in the white coat cutting the beef might pass the time of day. But the man was too busy slicing. Maurice stared at the jars of pickled cucumber and the tins of olives, chewing on a sandwich he no longer fancied, unable to gather his melancholy thoughts. Why was he feeling so low? Perhaps it was medical. Perhaps he should find a specialist. Maybe it was his heart. Before he had the opportunity to develop that line of thinking, however, he was relieved by a diversion: raised voices at

a table just behind him, a little to the right. A petulant child
was driving his parents mad. Without turning to see, Maurice
strained to hear what was going on.

'Drink your lemonade!'

'Don't want to'. The child sounded plaintive. Maurice
could not resist the temptation. He turned. The child – a boy
of about six – was starting to cry. Real tears. He was gulping
down sobs. His nose was running.

'Drink your lemonade!' his father shouted again.

'Don't make him do what he doesn't want to do, dear,'
the young mother pleaded softly, placing her hand over her
husband's. Maurice saw she hadn't a chance of influencing
the man. He was scarlet in the face. He was ready to explode.

'He can't go through life doing what he wants!' the father
shouted. 'Take me! Have I ever done what I wanted?'

His mouth filled with salt beef and rye, Maurice found
himself having to concentrate to swallow. He was not enjoying this sandwich. He slid off the stool, took his wallet from
his back trouser pocket and paid at the till. As he slipped back
into Golders Green Road, he found himself muttering aloud,
'Never done a thing he wanted in all his life. Like me. I've
never done what I wanted. Never!'

He did not have to consider where he was going. His feet
did the thinking for him. There, in the newsagents, he sorted
through the shelves until he came to the sports section. He
picked out the *Racing News*, the *Racing Times*, the *Racing Gazette*,
the lot. A frisson of excitement shot through him as he felt
the thick, warm bundle under his arm press against his side.

'Gina! I'm home!'

'How's it been?'

'Fine. Just fine.'

Gina appeared not to hear the more optimistic note in her husband's voice. Calling from the kitchen, she informed him that Linda had bought a microwave.

'And for your information, she says to tell you she's been reading books all her life.'

'Did she say what she got from them?'

'No. But I can't say I enquired.'

Gina was at his side, setting down his lemon tea. 'I hope you're not thinking of doing the horses,' she said ominously, noticing the pile of racing papers. 'We can't afford that.' Looking at him intently, 'You've always had that hankering, haven't you?' Receiving neither confirmation nor denial: 'You know what Father said before he gave his consent: "No horses, not if it's my daughter you want." He only gave us the house because you promised. So don't you go starting now he's gone.' And she turned on her heel and went back into the kitchen.

He thought the ninety days before he could remove his savings from his building society account would give him the time he needed to draw up foolproof plans. There were only two routes out of his desolation. Both brought him out in sweats and palpitations but things couldn't go on the way they were. He could play the horses and if he won he could disappear. He had seen a programme on TV and read two accounts in the papers of men – quite important figures – who had done this: left the house to buy a packet of cigarettes and never been seen since. He'd lay his plans very carefully, make it seem he was dead. He'd disappear to the south of France and find himself one of those slim, bronzed young ladies.

And if he lost? A lump formed in his throat. He could hardly breathe. Well, in that case he'd have to end it all. Gina would have the house; it was hers, after all. And she'd have the pension.

It was a peculiar peace that descended on him when he left the bookies in Golders Green Road for the last time, his wallet empty, his pockets too. *Well,* he said to himself, *at least I did something I wanted to do.* The familiar, brown, tired wave of boredom broke over him. The bronzed young lady on the promenade disappeared in the undertow. The peace of oblivion dissolved. Everything was back where it had been. Risk-free. The menu would be the same, the words exchanged would be the same. The routine ... The English classics in their navy Morocco bindings would stay forever unopened behind their glass doors.

Maurice found it an effort to put one foot down in front of the other as he climbed the stairs to bed. Gina was rubbing cold cream into her face. While she fixed a hairnet over her newly permed, dyed blond hair, she watched Maurice through the looking-glass on her kidney-shaped dressing table.

'Fold your trousers over the chair! Don't just drop them on the floor. How many times . . . Really!' Everything was happening in agonisingly slow motion. In his mind he heard the thundering finality of doors shutting out the thrill of what might have been.

Gina hung her eau-de-Nil candlewick dressing-gown on the hook behind the door and kicked off her mules. She was getting into bed. She had her back to him. When he slipped in bed beside her she was turning off the bedside light and settling down to sleep.

Maurice moved into position.

'D'you mind, Gina?'

'Go ahead,' she replied.

Supporting Roles

C live took from his pocket a smooth, egg-shaped stone wrapped in a handkerchief and thrust it against the window pane. Glass shattered, fell onto his hand and pierced the skin. He watched the blood creep furtively towards his fingers. A sense of intense excitement passed through him.

———

It was his GP, to whom he had turned for tablets to relieve his depression, who had referred Clive to the local hospital for a course of cognitive therapy. Anti-depressant tablets had made no inroads on Clive's mood and he had become increasingly despairing. He was not sleeping, he was not socialising, he was out of work and short of money.

Dr Anderssen was one of a team at the hospital at which the comparatively newly introduced cognitive therapy – the Christian Science branch of therapy, relying as it does on positive thought – had become central to the Trust's commitment to cost effectiveness. The Trust held that most patients undergoing this treatment could be relieved of symptoms such as depression, anxiety, obsessive-compulsive disorder, even phobia, in six to ten weekly sessions with a trained therapist.

Clive had had no experience of doctors whose area of interest was the psyche. Given that those of whom he had heard, Freud and Jung, were both foreigners, he was not surprised when he received a letter from the hospital with the date of his first appointment that the therapist, Dr I. Anderssen, was Swedish. However, on meeting Dr Anderssen he was thoroughly disorientated. He had expected a male, someone a lot older than himself, and, for some ill-defined reason, someone ugly. Dr Ingrid Anderssen was a strikingly beautiful woman in her mid-forties.

Clive Fraser had taken the hazardous path on to the stage via one of the lesser known drama schools and provincial repertory, a route that had led to cameo roles in the commercial theatre in the West End. He was in his early thirties when he was singled out by an influential critic for an accomplished performance in a supporting role in a Russian play. With the looks of a matinée idol, and a particularly well-modulated voice, he was kept in work that suited him. Clive was by nature lazy, and preferred to do what was within his capacity rather than attempt something that might require his stretching himself beyond it.

I had not met Clive at this juncture. I had seen him perform twice, quite fortuitously taken to both plays by an old school friend of his. I knew little about his childhood except that it seemed to have been a stable one. He had had no aptitude for academic subjects and although his parents had not been pleased that he had chosen the stage for his career, and would have been better pleased had he chosen accountancy, they could see some sense in it. I discovered later how reassured they had been when he married Alice, who had a steady job in advertising, and sorry when the marriage fell apart for reasons unbeknown to them. Fraser senior retired to Ayrshire prematurely at about the time of his son's marriage, and the physical distance he put between himself and London stood in my mind as an illustration of his moral distance from his only son.

At their first session, Dr Anderssen asked Clive why it was he thought he had been referred to her. Clive felt a spasm of unease pass through him. Was this a trick question?

'Because I am depressed, anxious and continually tired,' he said, but without much confidence. Dr Anderssen appeared satisfied by this response and quickly asked him how he imagined she might help him eliminate these symptoms. Clive had no idea and said as much, adding that he was desperate.

'You have told me how you are feeling: anxious, depressed and tired, but not what it was that precipitated these feelings.'

'I have failed as an actor and I have failed as a husband. I am a total failure.'

'A total failure!. Are you sure this is so? Is there no single thing in your life to which you can point as a success?'

'No!'

'Well, if I may, I would like to put it to you that going first to your GP, and then agreeing to be referred here, suggests you have succeeded in taking control of your mental wellbeing and that that is highly successful behaviour.'

Clive continued to stare down at his feet before eventually admitting uncertainly that he supposed it might be so.

'Shall we examine what you call total failure? You say you have failed in two roles: that of actor and that of husband. Can you say whether it is the temporary setback in your occupation or the more permanent breakdown in your marriage that is making you feel depressed? Or is it the sense of failure itself, which these events have generated?'

Clive's mind went blank. He could not distinguish the difference.

'It is very important, indeed it is the basis of this treatment, that you come to understand that what you think produces what you feel. You think you are a total failure; that is a shocking, unreasonable indictment of yourself. No wonder you feel depressed!'

Dr Anderssen tried throughout the session to urge Clive to say what he was feeling in response to the various suggestions she put to him. He was consistently negative. Above all he identified feeling stupid, unable to absorb her meaning, weak, unable to think of anything to say with which to fill the silences. Towards the end of the allotted fifty minutes, Dr Anderssen suggested that during the week that followed, Clive might list those things in his life that he regarded as having been successful, and how he had arrived at the conclusion.

—

'Excellent!' she said when Clive came into the consulting room the following week with a paper extended. 'Excellent! So you are not a total failure. That's a good start.'

Clive managed a short laugh.

'You brought two problems you judged as personal failures, problems to which you must find solutions because they are making you feel ill. You want to get back to work and you want to reclaim your marriage. Which of these two matters is the most pressing?'

'My work,' Clive answered without hesitation.

'Do you think these matters are connected in some way?'

'Only in that I have failed at both, and in the sense that I have failed to be supportive because I am just not up to either role. I've not been supportive to my wife, who accuses me of not being a real man, and I've let down the cast in my supporting role.' During this session Clive revealed that the symptoms he experienced on stage when he 'dried' and when he 'died' were much the same as those that overcame him when his wife accused him of being less than a man: his throat contracted, he sweated profusely and his heart thumped so hard it made him fear he might really die. This information encouraged Dr Anderssen to let the conversation proceed to the subject of Clive's marriage, despite his former assertion that it was not the first problem with which he wished to engage.

Suddenly, however, he started to speak compulsively, clinging as he did to the arms of the chair in which he was sitting, as if fearful of becoming uprooted, discharged into exile. He insisted that the accusation of his inadequacy as a real man was something he could not and would not confront. If that was what Alice had felt about him then it was right that she abandon him. He was a failure; he didn't want to go into it. The flow of conversation became a drip. He shuffled in his chair and then rose. 'If you don't mind, I'll go now.'

117

On arrival at his third session, Clive uncharacteristically opened the conversation, clearly determined to keep some control over it and not to have to account for having walked out the previous week. What, he wondered out loud, had happened to his hitherto excellent memory, his confidence on stage, his rapport with his fellow actors? How was it possible for all that to have evaporated?

'Have you suffered panic attacks in the past?' Dr Anderssen asked.

He had, and he had been remembering the occasions.

'How did you feel bringing them to mind?'

'Terrified. I sweated and felt dry-mouthed.' And then he described a school outing in Wales. He had been clambering down a cliff where there emerged, unexpectedly, a steep fall without any ledge to rest his foot on before he could gain the beach. He became stuck, able neither to turn back nor proceed, and he certainly did not dare jump the six or eight feet to the ground. It had been both frightening and humiliating. All the boys were egging him on, shouting, 'Jump! Jump!' but he was stuck, fixed as it were. On a further occasion his form had been taken to a country house in the grounds of which was a celebrated maze. He had become panicked, closed within the high hedges of blind turns, convinced he would never get out. He had wet himself and become the butt of the form, bullied, called a wimp.

'And how did that make you feel?'

He had wanted to die.

'Did you regard yourself as a wimp?'

'Of course. I was. What happened was in line with all the rest that singled me out as a wimp.'

'But you have told me what an excellent sportsman you were, how you won cups for swimming and archery, and that is to ignore the school plays in which you did so well. Did you never think that being called a wimp on account of such trivial matters, when you were clearly anything but a wimp at sport and on stage, was not only unfair but inaccurate?'

'No, I didn't.'

'Did you feel depressed at school?'

'I felt angry.'

'And how did you express your anger?'

'I didn't.'

At his fourth session Clive told Dr Anderssen that the sense of well-being acquired at drama school was due more to his improved physical appearance, which led to his success with women, than to his acting. He had been rather a pimply adolescent who had shot up too quickly and was ill-coordinated. By his eighteenth birthday he had filled out, felt more manly, applied himself to his appearance and found, at last, that he really had something going for him.

'You were thinking positively and as a result, you felt positive.'

'Yes, that was a better time for me.' Clive thought he might have chosen acting as his profession by default. Not only was he not clever enough to have gone to university, but up to then he had never enjoyed the role of being himself. At drama school he had developed something of a liking for himself. His description of his conquests animated his conversation and he started to notice the gulf between what he was feeling when he evoked his golden years and what he felt when he brought himself back into the present. It was annihilation.

'The trouble is, I have to turn in a first-rate performance six nights and two matinées a week on stage, and seven nights a week in the bedroom. And I don't, so I've lost my career and lost my wife and if that's not a description of total failure, I'd like to know what is.'

Dr Anderssen, careful never to take issue with her patient, suggested with consummate gentleness how it was that thought generated feeling. 'Your thoughts may not be wrong, in some respects factually correct, but they are unhelpful to yourself put the way you put them.' She told him it might be as well to stop examining the past too closely. From all he had told her, it was clear that he overreacted to the past in the present and was liable to be thrown off balance quite dramatically.

Dr Anderssen was concerned that Clive was chronically depressed, that his sense of worthlessness was isolating him, and his fatigue keeping him inactive. Daytime TV on a diet of cake and biscuits was unstimulating and unhealthy and contributed to his negative thoughts about the world in general. She believed it was time for her to suggest a regime for Clive to attempt to follow.

'Try to get out of the flat and walk on the heath for half an hour a day and write down a list of things you see: trees, ducks, joggers and so on. Telephone at least two people during the week. Why not phone your agent first? It might not be wise to stay out of contact with her for too long. And then how about a call to a friend or fellow actor?'

Clive let out a deep sigh and clung to the arms of his chair. 'But what on earth would I talk about? I've done nothing for months.'

'Well, you could lead the conversation in the direction of your friend's interests. You could discuss world affairs – you've been watching TV all day – you must have a pretty good idea about what is happening in the world.'

Clive's silence persisted just too long and registered itself as hostile. Then suddenly, in an overloud voice he said, 'Well, I'm certainly not ringing my agent. It wouldn't be worth her career to keep anyone on her books with mental-health problems. What company would thank her for supplying them an actor who dries, shakes, sweats and bursts into tears? I'm done for, can't you see that?'

———

I was the friend Clive eventually contacted after this, his fourth session with Dr Anderssen. It came about because he had tried to contact our mutual friend, John James, without knowing that John was about to leave for New York and a run of at least twelve months in *Lear*. John told me that Clive was in some sort of trouble, although he did not specify what, and knowing that I had admired him as an actor, and had some spare social time since he himself would be away, suggested I might get in touch with Clive and take him out to dinner.

I was seated at the bar in La Brasserie du Pont when Clive entered. I hope I concealed my shock at his appearance. He had become rather fat and coarse in the face since I had seen him on stage. He looked as though he had slept in the suit he wore and his shirt was none too clean, nor were his nails. Although I am habitually at ease with people, I felt uncomfortable with Clive from the start. I discerned something unpredictable about him.

I spoke of John and how his talent had revealed itself when he was very young and had matured gracefully with the passing years. Clive showed little animation except to say he was glad to discover I was a solicitor: he might be needing one. He laughed bitterly. 'Matrimonial,' he explained.

I asked him whether he would like to discuss the matter while we ate but he said no, he needed to 'thrash out his feelings' before he took legal advice.

He told me he had been on antidepressants for many months but they had done no good, and he had come off them to try some new one-to-one psychotherapy. However, he complained that his therapist was cold and indifferent to his suffering. He appeared to blame her for his not feeling fully recovered after just four sessions. I was disturbed by the state he was in. He described it by saying he was one of the unlucky ones of this world, how everything in his life and work had gone wrong at the same time. Part of me is rooted in the pull-yourself-together school and he did not endear himself by the whine in his voice and his monotonous self-pity.

I do not imagine he really enjoyed his evening. He picked at his food and drank just one glass of wine. I identified something of spiritual famine about him. He was punishing himself, 'thrashing out his feelings', as he put it. I doubted the efficacy of such immolation. We parted in the street. Clive shook my hand feebly and thanked me uncertainly. I offered him my card. He took it saying, 'I'm on the dole', and I understood that his sense of shame had become a disease.

———

Dr Anderssen was not displeased by Clive's outburst, his show of anger, and between his fourth and fifth sessions she wrote up her notes in an effort to assess his progress. He had agreed to be referred, had described himself to her as desperate, yet he had barely made a single move in the direction in which she was trying to lead him. At each session he sank down in his chair as if it were the maternal lap, and gave the impression of handing over his problems to her to solve without his having to take part: his problems were to become her problems. But in addition to the maternal role he was assigning her was something else.

He had adopted a way of observing her which was neither frank nor passive but somewhat sly. It could have been taken for a manifestation of concealment, yet the concealment was not, she thought, related to his own life but the way in which he was reacting to her. He would let his eyes scan the floor, his own shoes, the papers that lay by the side of her desk, and then raise his gaze to settle on her face for just a second or two too long, or travel round her person as if to memorise what she was wearing or, worse, the contours of her body. The occasional undue attention had become uncomfortable. It was not the first time she had experienced interest of an unwelcome kind from a patient. It was, however, the first time she had registered unease.

By the fifth session Dr Anderssen was forced to admit that Clive had almost without exception been unable to do much more than repeat his mantra of failure. The automatic compulsion was so strong in him that when she attempted to question him outside his discomfort zone, he managed to reenter it automatically, either by responding negatively or by not responding at all.

'Try to imagine yourself . . .'

'I can't.'

'In what areas of your life have you ever felt really comfortable?'

'When I'm asleep.'

'What are your goals?'

'I have none.'

Nor would he entertain further suggestions of how he might pass his time. 'The only appointment you keep regularly is with me, here. Can you tell me how it is you manage to muster the energy, the interest to do so?'

'I come automatically, like going to the corner shop for the milk.'

'So you come here to satisfy a need? Were you to extend this metaphor, you would require to consider raising the cow, grazing it and milking it before you could expect nourishment. Solutions to the problems of mankind do not come pre-packed, cannot be bought, and reside within. I can help you with your search, but I cannot manufacture answers.'

Dr Anderssen was starting to face the possibility that she would have no success with this patient. Meanwhile, Clive was beginning to lose sight of the two problems with which he had come, that of his marriage and that of his career, and to focus his attention on her failure to cure his symptoms.

At this point Dr Anderssen initiated a suggestion she had found to work with a previous patient. First, Clive should head a sheet of foolscap with the message 'My Problems Are My Responsibility'. He should divide the paper into three vertical columns and to each apply a heading: Problem, Possible Solutions, Positive/Negative Responses. As an example, Dr

Anderssen suggested Clive deal first with his physical appearance, a matter he knew had deteriorated since he had been ejected from the stage. Under Problem he might write 'inactivity', under Solution 'exercise' and under Response 'no energy'. There it would be, in black and white, for him to examine day by day. He might move on to examine his emotional and social life in this way. She wanted to feel that he would confront things in an organised manner when he was on his own, and she wanted him to return the following week with at least ten examples.

———

Dr Anderssen's mother was in the terminal stages of her illness and Dr Anderssen wanted to be with her at the end.

When Clive entered the consulting room for his sixth session carrying a file of foolscap paper, she dared to imagine some movement in his condition. He sat down in his usual way, trying without success to sink into the unyielding chair. As usual he had done almost nothing, seen one unsympathetic acquaintance, watched TV, eaten Jaffa cakes and drunk lager. The spots on his pallid skin were erupting, his hands were grimy and there hung about his person a smell that betokened unwashed flesh.

'How are you feeling?'

'I think I have reached rock bottom. I can't imagine feeling worse.'

Dr Anderssen was obliged to tell Clive that because of her mother's condition she was going to Stockholm in a few days and expected to be away for three weeks. Clive turned white, the muscles in his face appearing to tighten against the imminent threat of total collapse. He turned his face up to the ceiling and then down to the floor. He kept his expression concealed while she spoke. She was sorry, she said, that her life had trespassed on his treatment. Despite her concern for his welfare, she had no alternative. She would arrange for him to be seen by a colleague during her absence if that was what he would like. Alternatively, she could prepare a number of projects for him to work on, such as the ones she noticed he had brought with him that day. Might he consider taking the opportunity of her absence to visit his parents in Ayrshire?

'Certainly not!' he said.

It was impossible for Dr Anderssen to gauge accurately how Clive would behave while she was away. She knew he was feeling resentful, abandoned and victimised. He might try suicide, although she doubted he could muster the energy. She suggested to him that sometimes a shock, even one such as this, could release something in a depressed individual and lead him to think imaginatively. She flattered him with references to his intelligence, his previous successes in the theatre and in his social life. 'I know you will sense a vacuum. Perhaps you will find the strength to fill it. Do try. It doesn't matter much with what you fill the void, just don't sit alone in your flat and brood.'

Clive felt a surge of violence erupting within him. How dare she abandon him and then patronise him with her pathetic suggestions? She really thought too highly of herself, looked down on him. She should have seen him in his days of glory. That would have shown her. Cold bitch.

———

I do not know what it was that led me to telephone Clive. I do not believe I was looking for work and I certainly did not crave his company. Perhaps it was a feeling of obligation planted by John. In the event, I was astonished by the conversation he pursued with me. Instead of the whine I half expected, he adopted a shrill fury against Dr Anderssen who, he felt, had had no right to leave him in his current state to be with her dying mother. This sounded more than a little excessive to me, but I realised it would be useless to put the good doctor's case to him. If that was the way in which Clive viewed a daughter's love for her mother, no words of mine were going to influence him to see sense.

On and on he went, his language becoming ever more intemperate. I knew better than to interrupt. My practice had taught me that. When he appeared to have exhausted his subject I simply enquired whether there was anything I might do for him. Would he like to meet? Would legal advice be appropriate at this time? But no, he did not want to meet and he could not be bothered to think about his marriage and no, he did not want to talk about John. He seemed to be closing down and fastening every available hatch. I felt anxious about him. Where, I wondered, would all this hostility lead? Had his narcissism morphed into madness? Defeated, I simply said goodbye and wished him well.

———

Clive had no difficulty in finding Dr Anderssen's home address. In the earliest stages of his treatment he had looked it up on one of those afternoons he spent channel surfing and opening packets of biscuits. The house was located no more than a mile from the hospital, in a wooded cul-de-sac. Built in the 1930s Modern style by émigré architects, the building had few English admirers. Dr Anderssen, however, had grown up with the Modern in Sweden and had been delighted to find the square, white-painted concrete box with windows placed as Mondrian might have placed them if faced with the task in London.

With the full force of his weight and his anger, Clive struck the package of egg-shaped stone against an eye-level window at the back and smashed it. He put his hand through and prised open the door, which turned out to be that of the utility room. It sprang open on some patent device and allowed him quite easy entrance. Once inside, he secured the frame. Shattered fragments of glass streaked with blood preceded him and he quickly sought and found a tap and held his hand under icy water, letting his blood drop into the stainless steel sink. He did not wait to staunch the flow but took a clean tea towel from a basket of linen and wound it round his hand. He winced; clearly there were shards embedded.

Keeping the beam from his torch at floor level, he wandered through the kitchen, the dining-room and on reaching the living room, in a state of tired confusion, threw himself down on a long leather chair that afforded him room to stretch his legs.

Little by little he accustomed himself to the dim light afforded by a single street light and the full moon. He made out walls covered with abstract paintings, shelves stacked with expensive books and, built into the ceilings, modern light fitments in blown glass clusters. Glass featured everywhere in this house, as tabletops, shelves, *objets*. Everything cool, tidy, sterile: Swedish, he thought. A stage set? A show house? Unlived in! Who kept this house so immaculate? Who polished the gleaming wood floors, kept the muted tones of the rugs as new? Not Dr Anderssen, surely; she did not seem to Clive to be the sort to drive a vacuum cleaner, flick a duster or don Marigolds. This thought made him tense. Would a cleaner arrive at dawn?

Clive's intention was to inform himself about the private life of a woman who knew far too much about his own. What she knew of his life she regarded as being purposeless and without any systematic organisation. Well, be that as it may, he was certainly going to show purpose and system in unravelling hers.

He went from room to room, opening every cupboard and drawer, looking for anything that might reveal something of his therapist's life. There were no photographs, no letters in English, no dedications in books. What he found was a superfluity of clothes and linens: silk underwear, linen sheets, down pillows and duvets. She kept her sweaters colour-coded in individual plastic bags in deep drawers. Her suits, dresses and coats hung in wardrobes similarly protected and ranged. She revealed herself to Clive as a shop-window mannequin in an exclusive department store. Such a considered way of living added to his anger. By controlling everything so keenly, she demonstrated such hubris! No wonder she expected him to keep charts and conform to her set of judgements. She must have found it untidy dealing with someone such as himself.

Having toured the house and established what he could of Dr A's domestic life, Clive returned to the kitchen and poured himself a gin and tonic from the bar that stood beside the fridge and freezer. He helped himself to an unopened tin of salted nuts and a container of olives. He lay back on the Mies van der Rohe leather chair and gazed from the window on to the patio where he could make out a table and chairs ranged as if for a party. He wondered about Dr Anderssen's social life. Could any man tolerate her military order? It needed mussing up, he thought.

Clive's mood was one of anger narrowly contained by anxiety. He had helped himself to more gin than he was accustomed to. He was unsteady on his feet and confused. He hauled himself up the stairs into the bedroom, drew back the bed cover, tore off his clothes and let them fall in a heap on the floor. He fell into the deep, soft warmth of the double bed and from under the pillow extracted a silk nightdress which he wound round his still bleeding hand and held to his face like a child with his comfort blanket. He fell asleep.

——

Following our rather dreary dinner and the brush-off I received from him on the telephone, I would not have contacted Clive again. I had only involved myself with him on John's behalf in the first place. However, such entanglements have their own momentum.

One afternoon I received a telephone call from the police station in Camden Town. Clive had been arrested and my card had been found among his personal effects when his pockets were emptied. When I got to see him the following day, I found a broken, barely coherent man in panic. He was quite unable to grasp the seriousness of what he had done or its implications.

I persuaded him to accept my professional help and advice. Eventually, as I prepared his case, he unburdened himself to me and detailed all he had experienced before and during his treatment and subsequent crime.

Dr Anderssen did indeed wield her own vacuum cleaner and maintain her domain without help in keeping its antiseptic cleanliness and immaculate order. Thus it was that Clive had remained undisturbed there in her house for five days and five nights. More's the pity! The havoc he wrought was appalling: in revenge for what he regarded as having been his therapist's neglect and indifference, he fouled what he could not destroy.

It was the uncontrolled, primitive aspect of his violence against Dr Anderssen's home, rather than what might so easily have been a physical attack on her person, that made it possible for me to have Clive sectioned rather than imprisoned. And the remarkable outcome was that after only two years of rather orthodox treatment in a none too promising hospital building, Clive was released, healed, to return to his supporting roles.

Dr Anderssen, on the other hand, reacted so profoundly and neurotically to the assault against her property – experiencing it as rape – that she not only abandoned the house but also her hospital post. She returned to Sweden and sought refuge with her aunt, whose house reminded her of her own childhood home. Her trauma, coming so close on the heels of her mother's death, had stripped her of all defenses. She wrapped herself in a duvet and the arms of a comfortable chair. And she sat, behind locked doors, sipping at *filmjolk* drizzled with rosehip syrup.

Carter

From somewhere distant, a train could be heard softly rolling itself along the lines, clicking over points and then braking, screeching and coming to a halt nearby. Carter looked up calmly towards the window and then out of the door and peered right and left along the tiny landing. 'Children?'

'There are no other children. Just you, Carter, and me, Edna.'

Miss Edna Broom had been living alone at number 14 Mafeking Terrace, Gorton, for four and a half years before she was joined by Carter, aged five. The town was not a place anyone coming from elsewhere would have chosen to visit, let alone put down roots. It was a low-lying dump in which you would have regretted having been born or, having been born there, lacked the money to escape. Edna had known full well what she was about when she singled out Gorton as an ideal location for her new life and the child's.

At the end of World War Two some towns in England were selected for immediate regeneration, others set aside to wait upon more affluent times. Gorton was among the latter. It had suffered steady bombing, for there had been small arms manufacture in the area and important rail links. Whereas the rail links had had to be revived, only the lightest of industries were reestablished: ComfySlippers, for example, and SweetNothings, an artificial sweetener for the soft drinks trade. These manufacturers provided some employment for the women but the men of Gorton had to get on their bikes and ride twenty miles to the mines for work. By day Gorton was the preserve of women, children and dogs.

Edna had been an embarrassment to her father, then a disgrace. He had kept the situation from his brother and sister in London and from the men with whom he drank at The Fox. He had had to cut himself off completely from the members of the small Christian community to which his late wife had owed allegiance, for he could not have borne their unspoken disapproval of his daughter. Edna herself concealed her condition from her two friends at work by taking sick leave for five weeks and then writing to Mr Henderson, the boss, to say that because of her father's frailty she had decided to devote herself full-time to his care; he was not managing well as a widower.

Having made the move and got things sorted in Mafeking Terrace, Edna marvelled at how easy it was to disappear in England. She was not a criminal; she was not being sought by the police. No creditors were after her; all bills had been settled. She had never been one for socialising: look where her one experiment had got her!

Edna had visited Carter four times a year at Springfield Orphanage, but because visitors were under instruction not to show preference towards any one child, she was to Carter simply one of a crowd of women who brought fruit, cakes and sweets and the occasional toy to everyone. So he gave no sign of recognising her when she came to collect him. She had been anxious about the effect of a long train journey on the boy. He would be making a journey away from what he had always known into the utterly unknown. In the event, Carter endured the ordeal by keeping his eyes tightly shut, his cardboard case clutched to his chest with both arms.

On arrival at his new home, Carter appeared dazed. Edna pushed him gently through the front door and into the kitchen where he stood stock still, clutching his little case. 'Come along, dear, you sit here!' and she pulled out a chair from a table laid with a generous spread placed under covers.

Carter waited to be served. He managed with difficulty to swallow a single biscuit and drink a mug of orangeade.

Edna overlooked his silence and vacant expression, his lack of appetite and unusual expressions of unease. She spoke to him as if he were listening, and in some mysterious way even answering her. She introduced him to Sam the cat and pointed to the box with high sides in which he slept when he was not out mousing. She prepared him for when they would go upstairs to see his room, and spoke of the stories she would read to him.

But Carter seemed distracted. Suddenly, he struggled off his chair and took from his case a yellow knitted creature, a bear no more than eight inches in length, well flattened by small hands tightly clasped through treacherous nights. Edna watched him with a faint smile of recognition and satisfaction. Then she rose, disturbed by Sam's entrance, and put down the food he mewed for.

Carter showed some interest. He watched the cat lick clean his saucer, then contort himself to wash the underside of his back legs and finally leap into his box. The silence in the kitchen was broken by deep purring. Carter walked over to the box and peered in.

'This is your room!' Edna called out, for Carter had lingered on the stairs to allow his hand the pleasure of slipping along the highly polished banister. He followed Edna into a small room. 'These are your things. Chair, bed, table and shelf of books. All yours!' she repeated with satisfaction. She wanted Carter to feel special, but sadly, it was not possible to detect whether he understood her drift. His face retained a vacant expression and he avoided eye contact. Perhaps he didn't understand the concept of possession.

The matron in charge at the orphanage had warned Edna that Carter might never want to communicate; but she was not to imagine he was physically unable. He was not deaf or dumb; he was obdurate. She might get a curt 'yes' in agreement or a curt 'no' in disagreement, but she should not bank on anything more. And there was another thing: his behaviour under stress. Edna was made aware that there was a problem.

But it was not one that would exercise her. To her mind there was a lot too much talk, much of it to no good purpose.

———

Edna's daily routine started early. She rose with the sun to prepare for a day to be much like the previous one. She bought and prepared food, she washed, scrubbed and polished, she knitted and sewed. Everything she did was with

Carter at the front of her mind. Money was short; she needed to eke it out so that he would have everything to which a boy was entitled.

For his part, Carter appeared to accept his new routine with the apathy he had manifested in his previous one. Rarely overjoyed, rarely anguished, he continued to pass through life hermetically sealed from it, like the contents of an impermeable bottle on the high seas. At school he sat quietly listening or, possibly, not listening. Sometimes he would nod, at others shake his head. Every morning, the first thing he did was to line up his pencils, rubber and notebook fastidiously, and every morning the pattern he made of these few objects was the same. Should one of the other children disrupt the uniformity, he would rise from his desk, sweep his possessions to the floor and groan. At playtime children crowded round him: 'Can't you speak? You deaf and dumb or something? Where's your mum and dad? Got none?' They poked at his arms and kicked their ball against his legs. He moved away to hide somewhere alone until the bell saved him.

No teacher witnessing such goings-on did a thing to intervene. They claimed that Carter's preference for silence was born of a determination to conceal rather than reveal. It made them nervous. They advanced no other theories; they had none. But they murmured among themselves, expressing irritation that they should have been expected to educate such a disturbed child.

After a month or so, help came in the guise of Barney, a ginger-headed lad a little older than Carter. He began taking it upon himself to account for Carter: 'I think he means this,

Miss,' Barney would suggest, or 'Carter wants to go along the passage, Miss,' meaning that Carter wanted the lavatory. And as Barney allied himself with the silent boy, the bullies in class found that not only were they unable to get a rise from him, but one of their friends was showing signs of actually being on his side.

Because he was reading earlier than the more vocal and had started to answer questions on paper, the Head said they must keep Carter in class. She was, however, aware that the boy's groaning and his persistent thigh-rubbing and arm-waving when distressed created a disturbance. She asked teachers to try to see to it that situations were nipped in the bud before Carter got upset, and explain to the bullies that it was their behaviour that made his so unusual.

Had Edna been asked how she felt since bringing Carter to Gorton, she would have expressed satisfaction. But it hurt her that Carter showed her no affection, and was demonstrably nettled if she touched him. She wanted him to know and feel her fondness. Sometimes, when he was sitting quietly – distracted, she imagined, by his thought – she would take the opportunity to tell him how happy she was to have found him, how special he was to have been chosen. Yet she knew that her words almost certainly made no sense to him.

———

The various sounds of rolling stock, passenger and freight, rumbled day and night, accompanied and interrupted by whistles and screeching. Edna had come to accept these sounds. It was reassuring to know that life was being led out there somewhere, and without her involvement. She watched to see whether Carter felt likewise. At the orphanage he had shared a dormitory with twenty-nine other boys, and Matron had told her that their noise, their squabbles and even their smells had been odious to him, a fact he had conveyed eloquently in a series of gestures of disgust. But he appeared to absorb the railway sounds as he absorbed Sam's purring. As if he, too, liked background music to which he did not have to contribute.

Edna woke one September morning to find the sun streaming through her bedroom window, bathing Gorton in an unfamiliar yellow light. She thought of sea and sand, of donkeys and ice-cream. She woke Carter – 'We're going to the seaside!' – and she took a book from his shelf, opened it at a page of flat blue strung with boats, facing another page of yellow sand and brightly coloured beach huts. 'That's where we're going!'

Carter showed no sign of comprehension. Would this alteration in his routine upset him?

Edna packed a picnic. Into her basket she put a wooden spade and little tin bucket. As she walked along the path to Gorton station, she remembered in fright the last time she and Carter had travelled by train together. But Carter appeared to have forgotten, and for forty minutes he stared transfixed by the changing pictures he saw from the carriage window.

On arrival at Gorton-by-Sea, Edna removed his sandals so he might feel the warm sand between his toes, and they settled together with their backs against a breakwater. The tide was retreating, and as it did, uncertain small waves left foam on the wet sand. Carter watched this ebb and flow closely while Edna went to buy him an ice-cream cone. He enjoyed the ice-cream, Edna could see that, and when he had finished she suggested he might paddle.

'Too big,' he managed of the sea, and declined her suggestion. He groaned and rubbed his hands along his thighs, yet Edna's disappointment was modified by the joy she felt at hearing the child manage two words, one quickly following the other.

———

One afternoon, Barney followed Edna and Carter home from school, chattering companionably with Edna along the road and into the villa while she made tea.

'Does Carter talk to you?' Edna enquired.

'Not much, but I know what he's thinking, so he doesn't have to.' Barney thanked her for tea and asked if they might now go out to play.

'Of course.' Edna wondered nervously what sort of play Barney had in mind. 'Don't go far!' She felt cold-shouldered. Did Barney understand Carter better than she did? She was losing the boy, who preferred to play with Barney rather than weed the garden with her or bake biscuits. But he still fed Sam, cared for Sam's bed and played with him and his house-mouse.

On the first afternoon Barney and Carter had gone out to play, it had been by the railway, which had in every one of its particulars become Carter's obsession. Before school and after, he would run from home towards the brambled bank below the railway or along the footpath in excited anticipation. He learnt the time of each train that passed, its name and where it stopped. For those trains that did not stop at Gorton, he went to the level crossing with his frayed red flag and waved, ecstatic when passengers or even the guard waved back.

Edna felt at one and the same time anxious when Carter was out on his own, beyond her sight, and delighted that he was becoming more independent and had an all-pervading interest.

'Will you take me to see the trains today?'

They set off along the path, through the covered steps with their filthy windows and littered corners, to a bench on the platform where Edna rested. While she sat facing the lines, Carter wandered off in the direction of the ticket office.

Time passed. What could possibly be the attraction of train lines? Edna wondered. Carter returned with a timetable in his hand. He pointed to the cast-iron notice signalling that this was Gorton. His mouth formed the letters he was silently spelling. He turned to Edna and pulled at her jacket sleeve, so she followed him into the waiting room, where the walls were hung with posters. One illustrated sea, sand and beach huts, the resort to which they had gone together. Simultaneously attracted to this colourful picture and disturbed by it, Carter started to groan and sway. He stood on a bench and fingered the blue that was not wet, the yellow that was not gritty. Was it possibly the too big sea that had returned to frighten him? Whatever the problem, it lay too deep for Edna. But the child had ceased his groaning, swaying and rubbing, and Edna stopped trying to solve what it was about the poster that had so disturbed Carter, or what reassurance he had wanted from her.

He turned to the chocolate machine and dropped a penny into the slot. A train drew in, doors were flung open and slammed shut. The guard fixed his whistle between his lips and blew lustily. A spent ticket drifted towards Carter on a little breeze activated by the wheels of the train. He ran forward to pick it up.

———

Little by little, Edna accepted that it was natural for Carter to prefer playing with Barney to helping her with her chores. She consoled herself with the thought that she had been right to settle in Gorton: it not only concealed them but kept them safe. And now she participated increasingly in Carter's obsession. She borrowed books from the library about trains and train memorabilia. She haunted the junk shops that spilled into the streets of Gorton and looked out to buy cigarette cards illustrating trains, signal boxes and brass station signs. She would have liked to have the money to buy the station clock she found, but it was too expensive and she bought instead red and black pencils with 'Gorton Station' written in gold along their length, brass buttons from a station master's jacket. She stashed these items in her stocking drawer and every so often withdrew a single object and produced it at teatime. Carter accepted each treasure with a nod; Edna thought she detected the ghost of a smile.

Below the shelf of books Carter kept nicely arranged in order of height were his cardboard case, on which he sat his bear, and a box with high sides like the one in which Sam slept. In that big box he kept a pile of smaller ones in which he stowed his railway treasures. A great deal of Carter's time, when he was not at school or out playing with Barney, was spent alone in his room. He kept the window open wide and his possessions spread out on the floor. Edna made a point of telling Carter the name of each object she handed him: 'This is a ticket, Carter.' 'This is a button from the station master's jacket.' Passing his door, more often than not kept firmly shut, she would hear the child rehearse aloud words he never uttered in her presence.

She was used to Carter's habits, how he relied on strict routine, how his books and treasures were never to be meddled with or moved. It was painful to her that he resisted her touch, but she avoided displeasing him because she could not bear to see him distressed. He would no longer let her bath him or wash his hair. His attachment to Sam was such that he appeared to object to Edna's showing the animal her affection, and he carried Sam away from her, up into his room. He refused to eat meat and ate vegetables with his fingers. He had a strong reaction to smells and a particular aversion to all washing and washing-up products. Edna found him emptying the bleach and the Persil down the drain. These were small inconveniences, an expression of Carter's individual personality: 'Everyone has his funny little ways!'

———

A letter addressed to Miss Broom arrived at number 14, informing her that Carter was to be assessed. Edna ignored the communication. She was not interested. She did not understand precisely what assessment involved, or what its implications, but she rather imagined she was against it.

A psychologist came to the school and sat at the back of the class to observe Carter's behaviour. In the playground, she sat on a wall and watched him from there. Most of the children had come to ignore Carter by this time, and Barney's role in his life had become much more entrenched.

'How is it that you understand so much about Carter?' the psychologist asked.

'I am his friend, that's how!'

'And how did you make friends with a boy who doesn't speak?'

'I smiled at him.'

'And what do you do when he gets upset and behaves oddly?'

'I leave him to get over it.'

The psychologist came several times to study Carter and discuss his behaviour with his teachers. They insisted that despite the child's refusal to communicate verbally, he was learning – and he was not disruptive, if one ignored the odd signals he put out when distressed.

At home, the psychologist was struck by Edna's apparent acquiescence in Carter's behaviour. She was doing nothing to socialise him. To a number of searching questions, Edna replied curtly that she had chosen Carter for his difficulties in communication. She identified with this trait.

'But would it not be more desirable for you and the boy if he were more like other children?' The time had come, the psychologist announced, for Carter to be considered for a different type of education: he was a candidate for a 'special' school.

Edna objected; Carter must not be taken away from Gorton or from his friend, Barney. He was fine just as he was.

'But what of the future, Miss Broom?'

'The future will take care of itself.'

Edna was asked to let the psychologist accompany Carter at teatime. At first, she tried the uncontentious observations with which Edna had lost all patience and to which, of course, Carter never responded. How long had they lived here? Did they like Gorton? Where had they come from? The weather is rather unsettled hereabouts, is it not? and the town neglected? . . . Had she not persisted, tea might have been taken in total silence. As it was, Edna measured her words and paid undue attention to passing cake and filling the guest's cup.

On a subsequent teatime occasion, Barney was one of the party and the specialist was able to observe the role he played in the management of Carter. Here was real, non-verbal communication at work at an affective level. Carter had an emotional life – but it was not with Edna. What was the relationship with Edna? How was it to be described? Was she no more than a structural element in the armature of his being? Nothing she did or said contributed in any way to Carter's understanding of life. She appeared to be making no impression on him at all.

Having been told that Gorton station was his favourite haunt, the psychologist determined to go there with Carter. They took the footpath and the covered steps but Carter ran ahead, ignoring her. He made for the waiting room where four

new posters were on display, modern and optimistic induce-
ments to visit the sea for its ozone properties, the countryside
for its farmyard beasts and the city for its opportunities to wor-
ship in the great cathedrals. The largest poster of all displayed a
man and woman encircled by a wedding ring, exhorting travellers to 'Visit Mum and Dad!'

The specialist watched while Carter struggled to absorb
those words. The subject of his mum and dad was one he had
had to take on board, along with taunts of his being deaf and
dumb. On the playground, Barney had reported, the children
called out: 'Where are your mum and dad? Why don't you have
a mum and dad?' and Carter saw that other children had these
creatures back at home; he must have queried his lack. Certainly,
he was up to that sort of thinking: his reading books all told
of girls and boys living under the same roof with one of each.

The atmosphere at Mafeking Terrace had been thoroughly
upset by the intervention of the psychologist. The routine had
had to be interrupted to make time for her and her intrusive
questioning. Eventually, Carter refused to sit at the tea table
with her and would disappear into his room with the door
tightly shut. But she would have none of it. She knocked, she
entered, she said what a lovely room it was and listened with
Carter to the sounds from the railway and remarked on them,
hoping for a response. When she picked out a book from his
shelf, he became agitated and took it from her and restored it
to its proper place. She talked about railways, school and how
fortunate he was in his friend Barney.

Carter was probably not listening. He did not even face
the woman, and certainly made no eye contact. As with Edna,
he chose to look towards a shoe or the arm of a jacket.

In desperation, the psychologist suggested they go to the level crossing. Carter picked up his flag and they set off together. Once the boy appeared settled in his mind again, the psychologist led him to the waiting room and joined him on a bench facing the poster exhorting travellers to visit Mum and Dad.

'What do you think that means, Carter?'

———

Edna was relieved when the psychologist announced that she had paid her last visit to Mafeking Terrace. She and the boy could now get back to normal.

One morning soon afterwards, she went to wake Carter and found he was not in his room. His cardboard case was gone and so, too, his bear.

She threw on a coat and ran to the station. Three trains had stopped to pick up passengers that morning: the milk train, the slow train to London and the fast train to Glasgow. Neither the ticket collector nor the lady who ran the buffet had seen the boy.

Edna ran to the school, but Carter was not there. The Head came out to console her, assured her that Carter was not the sort of child to stray. Edna asked to see Barney.

'Carter's missing. Do you know what's happened to him?'

Barney did not answer.

'Where d'you think he could be?'

'I dunno.'

'Where might he have gone?'

'Anywhere.'

'But why would he go off like this?'

'To find his mum and dad.'

'Did Carter have the faintest idea of what a mum and dad were?'

'Of course he did. He saw my mum and dad. He liked them. Thought he'd like some of his own.'

Edna stood staring at Barney. She felt sick, and somehow could not move.

The Inquest

The silence in the courtroom is made palpable by the ticking of the clock on the wall above the coroner's head. There is something wrong with the mechanism, something that has proved irreparable, nothing so simple as a loose screw or want of lubricant. With each tick, with each tock, the case rattles. But whatever the irritation it arouses in witnesses, the press and other members of the public congregated to hear a good story unfold, it passes unnoticed by the coroner. His head is down; he is writing. When he has finished noting an observation and is ready to address the witness, he does so without preamble.

'Your name?'

'Albert Hodges, my lord.'

'Sir will do.'

'Sir.'

'And your address?'

'The flat, 2 Paddington Buildings, Harrow Road.'

'That would be W9?'

'W10, sir.'

'And your occupation?'

'Caretaker, sir.'

'Caretaker. Perhaps you would elaborate: what precisely are your responsibilities in your capacity as caretaker?' The coroner is writing. Still he does not take his eyes off his notes.

'I take things in, sir.'

'You take things in! And what exactly do you mean by that?' Now, for the first time, the coroner looks up and stares at the witness.

'Well, sir, when parcels and letters come, I sign for them, take them off the delivery man, sort through them and put them in the right cubby holes. Sometimes I deliver things personally to the doctors. I keep the waiting room and the doctors' rooms clean and tidy. I sweep up, even scrub where necessary. Some patients are given to throwing up and wetting themselves. I'm there to keep things ship-shape. And then I see to it that the windows are closed fast at night and the doors all locked. I get there first thing in the morning to open up. I'm very safety conscious; you can't leave things unattended, not in the Harrow Road, you can't, it's never safe.'

'And for how long have you been employed in this responsible capacity?'

'Thirty years, sir, since I was demobbed in '46. I took the job for the accommodation. My wife Bess liked the flat the minute she clapped eyes on it. Just after the war we couldn't be too choosy. "We'll be cosy here," she said. We'd got no kids, just the cat, and it was convenient for him what with it being at ground level.'

'Thank you, Mr Hodges, I think I have the picture.'

The coroner is now staring at the witness. Whereas some seek inspiration from a distant horizon, the coroner seeks his in the gap between the limpid tick and the turbid tock. What can thirty years of scrubbing, locking and unlocking, signing and sorting have done to the man before him?

The reporters in the gallery are becoming impatient; they rustle their papers. The public is shifting on the benches. The noise of papers and of feet scraping the floor is accompanied by the peculiar, unyielding complaints of mackintoshes.

'Would you be so good as to tell the court what you knew of Miss Alton?'

'How do you mean, sir? I didn't know her – not really, not personally.'

'No, Mr Hodges, but you saw her regularly, did you not?'

'That I did, sir, every day, Monday to Friday, at ten minutes to three when she arrived and at four o'clock when she left. She was Dr Neustadt's patient and I'll tell you a peculiar thing, sir: she'd even come when the good doctor was on his holidays. She'd sit in the waiting room for exactly fifty minutes, as she would have sat with the doctor had he been there. She was a lovely young lady, about thirty years old, I'd say. Stood out from the rest, she did. Her name was Magenta. I'd never heard that name before. She was exceptionally tall, had long black hair and big blue eyes. She was always polite and thoughtful. Our patients come in all shapes and sizes, but the odd thing is they tend to look alike. Dr Neustadt explained to me why that was. It's what their problems do to them, make them bent and slow and out of control of their mouths.'

'What do you imply by "out of control of their mouths", Mr Hodges?'

'Well, sir, for one thing they tend to dribble. For another, they often shout without warning and use terrible language. Some of the rough sleepers and druggies come out with words I'd not even heard uttered in the forces. Some think they're Jesus Christ and want to wash everyone's feet, others think they are King this or that and expect to be bowed to, and if no one does respond, all hell breaks out.'

'And was it part of your responsibility to control this mayhem?'

'It was in the waiting room. I'd frisk the dodgier ones for sharp instruments and syringes, but I never interfered in their nasty personal habits, the nose-picking and scratching of one another. I was firm with the ones who took off their clothes, or unbuttoned to expose themselves, that sort of thing.'

'Did you experience difficulty in keeping order?'

'Yes and no, sir. One of the other doctors showed me how best to deal with the violent ones and the awkward ones: not to get involved physically but to "catch them by the eye". It worked with most. It was the women who tore off their clothes I found the trickiest. And I didn't want Miss Alton to be upset.'

'And was she?'

'Funny thing was, she didn't seem to notice what was going on, seemed to be in a sort of dream. She sat quite quiet in a corner. I think she must have known I was keeping an eye out for her.'

'Indeed, that would have given her confidence. Tell me, in what other ways was Miss Alton different?'

'Well, she was an educated lady. Spoke nicely. She made quite an impression on me, the first day I saw her. She came in carrying a bunch of daffodils tied with grasses. She had a jam jar with her and she asked me whether I could fill it with water. She smiled and thanked me. Later that same day, Dr Neustadt asked me whether I had seen his new patient. Said he was going to make her better. I was struck by this: he never said that about the others.'

'Really? A fine pass it has come to when a psychiatrist does not so much as imagine he is going to improve the mental health of the majority of his patients. Hardly a consoling thought for the rest of us.'

'Beg pardon, sir?'

'Just an aside, Hodges. You carry on!'

'She wore pretty things in the modern manner, two or three skirts one on top of the other, shawls over her shoulders. And hats! Straw in summer with flowers pinned at the brim; velour with silk bows in winter. Quite a stunner, she was. But later she got to wearing grey and black like the other patients, and her skirts got torn and a bit dirty. It was sad to see the change.'

'So, despite Dr Neustadt's confidence, Miss Alton went downhill?'

'She did. It started when she read on the noticeboard that he was going to retire.'

'So, to sum up: this was an attractive woman in her early thirties who, during the course of her treatment and before she was apprised of her doctor's imminent retirement, maintained herself, was somewhat withdrawn – aloof even – well mannered, and apparently well disposed towards yourself. Would that be a fair résumé?'

'I think that sums it up, sir.'

'But you understood that Miss Alton could not have been entirely well balanced, or she would not have been attending the clinic? And despite Dr Neustadt's confidence in the permanence of his healing powers, she deteriorated.'

'Well, sir, it's not for me to say. I don't understand these things.'

'Quite so. What can you tell me about Dr Neustadt himself?'

'First and foremost I'd say he was a proper English gentleman for all that he's a foreigner. For twenty odd years he was my boss, and it was a real pleasure to work for him. Always remembered his pleases and thank-yous, treated me same as everyone, not like some of the other doctors – I'm just a workman to them: "Bring me this! Take that! I've not got all day! The room's a mess, Hodges, hasn't seen a mop or duster in weeks!" Some used to try to get my Bess to do a bit of washing and ironing for them when their wives were on holiday. But that's something I'll not stand for, them making use of my Bess.'

'All right, Mr Hodges, those details are more than I need to know. Let us get back to Dr Neustadt.'

'He treated me more as a friend, talked to me, told me ever such a lot about himself and his past. He's what they call a survivor. All his family was killed in the war, in Germany, and all their property was stolen. He's got no one of his own. He lives in two rooms, as we do, just has a bed, a table and two chairs: nothing superfluous, he explained to me. It's been his patients who are important to him since them days.'

The coroner looks up at Albert Hodges and slowly considers what he sees: a man who will report things as he found them, as he had them reported to him, would see them with an unimaginative eye. Not a man to indulge in flights of fancy.

It was the police reports that had not made sense; the witness seems straightforward enough. An ordinary working-class man. A Londoner. Salt of the earth. A man whose western horizons would stretch to Slough and whose eastern horizons would terminate at Clacton-on-Sea.

'Mr Hodges, would you remind me how old you are?'

'Seventy-five, sir.'

A man of seventy-five, living in the caretaker's flat in a concrete, custom-built, council-provided slum on the Harrow Road, a drab neighbourhood ignorant of any natural feature. No greensward, blueberry-clad hills, no dew pond, no carpet of bluebells, no stream glistening with trout. Distant from the song of the lark and moan of cattle. And every working day within both sight and sound of the mentally deranged. Yet here is a man who can cope, an uneducated man neither shocked nor threatened by the uncertainties of mankind.

'Do you attend the cinema, Mr Hodges?'

'Not these days, sir, we don't. It's become too expensive. We watch the telly.'

'And do you do much reading?'

'The *Mirror* most days and the *People* on Sunday.'

'No books?'

'No time for books, sir.'

'Quite so. I don't mean you to think I am suggesting you ought to read books. It is only that I have been impressed, even confused by the extravagance of the descriptions of all that took place at the clinic as you recounted each event to the police.'

'Extravagance!'

'Should I perhaps have said "imaginative"?'

'I don't have imagination, sir. I don't hold with it. I keep my feet firmly on the ground.'

'I'm sure you do, Mr Hodges. However, I am also some-what bewildered by the fact that Dr Neustadt, himself, in accordance with the strict rules governing doctor-patient relations, has refused to verify the evidence you provided the police.'

'I don't lie, sir.'

'No, Mr Hodges, nor am I accusing you of lying. It is simply the case that it is unusual for a man of your type to come forward with the particular class of narrative you have unfolded. Let us say, the stories you have told the police.'

'They are not stories, sir. I don't tell stories.'

'Allow me to rephrase: tales.'

'There you go again, sir! I don't tell tales. I can't make up stories and I don't lie. I leave imagination to them that can afford it.'

'That is what I like to hear, Mr Hodges, for what I need are facts. These descriptions of yours that I have before me in the police reports strike me as being more highly coloured than I would normally expect from a man such as yourself, a man whose feet are set firmly on the ground, a man who does not invent, a man who does not lie. At best they strike me as fanciful delusions.'

'Delusions? What are delusions?'

'Well, we need not go deeply into that. Shall we say dreams? Certainly not the sort of happenings normally associated with daily life in the Harrow Road. In addition to which, I am bewildered by the account of the close relationship you formed with Dr Neustadt. Surely you would admit that what you had to report of both Miss Alton and Dr Neustadt was unusual?'

'They are not your usual sort of people, sir.'

'Quite so. Perhaps I meet fewer unusual sorts of people than you, although I doubt it. However, let us leave that aside for the moment. I have to get to the heart of this matter. That is what I am employed to do; like you, I have to take things in and sort them out and deliver each to its correct cubby hole. Now, I think, we should adjourn for luncheon. We shall take up where we left off at two-thirty. Be back on time, Mr Hodges!'

———

Reporters hurry to the Canal Inn. Members of the public gather to compare notes. Albert Hodges walks out of the court slowly, alone, and settles on a bench he finds overlooking children's swings set in a concrete square where pigeons loiter to be fed by the old and the lonely. He takes a packet of sandwiches from the pocket of his coat and eats, if only because it is time to eat. And when he has finished, he stands up and stretches, and then, because there is nothing else to do, sits down again. Bess believes him. And the good doctor is not a man to lie. He himself has not discussed Miss Alton with a living soul bar Bess, with whom he discusses every item of the day because what else is there to talk about? It is only in the peculiar circumstances of the deliveries that he is in court. And, of course, Miss Alton's passing.

Albert Hodges closes his memory against things unpleasant, things that cannot be borne and things that defy description, and picks his teeth. Why don't these bloody NHS dentures fit? He looks about him for a bin into which to throw the grease-proof bag in which Bess packed his sandwiches. Having found one, his thoughts turn back to those matters that have defied the imagination of the police. How is he going to tell it as it was, pass on what he saw and heard and get the coroner to believe he is telling the truth? People don't believe what you tell them if they haven't had it happen to them. Take the young: they don't want to know, because they weren't there and the war's been over thirty years. Same after the first war: no one wanted to know. Not those who hadn't been in the trenches. They passed by those poor men on crutches, a tray of matches round their neck and didn't give them so much as a good-morning. He does so wish he didn't have to go back into the courtroom.

In fact, he is among the first to return. As others follow and the small room fills, he feels caught by the incoming tide. Now the coroner is shuffling in, returning in the same mood in which he recessed.

'Well now, Mr Hodges, I hope you feel replete and can provide me with your full and honest description of the events that occupy us here in this court. You do understand how important it is for your testimony to cleave to the facts? Perhaps I may take you back to the first day on which British Rail unloaded a mountain range at the clinic. It was the Alps, was it not? And it was British Rail?'

'It was, sir. Only British Rail had the capacity.'

'Quite so.'

'It was a nice morning. The sun was up. It was about seven-thirty. The British Rail driver sounded his horn for me to open the gates. Soon as he was into the yard, he jumped down. "This the Klein Clinic?" he asked. I said yes, it was. "You got a Dr Neustadt here?" I said we had. "Well," he said, "the delivery's for him." "What am I signing for?" I asked. "Mountains," he said. "Beg pardon," I said. "You heard," he said. "And where d'you think I'm going to put mountains?" I said. But I wasn't really speaking to him, more thinking to myself out loud. Then he started to get nasty because he thought I was going to refuse to take them off him. "All right," I said, "you unload them here." And that's what him and his mate did: unloaded the range on my yard. I went straight to my lodge and rang Dr Neustadt at his home, because it being so early, it wasn't time for him to be at work yet. I told him about the delivery cluttering my yard. "Have it put on the roof, Hodges!" he said, as if it were nothing more than an aerial or two, or some lagging. I rounded up three of the porters that do our rough work and they got the thing onto the roof. I had other jobs to do, to get ready for the early appointments. But I did worry about the weight and whether the sun might melt the snow and we'd have the problems with leaks we get when there's thunderstorms. No amount of buckets was going to cope with an avalanche. I could see that. These buildings were put up after the war, sir; they're not sound, not sound at all.'

With dutiful indifference the coroner finds his voice. 'So, Mr Hodges, we are now faced with a mountain range, the Alps no less, on the roof of the Klein Clinic in the Harrow Road. That is what I understand you to be asserting?' *They do say that dreams move mountains*, he mutters to himself. His patience is being tried beyond the obligations of his profession. 'And did you attempt the climb?'

'No, sir. But that evening before Dr Neustadt left the clinic, he thanked me for the trouble I had taken and gave me a bunch of those blue flowers that grow in the mountains, said to give them to my Bess. Said when he was a boy he used to climb those mountains with his father. So when I got back home and told Bess the whole story she said I was daft, that I'd been working at the clinic so long I was getting like the patients.'

'Following this delivery, I believe there were others?'

'Oh yes! Every week things came: books, pictures, musical instruments. Miss Alton sent the doctor all the things that had been stolen from him in the war. It was to show her appreciation, Dr Neustadt said.'

'And you saw all those things with your own eyes?'

'Not exactly, sir, I just took in the containers, saw what was written on the outside, signed for them and had them put where the doctor wanted. I never unpacked anything. I don't go rummaging about in other people's belongings.'

'Did Dr Neustadt remark on Miss Alton's generosity?'

'He told me it wasn't a question of generosity, said he and Miss Alton gave back to one another what they could of the past.'

'And what did you understand by this enigmatic reply?'

'I didn't, sir.'

'Nor, may I say, do I.'

'But he made a point of always telling me what was in the containers. Said there were sights and sounds and places, not to mention treasure. There was no point in my looking into these crates. I wouldn't have recognised such things. You see, sir, I have very little in the way of knowledge: I had no education. I needed the good doctor to explain things. On one occasion he told me about trees turned into ordinary men and women, and wild creatures that gave birth to human babies. There is nothing that's impossible, he told me. He and Miss Alton had experienced wonders.'

The coroner's thoughts derail. Hodge's testimony has moved him by a frank simplicity that delivers much more than words. It arouses in him memories of what had been of substance in his own life many years ago – and what might have been. Who and what is this decent man whose youth has been devoured by the enemies of war and whose adulthood confined to the soiled streets and mephetic fumes of west London, among the destitute and insane? Like himself, would Hodges not have been better served returned to his long lost peasant roots, that of bodger or charcoal-burner, farm labourer with time to hang on a five-barred gate to watch the horses stamp the ground? He, too, might well have been open to the messages of nature.

The tick-tock of the clock asserts its influence and the coroner casts his attention back to his list of questions.

'And now we must come to that sad day in November. Would you kindly explain, clearly and accurately, what it was you experienced?'

'I came into the clinic as usual at seven o'clock, but as soon as I turned the key and stepped into my lodge I knew there was something had happened, something not right, you could say.'

'Different?'

'Yes, sir, very different in the atmosphere. It was all quite dead.'

'Was that not the usual atmosphere you experienced first thing in the morning, before the patients and the doctors arrived?'

'No, sir, that is, not since Miss Alton and her presents for the doctor started coming. I'd turn the key and get the sweet scent of spices and the gentle sounds of music and all about me a friendly presence.'

'What do you mean by "presence"?'

'As if all were in the hands of something that meant well. The morning you are referring to I knew at once all was not well. Something was terribly wrong and bad. The silence was alarming. My first thought was we'd had burglars. Then that there had been a fire or a flood, some accident or other. I got very agitated.'

'What action did you take?'

'I don't remember taking action, sir. I think I might have slowed down a bit and told myself to pull myself together and just carry on as usual. I took the keys from the safe in my lodge, opened up the waiting room and tidied the magazines, watered the rubber plant in the entrance hall, that sort of thing. I just kept to my routine.'

'Very sensible, Hodges. And were you still feeling agitated, as if something dreadful had happened?'

'I certainly was, sir. It was that that made me go and check to see there were no broken windows, no forced doors, no leaking taps, no trouble with the boiler ...'

'And did you find any problems?'

'None, sir. It was that that drove me to climb the stairs right up to the roof. I never go up there normally. The roof's not part of my job. And I certainly wasn't going up there once the containers for Dr Neustadt started to arrive. It would have looked as if I were being nosy.'

'So, most uncharacteristically, Mr Hodges, you went up to the roof that day?'

'I did, sir. And what a shock I got! Never experienced anything like it. There was nothing there! Not a single container! Nothing! Nothing at all.'

'Nothing?'

'Nothing! Just the bare lead spattered with pigeon droppings and the remains of their sodden, empty nests. And, of course, the water tanks. They looked a sight with their insulation escaping. The pigeons use the wool for their nests. I stood up there in a daze, deafened by shrieking traffic. It seems to collect up high in the petrol fumes and soot. I was in a sort of nightmare. I couldn't put things together, I was so confused. What was I going to tell the doctor? Had everything been stolen? I was stuck to the ground, as it were. I wanted to get away, but I couldn't move my feet.'

'For how long were you stuck up there?'

'I couldn't say, sir. It seemed a very long time. Eventually I got my legs working, but I remember I took the lift down. Still very shaken. It was not long after that I heard the unmistakable sound of a British Rail lorry at the gates to the yard. I rushed out to unlock and I could see the driver was the same man as usually came, but he was on his own. He beckoned to me, mouthing he wanted me to give him a hand. Once he'd stopped, I went to the back of the lorry and helped him pull out a long, narrow box addressed to Dr Neustadt. The box wasn't heavy, but it was an awkward shape for one man to handle. I had the driver come and put it down on the carpet in the doctor's room.'

'That was not your usual practice, was it? Do you think you had some premonition of what was in that box?'

'I don't know that I did, sir.'

'Well, in that case, why did you not have it sent up to the roof as you had done with the other deliveries?'

'It must have been because of what I'd seen. The roof looked so ugly, so dirty and deserted. And there may have been robberies up there and it may have gone missing like the rest. Anyhow, I wouldn't have wanted the good doctor to have seen such desolation.'

'Once the box was in the doctor's room, did it occur to you to lift the lid to see what was there?'

'It did. I wanted to drive out the horrible thoughts that were coming to mind, so I reminded myself of a patient who always came to the clinic carrying a violin case with him. It turned out that there was no violin, just his washing. It was something along those lines I was hoping for.'

'But in your heart you knew otherwise?'

'I did, sir.'

'And subsequently the police were called and you were interviewed over the course of several days and, therefore, in much greater detail than we have had time for today?'

'Yes, sir.'

'I want you to know, Mr Hodges, that I am completely satisfied both with your account to the police and what you have reprised here. I am grateful to you for the straightforward manner in which you have accounted to me. Court Dismissed!'

The Life She Chose

Miss Paternoster had made a life for herself and sighed the way some do when they experience a feeling of deep satisfaction.

The injury benefit was derisory, but together with her pension and the money left from the sale of her mother's house it was adequate; she had never been a spender. Of course, had she not suffered the accident, had she been able to work until she was sixty, she would have been better off. On the other hand, she might have become too frail to have taken on this sort of life.

Isolation – the enchantment of solitude – had always attracted her. Perhaps it was a reaction to the pressure of her dual role as public servant from ten to five and domestic drudge from six to nine. The non-stop obligation to be at the beck and call of an increasingly ill-mannered adult public at the library was one thing, but she had not contracted to bear the cacophony produced by the mothers-and-toddlers mornings. Nor had she bargained for her own ageing mother's needs. In her mind's eye she saw the look of relief on

165

the carer's face when she got back to take over from her. She barely had time to take off her coat before resuming the roles of cook, gardener, electrician and financial manager.

Mrs Paternoster had married late and been surprised to produce a daughter at the age of forty. Mr Paternoster, a traveller in malt vinegar, died not long after in a pub in Blackpool – in the company, if not the arms, of a trapeze artist. A combination of financial deprivation and social humiliation had combined to transform his ordinarily sociable wife into a reclusive widow. Whilst not being unkind to her daughter, she became distracted, indifferent, incurious, fearful and dependent. She was overwhelmed by the sense of things at an end, indeed that the end of her own life had arrived, and was resentful to have to carry on as if it had merely entered another phase. The word 'end' took on a significance it had not previously borne, and haunted her as she repeatedly intoned her fear of not being able to make ends meet, her regret as to the end of visits to the cinema, her sorrow that a death blow had been dealt to her plans for the garden and sabotaged any future day trips to the coast. The widow Paternoster had reached a terminus from which all outbound transport had been cancelled, yet she was obliged to journey on.

She pressed her bookish daughter into taking a Saturday job as a helper in the local branch library. She nagged the shy girl to apply herself diligently, so that she would be kept on when she left St Mary the Virgin at sixteen. Miss Paternoster had been kept on – for thirty years – when she slipped from a ladder in the stacks and did something to her back. Eventually, after days sitting in hospital waiting rooms, she was advised that nothing much could be done for her slightly awkward gait and her pain. She should not, however, carry weights or stand for hours on end. Such restrictions being incompatible with work in a library, Miss Paternoster found herself invalided out of her job.

The widow trembled with anxiety; she could not tolerate the strain of seeing her daughter, her support, at an end of her own, without salary or prospects. She indicated that her curtains should be drawn against the light, she resisted solids, she stopped speaking: she was at the end of her tether. She died.

The future for Miss Paternoster had never looked more promising.

As a girl, Miss P had been introduced to the pleasures of outdoor life under canvas, to sausages charred over an open fire, to the fleeting sight of deer hiding stock still in the forest, and to the sound of the dawn chorus. But these delights had been taken *en masse* with the Guides, in suburban Epping and Burnham Beeches, and lacked an essential quality for which the young girl yearned, but which she failed to identify. As soon as her school days were over, however, she abandoned the Guides and pursued a course of her own. Her library contract had entitled her to three breaks a year. While her mother was alive, she devoted the Christmas break to her, but not the Easter or summer holidays. Those she guarded jealously to explore places as remote as her meagre earnings would allow. She filled a rucksack with a one-person tent, a primus stove, a sleeping bag and little else. She took the train, stashing her bicycle in the guard's van and making for those areas of England lacking main roads, with towns widely spaced, wooded countryside and snow-capped mountains.

It was on one such summer's break – long before her accident and her mother's death – that she had happened upon the abandoned croft choked with ivy and buddleia which, transformed, had provided her with the home in which she now exalted, in which she led the life she chose. Year after year, she had returned to the deserted croft and set up her tent in the open beside its walls when the weather was clement, and when the weather turned wet and the wind gusted she pushed inside to sleep on the mud floor. She sensed the place welcoming and the landscape familiar, as if she had known it in a previous life, or in a dream.

The croft stood overlooking sheep-cropped grass and a track that led down to a farm two miles away and on to a river. Behind, it was overseen by swollen hills that sheltered a sable tarn and above them rocky, slate-grey mountains. This was silent country: no trains, no overflying aircraft, the nearest market town ten miles west. Apart from the sheep, the night owls, the flights of migrating geese, an occasional dog bark and the weekly rattle of the farmer engaging second gear to climb the track on his way to the market, there was little to interrupt the serenity.

Miss Paternoster brought nothing from a life desiccated in duty into her new life. A new immigrant bought number 23 Butt Villas but rejected its contents. These Miss P. consigned to Mr Crump, the man who cleared houses. As with the house and its contents, there was nothing in Miss Paternoster's emotional or physical past worth preserving and examining. The past, threadbare, disintegrated and turned to dust along with the contents of Butt Villas, which Mr Crump deposited on the pavements of south London.

—

Miss Paternoster had never been warm enough in Butt Villas. The musty-smelling kitchen had been damp and steamy, the heat from the four-bar electric fire in the front room burnt her legs to the knee but never penetrated her body, and when she bound her arms about her chest and shuddered with the chill her mother advised her to go and fetch her cardy. The coat she wore from September to May had been ample enough to accommodate the extra sweaters demanded by mid-winter, but it was permeable. Her bedroom, with its linoleum floor covering and small rag rug by the side of the bed, was frigid throughout the year; the windows did not fit tight and the rotting gutters caused damp in one corner. She always took a hot water bottle to bed, but often in the small hours woke cold under the lean army blankets to which, for some unexplained reason, her mother seemed to owe some loyalty. When one Christmas she had suggested to the widow that they might exchange them for thick Witney blankets, the widow shook from the shoulder in her alarm.

All unnecessary expense had been anathema to her, an aversion that extended to the food she provided. In the kitchen, the widow had come to rely almost exclusively on the tin opener and her dexterity in tearing open plastic. Such green vegetables as found their way to the plate did so enfeebled and tasteless, and such fruit, jet-lagged. Since Miss Paternoster's experience of food had been limited to that which her mother provided, that which the dinner ladies at St-Mary-the-Virgin deemed adequate for the soul if not the body, she herself had developed indifference towards what she ate.

All that had changed now that Miss Paternoster lived the life she had chosen, a state of affairs brought about by her mother's demise, her own financial independence and the cooperation of Mr Tyson, the farmer. He not only sold her Kimble Croft for a modest sum, but arranged to have it made habitable by employing casual labour out of season, and overseeing the work himself.

———

Miss Paternoster's access to books and magazines at work had been a scourge. The sheer quantity of material devoted to the embellishment of life sickened her, its prospects being so unattainable. Added to which she had no need to diet, learn how to pleasure a husband or wean a baby. She had had no leisure in which to acquire a skill, no money to be fashionable. Number 23 Butt Villas, to which Mr and Mrs Paternoster had returned from honeymoon in Brighton, had been in stasis for three-quarters of a century, and glossy magazines illustrating exquisite furnishings were just one in a series of irrelevancies. But once Kimble Croft became Miss Paternoster's own, the scourge became a blessing and the sea-change all-embracing; she went from an absence of comfort and a denial of pleasure to a consummate surveillance of both. Having pursued the life of an automaton in the past, it was inevitable that now she would programme herself just as closely.

During the first year of the life she had chosen, Miss P. applied herself to equipping the croft and her own wardrobe with beautiful, functional things. Expeditions on foot and cycle were made feasible by her choices: a mountain bicycle and specialized climbing boots and clothes. And so she rejoiced in every aspect of the weather, glad to hear the wind moan and to receive icy blasts that starched her face, amused by the little gusts that in their agitation threw up mud. She welcomed the impenetrable walls of rain and mist that made her feel more estranged than ever. As for the snow that laid siege to the croft, she regarded it as a comfort blanket and rejoiced in hibernation. Her senses were becoming increasingly acute: she watched, she listened, she breathed in the scents of the land. She was intoxicated. In the sanctity of the croft she read the books she had once avoided and listened to the music her mother had outlawed, finding it too searing in her widowhood.

The only person with whom she kept up some contact was the farmer, Mr Tyson, from whom she regularly bought her milk, butter and eggs and the occasional old hen for the pot. From time to time, Mr Tyson would provide a trout he had fished or offer her half a lamb from his flock. Miss Paternoster understood that being like her, isolated, the farmer was no more fluent in conversation than she. Out of embarrassment, he would occasionally detain her in small talk by mentioning that someone had arrived to help with the sheep, service his truck, or that the weather was turning, but once she had paid him for what she owed, both were ready to take their leave.

It was some years into her new life that Miss Paternoster became fascinated by the riverbed to the far east, for there she had been rewarded by the sight of an otter with an eel in its mouth. Not knowing that this was a rare sighting, she returned to the same spot time and again at the same hour in the expectation of seeing the otter again.

On a later afternoon, she made another unusual sighting: a man decidedly not the farmer, picking wild watercress. Was he, she wondered, the casual labourer working for Mr Tyson? Because the track to the croft only continued its way down to the farm, it was rare to see anyone further east, for all that lay that way before the rise of Great Hill was Great Wood. She feared wild boar and snakes and something incorporeal she could not name, and she always skirted its boundaries, keeping to the narrow path that circled the trees and gave way to pasture. One autumn, under an unexpectedly warm sun, she had seen a herd of deer leave the security of the wood to graze on the soft ground of succulent shoots at the fringe.

It was winter, and Miss Paternoster knew how to prepare for it. Once the land and its boundaries were whited out, she would not need her bicycle, and so she oiled it, stood it at the back of the barn and threw a tarpaulin over it. She counted the logs stacked in perfect alignment and checked to see the roof was weatherproof. She counted her stores and drew up a final list of what she would need to see her through the months of siege.

Since her first sighting of the man who was not the farmer, Miss Paternoster found herself looking out for him, catching a fleeting glance of him on the fells, emerging from the farm with a cup of something, fishing, and once carrying a rabbit and some wire from the trap he must have set. Her curiosity upset her composure; she was not accustomed to being invaded by speculation. So, too, did her physical reaction, for on catching sight of the man a peculiar sensation gripped her stomach, combusted her cheeks and weakened her knees. It was as if some spell had been cast. Mr Tyson did not volunteer any information about the man and she did not like to ask, although she thought she remembered his mentioning that he could not afford to keep him on. He was clearly not lodging at the farm. Where else was there for him to shelter?

Miss Paternoster had made no practical changes in the life she had chosen in spite of which she noticed that the tone of her life had subtly altered, as if a small corner had been lifted to expose a deficiency. Until recently, she had been utterly content, all her desires met in the croft and its arrangement, her excursions, and her deep submission to the books she read and the music to which she listened. She had never had cause to ask herself what more there was to hope for.

But now, quite suddenly, her sleep was interrupted, she was made anxious by the sobbing wind and the creaking in the old timbers. She would rise in the small hours and look out with awe on the empty pasture, the overpowering black mountain range and the infinite sky. Soon the snows would arrive.

One evening she did not go to bed, but sat in the dark at the kitchen window, wrapped in a blanket. She felt as bleached as the moonlit landscape. Towards the end of night, her attention was caught by a shadow moving at the far end of the barn. Probably a vagrant sheep; sometimes one or two sheltered there when they got separated from the flock. She dressed early and went to investigate. There, thrown across some bales of straw, she found a thin, dirty army blanket.

Late that afternoon, as Miss Paternoster prepared her food, she made enough for two and left one portion in the barn by the side of the straw bales. When she was ready to go upstairs to bed, she bolted the back door, as she always did, then paused before slipping back the bolt and leaving the door on the latch.

Take Care

Every morning, the second thing Reg did (the first being to take Maisie a cup of tea in bed) was to collect the rubbish from the grass struggling to survive outside their pre-fab, and give the windows a shine. The third was to wipe the plaque at the side of the front door registering the history of Winston's Harrowton. Reg was proud that it was his of the four prefabs still standing which had been chosen to display this commemorative tablet, and he kept it clean and polished whatever the depredations it suffered.

Anyone watching the couple cross the wasteland enroute for the shops or the dance-hall or on any other of their little forays, might have registered the gender of the two but not the sex. There was nothing of the woman evident in Maisie, nor of the man in Reg. They seemed to have had the qualities involved in such distinctions ironed out, had they ever existed. They moved in tandem, like synchronised swimmers.

The routine in the Brunts' life was immutable. Without consulting a clock or calendar, each knew instinctively the day of the week and the time of the day and what they should be doing. And because it was Wednesday or Sunday, or any other day between the first and last of the week, what they should be eating and to what chores they should be attending. They allowed themselves to be carried through life hand in hand, underreacting on a reliable tide of habit.

It had been the same throughout their employment at the builders: Reg as stores' manager – always dressed in a cinnamon-coloured calico overall – and Maisie in accounts. 'They're alike as two peas in a pod,' some said, others – more demotically – 'two buttocks on a single backside'. Reg's thoughts were conditioned by what the TV brought into the home, the weather, and the dailyness of the soaps, which coincided with the dailyness of their own life. Neither he nor Maisie had any idea that other people lived otherly: only celluloid people, not real people like themselves. True, there were those with a lot more money, but even they had to get up in the morning, prepare for work, work, return home, eat and sleep. They had no more time than ordinary people had. 'That's what it's about, isn't it Maisie.' Neither had any curiosity; their education had done nothing to stimulate or inform them, only to ensure that they 'knew their place'. Reg spent too much time polishing the commemorative plaque, and Maisie on ironing tea towels – being normal, like everyone else. They shared their flavourless existence unimpeded by ambition.

The long, unpleasant path they had to tread to the shops was one made by their own feet disturbing the rubble. It led north for a quarter of a mile to Fish 'n' Chips, the sub-post office and the Co-op (Alex's Discount Store, where they bought the plastic flowers for their window box, had closed), and south to the bridge over the canal and a view of Badger's

Green. Occasionally, they idled uncertainly across the bridge to the High Street beyond the Green, but the shops which served the residents of Badger's Green did not stock the provisions the Brunts required – indeed several shops sold vegetables they had never heard of – and it was all a bit quiet, they found.

'What are we going to do?' Maisie was crestfallen. It was Thursday – fish day – but a notice on the window of Fish 'n' Chips announced that DUE TO REDEVELOPMENT THE SHOP WILL BE CLOSED FROM MARCH AND WILL NOT REOPEN. WE WOULD LIKE TO TAKE THIS OPPORTUNITY TO THANK OUR CUSTOMERS FOR THEIR LOYAL SUPPORT.

'What d'you think, Reg?' They sat on the bench in front of the boarded shop until they agreed that Thursday would never be the same again, and would have to become ham day. 'Won't be the same, of course.'

'Ah, well, there's worst in Russia,' Maisie said, adding, 'I hope the post office's still there!' They chortled together at the thought of the post office not being there.

'What do you make of it all?' They opened their shocked conversation with Marjory, the sub-postmistress, who already that morning had several times rehearsed her own shock and disappointment with the changes taking place.

'That nice Mr Barton – been here since the estate was built – given no alternative but to go!' Neither Maisie nor Reg had letters to post (it wasn't Christmas) but did as they always did on a Thursday and withdrew ten pounds from their Post Office Savings, and then went to consult the board on which locals left messages, people who seemed to spend their lives buying and selling their belongings, getting their dogs walked and learning foreign languages! The Brunts chewed over these requests and consulted one another about them, as they did the adverts in the *Harrowton Gazette*. They were much more taken by the adverts than by the dramas in the body of the paper. 'Did you notice the card at the bottom from Take Care?' Marjory called out. 'I think you'd be perfect for that now you've got the time.'

It was not long before Saturday was demolished for them: the pensioners' hall was closed, prior to demolition, and bingo went the way the fish had gone. Thursdays and Saturdays had become a hollow maw. What next, they asked? Their question was soon answered: the Phoenix was to be redeveloped to become a six-screen multiplex and until such time as the modernisation was completed, it would be closed.

'There go our Mondays!' Reg said, remembering lovely afternoons sitting close to Maisie in the warm, with a bag of popcorn and a view into the extraordinary lives Americans led.

———

The card Marjory had mentioned was one pinned up by Take Care, a local charity that relied for its existence upon voluntary workers and a small grant from the Rotary Club. Their brief: to identify the old and lonely abandoned in Winston's Harrowton, isolated in the cracks between the new high-rise flats, the council offices, estate agents and banks. Marjory, always in the know regarding local matters, was keen to offer information about a particular case. 'There's a nice lady living behind the Green, a Miss Corringer. She used to be Head of the primary school. I've heard she's a bit lonely, needs company, can't get about with her leg, always forgetting things, sometimes imagines she should be in Australia. I think they have her in mind.'

'Sounds a bit posh for us,' Reg said.

Maisie bit her lip, consulted the floor and agreed. 'Mm,' she said.

'Well, you think about it!' Marjory said. 'Shall I give the lady at Take Care your particulars?'

'What d 'you think Reg?'

'Well, I'm not sure.'

'Me neither,' Maisie said.

———

Harrowton had been a prize-winning development in the 1930s, recognised as an architectural model owing its inspiration to Voysey. However, situated as it was in northeast London, it had not qualified as a priority for redevelopment when hostilities ceased. Instead, hurried use was made of the availability of German and Italian prisoners of war to erect an estate of prefabs, where the mains electricity, gas and water of Old Harrowton could be accessed. Each little factory-built house was set down on a concrete slab, where it was allowed a three-foot surround of grass to separate it from its neighbour. One could not have called the result aesthetically pleasing, but each house had a bathroom and a separate lavatory (something few council tenants had enjoyed pre-war) and, as an imaginative response to need, brought with it something of the indomitable spirit of the

Britain that had won the war. The estate enjoyed the blessing of Winston Churchill himself, and so it was that Old
Harrowton was renamed Winston's Harrowton.

It was not until well into the 1970s when the prefabs, put
up to last one year, yet still looking sound and well maintained
by residents who were thought to love their detached houses,
attracted the displeasure of local councillors determined to
effect a redevelopment of the estate and bring glory upon
themselves for their initiative. After all, this part of London
had once been internationally revered and students had come
from as far away as Africa to see what was being done for the
bombed-out homeless.

Councillors convened meetings, distributed leaflets and
consulted residents of Winston's Harrowton, in fact only to
reinforce decisions previously agreed. Developers in cahoots
with the council had by now got the go-ahead to raze the
estate to the ground.

On the far side of the canal, Badger's Green, fringed
with Georgian houses neglected pre-war for their location
on the wrong side of the city and within sight of industrial
buildings, had been discovered by a new breed of architects,
university teachers and solicitors. They restored these houses,
some by their own labour, determined to maintain the vestiges
of what remained of a village atmosphere. On learning what
was being planned for redevelopment across the canal, they
were torn: on the one hand, some of the architects would
no doubt find employment with the developers, would take
part in the design of modern glass and steel buildings, and
the solicitors on the conveyancing. On the other hand, razing
the prefabs to the ground was unthinkable: they had been an

important contribution to Britain's housing supply and their simple design and study build deserved better. Something had to be done to conserve them, not all of them, but certainly a sample.

Their lively conservation society approached the council, only to discover that the council had interest in the preservation of neither prefabs nor their inhabitants. One joker went so far as to suggest that the prefabs and their occupants be loaded onto lorries and deposited in a field somewhere. 'Anywhere. But far from here!'

The conservationists had meanwhile discovered a loop-hole in the planning law, ascribed to Winston himself: it forbade the council from evicting anyone from a prefab on Winston's Harrowton without their agreement. At once they put together a team of researchers to visit every householder on the estate to ascertain who would be willing to move into a high rise block with modern bathroom and separate lavatory, fully equipped kitchen and underfloor heating, and who would not. They were in for a surprise: all but three households took the carrot. Among those who did not were Maisie and Reginald Brunt. 'No, we don't like change,' they said. 'We're used to being here.'

It was put to them conscientiously that only a handful of others were of the same mind. Would they not feel marooned? 'You won't have your paper shop or your pub while the site is being cleared. The market will go! All your nice little shops will go. And they won't come back. They won't be able to afford the rents. All you'll be left with is Tesco's!'

Perhaps it was that they refused to be threatened, or was it that they could not imagine themselves in a future that was unlike the past? In the event, numbers 31-34 Winston's Harrowton were conserved, while all the paraphernalia of demolition took place around them. There was deafening noise from pneumatic drills and diggers, and danger from cranes depositing blocks of concrete. Clouds of dust filled the air from the stream of lorries coming and going. There was the constant stench of chemicals, the removal of familiar landmarks such as the telephone and post boxes, and, to top it all, interruptions from the labourers requesting use of their bathroom.

Maisie and Reg did wonder whether, since these new conditions were not ones to which they were used, they were going to be able to endure them. 'There's nothing we can do about it, dear!' Reg said. 'I suppose it can't last forever. And then we'll be back to normal.' Maisie agreed. Nearly all their conversations led into a cul de sac.

———

Rhoda George knocked on the Brunts' front door, said she had heard about them from the sub-postmistress and asked if she might pop in for a moment? There being no way that Maisie could think of to keep Miss George out, she let her in.

Rhoda George followed Maisie into the sitting room, looked about her and registered plain, clean surroundings accompanied by the mingled scents of pine lavatory cleaner and washing-up powder. Most satisfactory!

'I've got the kettle on,' Maisie said, 'would you like a cup of tea?' Rhoda said she would, if that was no trouble, and as Maisie returned to the kitchen, Reg, who had been doing the pools on the kitchen table, got up from his chair and commented to Rhoda how changeable the weather was, and she answered him with regrets that Fish 'n' Chips had closed.

'Yes, it's meant we've had to change our routine,' he said.

'And so do you have Thursdays free now?' Rhoda tried.

'Oh, no, it's not that. It's just that it's had to become our ham day.'

Rhoda said she understood, although she hardly did. She would need to check with Marjory.

Two weeks later, on a Monday, Maisie and Reg were waiting in the kitchen for Rhoda to come and show them the way to Miss Corringer's. Maisie was wearing her pale blue polyester dress and matching coat, the hat she had bought for the foreman's wedding and a pair of beige cotton gloves, Reg his only suit and well-polished shoes. 'Now Reg, go careful on the Brylcreem!'

'I thought you might like to take these to Miss Corringer!' Rhoda said, handing Maisie a bunch of daffodils. 'I'm just going to show you her road and then I'll disappear. She knows you're coming.'

Victoria Terrace, a row of ten five-storied houses, stood to attention in conformity. Only the so-called front gardens, a matter of three square yards to the right of the steps leading to the front door, identified differences in the character, the ethnic origin, social status, even the health of the inhabitants. And this they achieved with greater accuracy than any written report could have.

Miss Corringer's pebbled plot was enclosed in laurel gloom. Industrious Victorian builders would have applauded her attention to the damp course, the unblocked gutters and repaired grouting. Today's passers-by would register only her dustbins and the absence of ornament and embellishment: no window box, no potted plant, no stone animal or bird, no colour, no scent, nothing for the bee to buzz about, no turned earth for the blackbird to explore, no berries for the sparrows, but a place of solid, silent resentment, reminiscent of a chapel cemetery. It takes a particularly unseeing individual to live enclosed by laurel, and this cheerlessness carried itself beyond the stained steps to the painted front door on which the flaked black paint revealed that once, in happier times, the door had been dressed in primrose yellow.

Reg reached the door and then stood back. Keeping his feet planted a yard from the threshold, he bent forward from the waist, extended his arm and rang the bell. Maisie pressed her face into the daffodils. Hand in hand they made to step away from the door but immediately found themselves in danger of toppling back down the steps. They shuffled their feet and repositioned themselves.

Moments passed. From behind the door came the sound of locks unlatching, bolts withdrawing and a chain swinging. The door opened a crack. 'Ah! You must be Mr and Mrs Blunt,' Miss Corringer noticed. Neither Reg nor Maisie thought fit to correct her. 'You've come to tea, haven't you?' and she opened the door a little wider to allow the Brunts to enter the half-dark hall.

Tea had been laid on a mahogany table in the parlour. 'Oo, isn't it lovely!' As it was a round table, Maisie did not know where she was meant to sit.

'Yes, it is lovely,' Miss Corringer agreed. 'That's why my parents left everything exactly as their parents left it to them. Of course, they put in electricity, but they never bothered with a refrigerator; no need for it in this climate, they always said, seeing the lovely larder we have. I'll show you later.'

Maisie sat on the edge of her seat, fingering the napkin to the side of her plate. Reg tried his best to drink his tea noiselessly. Both refused the Eccles cakes, which might have led to crumbs, but accepted a Bourbon cream.

'I don't get out much these days,' Miss Corringer said, and Reg explained that since all the changes, neither did they.

'Do you have to visit the hospital?' Miss Corringer asked.

'Oh, no, nothing like that!' Reg said.

'I go quite a lot, what with my leg ... and my memory,' Miss Corringer said. 'Would you believe it? I can't remember what happened yesterday! Something surely did, but I've no idea what. Yesterdays are finished for me. But I'm fine on the dim past: Mum and Dad, the war, sleeping on the Tube platform, rationing and the children. I remember all of that.'

'The children?'

'Yes, my pupils. I'll show you their drawings after tea.' Miss Corringer pushed back her chair, and hanging on to a solid surface to her side, used both her hands to lift her right leg to an upright position. Her sticks, which she had hung on the back of her chair, fell to the ground. Reg dived to retrieve them.

All the while Maisie sat at tea, she itched to turn her head to examine the contents of the parlour. But she felt it might be rude, and that she should be attending to what Miss Corringer had to say and finding something suitable to say back. However, even by keeping her face firmly fixed on Miss Corringer's, she was able to catch sight of an array of objects from the corner of her eye. Miss Corringer's parlour was like an antiques shop; the curtains made from heavy magenta velour held back by fringed swags, the doorstop a large white china King Charles spaniel, the brass lamps with shades from which coloured glass baubles hung. Each table – and there were three – was covered with little papier-mâché boxes in various sizes, with Tunbridge ware, glass scent bottles, card holders, ink bottles … There was a tall candle stand with a rubber plant atop, a fire screen decorated with a child's sampler and on the chaise longue, cushions covered in petit point. But for all the colour in the objects, the cold dust of time subdued it and the room was half dark, although it was only four o'clock on a late March afternoon. Maisie was not at all sure she liked the dim. It was a bit gloomy, but it was also a little mysterious: was it really fitting to have a donkey on wheels alongside these valuable antiques? She wanted to ask Reg what he thought, but it was impossible to compare notes just then. Anyhow, she was quite sure he would be asking himself the same questions she was asking herself.

Miss Corringer appeared more at ease in the sitting room than in the parlour. She tumbled into a large winged chair, hoisted her right leg on to a leather pouf and motioned to Maisie and Reg to sit down. 'You see!' Miss Corringer said, pointing with one of her sticks, 'my children's works.' Maisie and Reg followed the arc of her stick. They were dumbstruck, even horrified. What was there to say about daubs of paint on pieces of torn paper Sello-taped to the wall of such a beautiful room where, in pride of place, hung a photograph of the Queen?

'Proper little artists!' Miss Corringer purred with the pride normally reserved for birth parents. 'Of course, it was all beaten out of them as soon as they got to secondary school. Artists,' she continued, warming to her theme, 'should not attend secondary school.'

Once again, neither Brunt had anything to offer in response to this point of view, and each continued to stare speechless at the walls.

'And I'll tell you another thing. In my opinion, some of my children could have become famous artists if they'd been given the opportunity.'

'And would that have been a good thing? Would they have earned a lot of money?'

'It would have been a very good thing, my dear, even if they had not earned a lot of money.'

'Well,' said Reg, 'one can get along without much, can't one?'

'Indeed one can!' said Miss Corringer, with applause in her voice.

'May I ask you something?' Maisie tried.

'Yes, what is it?'

'Would you like to go to the seaside?'

———

Several Monday visits followed, on each of which Miss Corringer led the Brunts to another room in her house. First the kitchen, and then the larder that led from it and was icy cold 'even in a heatwave, but we don't get many of those, do we?' In her mother's and her grandmother's day, the slate shelves had been lined with bottled fruit, vegetables and jam. Today there was a sole bottle of milk and a packet of Flora on the nearest shelf, and nothing on any of the others. 'Since my retirement, I seem to have lost my appetite,' Miss Corringer confided uncertainly. 'I used to have my midday meal at the school – sometimes I would take it with the children. A nice woman who worked in the kitchen made me sandwiches to take home for the evening,' she added, and, having said that, with the glimmer of a smile on her face, Miss Corringer mumbled to herself about forgetting to eat, forgetting most else, regretting the past, losing her friends and being alone.

Maisie and Reg felt they should not be listening to such private matters; it was like reading someone's letters, they agreed, when sharing their thoughts about Miss Corringer later in the privacy of their own sitting room.

Miss Corringer did not appear much interested in Maisie and Reg other than in their role as listeners. Her subject was the past, which for her went back to her grandparents' time and forward to her time with the infants. But even her professional life left craters of time forgotten. Whereas this in no way disturbed Reg and Maisie, it clearly upset Miss Corringer, who felt she had died several times in the course of her life. For her, remembering was living, forgetting a sort of death.

'I am sure you would like to see the upstairs!' Miss Corringer's assault on the stairs was ungainly and would have aroused merriment in a watching child, but for Maisie and Reg it produced embarrassment. When Miss Corringer was not mumbling, she was grunting, particularly when obliged to make some physical effort, such as raising her right leg to a standing position, mounting a step or hauling it on to a pouf. At other times, seated comfortably with a cup of tea and a biscuit, she seemed perfectly normal – a rather superior woman. A lady, not the sort of person with whom it had been the Brunts' habit to take tea in the past.

The Monday following Miss Corringer's invitation to the Brunts to view the bedroom and bathroom on the first floor left the pair uneasy: why did Miss Corringer have such a huge bed? It occupied half the room and was covered in several lush oriental bedspreads in glaring and contrasting colours with embroidered birds, flowers and leafy trees dipping their fragile branches in streams of undulating water. Miss Corringer parked her sticks in a great Chinese vase to the side of the bed, took one of the covers into her hands and threw it over her arms: 'See,' she said, 'how wonderfully the Chinese depict their land! I wonder, is it that theirs is so much more beautiful than ours, or do they use their eyes to greater effect?'

Neither Maisie nor Reg felt able to say.

'Some of my children saw our world as beautiful,' she said. 'You must look more closely at their pictures and you will see what we adults ignore.'

'You have a very large bed,' Reg observed.

'Yes,' Miss Corringer agreed, making the small affirmative longer than its three letters.

'I've never seen a mirror like that one before!' Maisie exclaimed, pointing to a cheval looking-glass.

'They were quite popular years ago,' Miss Corringer said, adding that their great virtue was in reflecting the whole of one's self.

'Oo, I don't know about that!' Maisie giggled. She looked at fat Miss Corringer with her unresponsive leg, her brown-grey bun with its pins sticking out in all directions, her petticoats leaking from her dirndl skirt. Perhaps Miss Corringer no longer used the mirror.

Two sides of the bedroom were lined with floor-to-ceiling wardrobes. Miss Corringer threw open their doors to show Maisie her collection of clothes. 'I have kept the nicest from my earliest days to the day I gave up teaching,' and she pulled from their hangers little girls' smocks, ball gowns in shot silk cut on the cross, country tweeds, waxed jackets and school uniforms, and from drawers and shelves patent leather pumps, long fishing boots, embroidered evening bags, kid gloves, and all manner of other accessories. While Maisie gasped at the extent and variety of Miss Corringer's wardrobe, Miss Corringer, in something of a trance, described salmon fishing in Scotland, balls in country places, playing centre forward for the Bucks Ladies' hockey team (of which she had been captain), how her mother bought Liberty prints and smocked them for her daughter, and how she had always dressed with care in her role as headmistress so that 'my children had a good role model. Their mothers were not always so careful, you see.'

Meanwhile, Reg stood at the window and looked out on the row of well-tended back gardens, with their budding lilacs and laburnums, their birdbaths and feeding tables, potting sheds and neatly stacked piles of logs. 'Do you lay a log fire in winter?' he asked, not because he was interested in whether Miss Corringer did or did not, but because he thought it time he entered the conversation.

'Not now. I wouldn't be able to carry the logs. But in the past …' And having introduced the Brunts to every piece of furniture in her bedroom, and shown how the plum of the paint on the walls was picked up in the William Morris curtains, which she had felt free to choose herself 'once Mother had gone', she led them into the bathroom. An old, stained bathtub stood at the centre of the green linoleum-covered floor. Brass taps and a long brass stopper excited the attention of both the Brunts.

'That's an old one if ever I saw it!' Reg exclaimed.

'And still performs very well indeed!' Miss Corringer was quick to add.

Reg examined the furniture: a white-painted, free-standing cupboard, a wood towel-rail to match, an airing cupboard built round the water tank, a couple of wicker armchairs and a foot rest and a wicker table piled with magazines.

'I've never seen chairs and things put in a bathroom!' Maisie said.

'Well, there's not room in ours,' Reg explained quickly, in an effort to prevent his wife's observation being taken as criticism.

'I like a nice long rest after a nice long soak.' Miss Corringer's expression was wistful as she gazed at the wicker chairs. She hesitated before them as if considering whether to sit down, but before reaching a decision she gave way to impenetrable low mutterings. She led the Brunts downstairs again, but as the last to leave her bedroom and close the door behind him, Reg noticed that there were further doors up a single flight of stairs on a half landing.

'Are there more bedrooms?' he asked.

Miss Corringer turned to face him. 'Oh yes, of course. We had to have somewhere for Uncle Harry when he visited. You see, he lived in Australia. Came over every summer. That was long ago. Must have been before the war, when I was a child. Then there's my assistant's flat in the attic, at the top.

We won't go there.' Miss Corringer clutched the bannister. She had started to shudder. She let out a persistent, drawn-out moan and slowly slid from a bent standing position to sit on the stairs. She covered her face with both her hands, letting her sticks tumble from reach. 'Oh dear! Oh dear! Oh my! All so long ago, the past! Did it happen? Does it matter? Pain! Such pain!'

Miss Corringer's behaviour – her sudden expressions of intense pleasure and unbearable pain following quickly one after the other, her forgetfulness in not being able to recount for what happened yesterday, but being able to reconstruct whole passages of time before World War Two – led Reg and Maisie to regard her as not normal, even slightly mad. There had to be some explanation!

'Would you like to go to the seaside one day?' Maisie asked Miss Corringer, by way of a change in the conversation, and not for the first time. The old lady had not replied to her previous question on the matter. Whether she had not heard Maisie, or whether she had not wanted to commit herself was hard to gauge, and so Maisie risked another attempt.

This time, Miss Corringer, rousing herself from the torture of the past, said she would like to, 'very much. And let us have crab sandwiches!'

At home, the Brunts discussed the forthcoming expedition. 'It's going to be quite expensive.' Maisie tucked her knitting under her arm to give her whole attention to the subject.

'Don't you worry, dear,' Reg said. 'We can manage, and a breath of sea air will do your chest a power of good, clear your lungs and that.'

Maisie fell to remembering the old days, when they were young and took their annual week's holiday in lodgings in Birchington, a quiet spot rather like Walmington-on-Sea. Before the war, when the sun used to shine from dawn till dusk in summer. 'Supposing her leg gives up, how would we manage?'

Reg needed time for that one. Luckily for him, this mulling over of a thorny topic was interrupted by a knock on the door. It was Rhoda George.

'May I come in?' she asked, one foot already placed firmly on the mat. 'Just passing, thought I'd drop in and see how you and Miss Corringer were getting along.'

Maisie moved into the kitchen to put the kettle on, leaving Reg to deal with Miss George.

'Very well indeed, thank you. We're going to Brighton together next week.'

'And whose idea was that?'

'It was Maisie's.'

'Well done, Maisie! And what was Miss Corringer's response?'

'Something about crab sandwiches, I think.'

'I shouldn't worry about that, she'll probably have forgotten by the time you get there. I don't think Brighton's celebrated for crab sandwiches anyhow. I suggest you head for fish and chips at Cod's Wallop. It's somewhat off the beaten track. Then, when you want to get down to the beach to paddle, leave her on a bench on the promenade with the paper. Don't let her think of moving onto the pebbles, or she'll fall and you'll never get her up!'

———

Miss Corringer said she had done no travelling for years. She asked Maisie what she should wear and what she should take along. She showed Maisie the suitcase she was preparing to pack.

'I don't think you'll need that. Just your usual bag and your tablets.'

'Will it be cold?'

'No, I don't think so. They say it'll be warm for the week. But you might take a cardy, just in case.'

'Norfolk's always chilly. There's nothing between the Steppes and the Wash,' Miss Corringer mused.

Reg got out a blue canvas peaked cap, a yellow short-sleeved shirt, brown trousers, white socks and brown sandals. Appraising himself in the looking-glass, he judged himself well prepared. Maisie chose her white cotton dress with printed red poppies and a large white plastic handbag and white sandals with heels. 'You'll not manage the beach with those,' Reg pointed out.

'I'll carry them,' Maisie quickly replied. 'I like them and I don't get much chance to wear them. Look,' she said, twirling a pair of sunglasses on her finger, 'I'm going to wear these, too.'

'You'll look like a film star!' Reg agreed. 'I wonder what she'll wear?'

'Now Reg, you've got to be polite. She's not young and she gets muddled, and she'll probably have something a bit out of date.'

'Yes, that's what I'd been thinking.'

Miss Corringer clearly had no memory of a day's outing at the seaside. However, she did remember that summers were long and that she'd taken them with her assistant in a rented bungalow near Cromer, and because – despite the unfailing sun – the east wind never ceased to blow across the North Sea, they packed for heat and cold. It was the fond memory of those times that had led her to get out the suitcase in preparation for a day in Brighton. And to wear, she chose a full pink skirt on an elastic waist band with a white cotton short-sleeved blouse tucked in, brown lisle stockings and white sandals. Her petticoat trailed under her skirt. Maisie squirmed: should she point this out to Miss Corringer or not? And on her head the old lady fixed a child's cotton hat, perched forward on her forehead, so arranged for her bun to support it. In her out-sized, straw bag she carried boiled sweets for the train.

'The children often get train-sick. They're not used to it, you see.'

'I don't believe the children are coming,' Maisie said.

'Oh well, no matter! We'll enjoy them.' Miss Corringer did not appear unsettled by the absence of the children. 'Sometimes the mothers don't have the fare,' she explained.

They boarded a bus to take them the short distance from the station to the promenade and settled Miss Corringer in one of the shelters overlooking the sea while they went for a paddle. The sea was neither in nor out but poised some thirty feet beyond the shingle and a nice, clean sheet of golden sand. Reg rolled up his trousers and Maisie lifted her skirt to a seemly position just above the knee, and they tested the water hand in hand. Around them, children with buckets and spades tried emptying the Channel, building fortresses to stay its incoming tide and pushing their fellows over while dogs, determined to show off, rushed headlong into the water. Gulls whirled overhead, reconnoitering for picnickers to divebomb.

Miss Corringer, holding tight to her bag and Maisie's, mumbled while staring out to sea. A few elderly couples imagined they could see France and took no notice. 'Beautiful day!' she managed.

'Mm, yes, but it'll rain before long. You mark my words,' an old man observed.

The sun shone, but shyly and not continuously, and a little breeze puckered the incoming tide. The beach was emptying as mothers retrieved children from their pleasures on the grounds that it was time for their dinner. Picnickers sought the protection of the breakwaters. Some of the old folk, who had spent the morning in the shelter, compared notes on fish and chip cafés. Maisie and Reg remembered Rhoda George's advice to search out Cod's Wallop on Fish Street, next to the charity shop in a cul de sac north of the promenade. 'It isn't far, and Reg'll carry your bag.'

Reg pulled open the door and Miss Corringer urged her way in. 'This is perfectly lovely!' she exclaimed. 'Could have been done by children.' She was pointing to the walls, covered with the outline of fish of different colours and sizes on a background of yellow sand, blue sea and red coral. Fish nets had been draped in folds across the decoration and half an old salvaged fishing boat, sliced longitudinally, served to disguise the till. The café was divided into sections by low walls on which menus were displayed, citing everything from cod fillet and mushy peas to fried Mars bars. Fish might be fried, grilled or boiled according to taste, and every Mars, Crunchie and pack of Rolos could be ordered wrapped in pastry or breadcrumbs and fried. Along the length of the waist-high walls stood painted plastic pots filled with artificial fuchsias, begonias, carnations and irises.

Reg pointed Miss Corringer to a place at the back, but she did not move. She stood firm, taking in the décor. 'This is how my children would have done it. It's most artistic!' Maisie was astounded by this reaction, having feared that it might all be a bit too showy for the old lady, and not to her taste. But not at all: she loved it. Eventually, she negotiated her way sideways, between the maze of cubicles fashioned by the low walls, to reach the back where Reg had chosen a banquette and two chairs covered in what had once been red leatherette but was now brown – dirty towards the centre of the seats and beige where the fabric had split with age.

Miss Corringer sank into her place in her usual manner, throwing her painful leg out to her right and letting out a sigh ending in a rattle. A few customers turned to see from where the commotion was coming, but looked away quickly when they identified the source. Miss Corringer's bun had collapsed and unwound when she took off her hat, leaving her grey-brown hair lying exhausted on her shoulders. Her petticoat had slipped further south beneath her skirt and she was sweating.

'I hope you're feeling all right!' Maisie said anxiously.

'I certainly am! And this is such a lovely place. I'll have crab sandwiches!'

'I'm very sorry, but we don't do sandwiches and we don't serve crab. It's not caught in these parts, you see: you need Norfolk for that!'

'Oh!' Miss Corringer appeared to choke, as if from something frightening. And then she gulped and her face tightened in a rictus of pain. 'Yes, I remember, now I remember,' she murmured.

'But we can do you just about anything else. May I suggest some nice fillets of plaice, caught this morning?'

Maisie joined Miss Corringer in fillets of plaice and tinned pineapple for afters. Reg chose battered cod, followed by fried Rolos. Each ordered a mug of tea.

———

It would have been impossible to say whether Miss Corringer derived pleasure from the Brunts. When she spoke in their presence, it was not to connect with them but to have them listen to her. She had near exhausted the patience of Ahmed, who delivered her groceries and was always in a hurry to get along with other orders, and of Gita, who did her chores, both of whom would have liked to confide their own problems to the old lady, for she was educated and would know her way round bureaucracy. Nor did Miss George have time to listen, what with all the form-filling expected of her and the meetings she had to chair. She allowed herself to feel confident that the Brunts had factored Miss Corringer into their routine with plenty of time to listen to her, and gratefully removed the old lady and those upon whom she depended from her list of obligations.

Maisie sometimes wondered to Reg where the children had gone. Surely some must have stayed in the area when they were grown up and had children of their own? Why did not one of them visit Miss Corringer? And what of relatives?

———

Six months had passed since the Brunts first came to tea, and Monday had assumed its place in the routine that was their life. Some small alterations in their relationship with Miss Corringer had taken place. Reg had fixed a washer on a tap in her bathroom and Maisie had taken home a little lace collar Miss Corringer had shown her.

'It could do with a wash,' she said, handing it to Maisie.

'Leave it to me!' Maisie said, and returned it washed and ironed the following Monday, nicely wrapped in tissue paper.

It was some weeks later that Miss Corringer failed to respond to the bell when they rang. They did not like to ring more than three times or knock hard: if she did not want to see them, that was for her to decide.

'But supposing she's not well?'

'Perhaps the bell's not working?'

The next day, Tuesday, Reg popped over to Badger's Green and tried the bell, and Miss Corringer opened the door. 'Where's Maisie?' she enquired.

'Well, it isn't our day. That was yesterday, and you didn't answer the bell.'

'Didn't I? That's funny. Why didn't I?'

'I don't know. Perhaps you were not feeling well?'

'I don't think that was it. Well, now you're here, I've a light bulb needs changing.'

Reg quickly unscrewed the old bulb and screwed in a new one, put the little steps back in the kitchen and left. Tuesday was Tesco day. Maisie would be waiting for him.

Little by little, things began to alter in the Brunts' attention to Miss Corringer's needs. On arrival, Maisie would brew the tea herself, look into the kitchen cupboards and make a note of items running out or beyond their sell-by date, and put them on Ahmed's list. She examined whether Gita, who came on Saturday afternoons, had done all that was required and done it properly, and where she had missed some dust, not only flicked a duster of her own but got down on her knees to give the kitchen floor the sort of going-over she gave to her own kitchen floor. Slowly, Miss Corringer's well-being was becoming Maisie's. 'I don't like to see the old lady being short-changed,' she told Reg. From time to time Reg or Maisie, or even both, slipped over to Badger's Green unannounced, to check on Miss Corringer and see whether there was anything she needed. Her memory for time was fast deteriorating, whereas the Brunts' was expanding.

Early one morning when Maisie had finished making the beds and was arranging her collection of knitted bears on her pillow, Reg, back from buying the paper, called from the kitchen that he had bumped into Miss George and she had asked him a lot of questions about Miss Corringer: was she needing more help than she was getting with just a cleaner, Ahmed's deliveries and their visits? 'I told her all you were doing.'

'I hope you told her all you were doing!'

'I did. I said we were pleased to be of use.'

Waiting one day for Miss Corringer to open the front door, the Brunts were overcome by a stench from the dustbins and the sight of a toad sitting menacingly at the edge of the laurels. While Maisie walked in haste into the kitchen to wash hands that had been nowhere near the offending dustbins or the toad, Reg examined the stinking bin, emptied it and cleaned it out with disinfectant. Then he investigated round the base of the laurels to locate the toad, but he failed, and feeling slightly nauseous, ran upstairs to the bathroom.

Perhaps it was being on his own for a few minutes that encouraged him to give in to his curiosity, for he found himself hastening to climb the short flight to Uncle Harry's room and once in, had a good look round. Uncle Harry's room was obviously a man's room, brown and dusty, and seemed not to have been in use for years. There were piles of old newspapers turning crisp, a moth-eaten Welsh hand-knit, and the bed on the single iron bedstead was only half made. There were photographs of climbers struggling to the summits of mountains and a stick with spikes, which Reg imagined might have been something Uncle Harry carried to help him on icy slopes. Masses of books, all about Australia, lined the shelves, and there were files stacked to the side of an ancient typewriter. A musty smell emanated from damp patches just under the ceiling, where the paper was coming away from the wall; the hems of the dark green hessian curtains were heavy with dust and the springs from what had been a sofa lay around its carcass like the innards from a recent kill. Staring out from under a glass dome, a mangy stuffed rodent the size of an alpine marmot was poised in mid-step. Reg noticed that on a saucer acting as a paper weight lay keys attached to frayed string. He recognised two as belonging to the front door, but there were others he did not recognise. He put them in his pocket. Later that day, Maisie noticed keys which were not theirs hanging from a cup hook in the kitchen.

'What are these?'

'I think they are hers. I found them in Uncle Harry's room.' And then the explanation came to him. 'One of these days she won't be able to open the door to us; she will have fallen or forgotten – or something or other – and they will come in handy.'

Maisie agreed. 'Should we tell her we've got them?'

'One day, perhaps. You know: when it's necessary.'

———

Miss Corringer's health had worsened. In her moments of lucidity, she acknowledged that old age was catching up with her and would confide to Maisie that whatever happened, she was not going to be moved from her house. 'I am not going to be put in one of those places. The ugliness alone would kill me. As for the food and the company – no!' She could just about manage the stairs from her sitting room to her bedroom and bathroom, but she no longer left the house on her own. She kept her clinic appointments at the London Hospital because the ambulance picked her up and put her in a wheelchair at the front door and carried her down the front steps and returned her with the same attention. She had become used to the pain in her leg, and now her back and arthritic hand. She walked bent, and would stop mid-pavement and, using one of her sticks, push detritus to reveal marks on the pavement she saw as pictures. Her right hand responded only imperfectly to what she required of it; she dropped most of what she picked up, and was unable to stoop to retrieve things. She relied increasingly on the Brunts and the telephone. Ahmed and Gita remained loyal, and she had her books and her wireless.

'Would you like to have a television?' Reg asked. But the moment was inappropriate, and she looked quizzical and asked him what that was.

Sometimes, having entered the house with Uncle Harry's keys, they found Miss Corringer sitting like a saint disturbed in contemplation. They would stand still and quiet for a few minutes while her eyes flickered, before addressing her. 'We mustn't give her a shock.' And then, after a little time, Miss Corringer would emerge from wherever her mind had taken her and enquire, 'And who may you be?' Maisie would go and sit next to her and remind her, and ask her if she would like a nice cup of tea. Meanwhile, Reg, embarrassed by someone who could turn from being normal, if not a little eccentric, to being mad in a matter of seconds, would stand at a window and take in the view. The view changed too, but according to rules he understood.

He was looking out on to the back garden and thinking it must be many years since Miss Corringer had felt the urge or had the mobility to work on her garden. The soil had been neglected, branches of trees trespassed and bluebells, wood anemones and primroses were thriving as they did in the wild. Reg would have liked a garden, would have enjoyed tiring himself out with digging and bringing Maisie bunches of flowers he had raised. And when it was sunny they would have sat in deck chairs together and Maisie would have hung the washing on the line. Perhaps he would have planted a fruit tree and raspberry canes ...

'You know what?' Maisie said. 'I wouldn't mind a house myself some day!'

'What, with all those stairs and a whole lot of rooms we don't need and wouldn't use? Whatever's made you think that? What's the matter with our place?'

'Nothing's the matter, it's just that ...'

'What?' In an effort to change the route to which conversation was pointing, Reg suggested they might go dancing up west that afternoon. 'You could put on your taffeta dress and that Alice band in your hair. I used to like that. And we could order a plate of those little sandwiches …'

'Oh, I don't know as I feel up to it.'

'Something wrong, dear? Something got to you?'

No, there was nothing wrong, exactly, but she had been remembering the old days and the nice routine they had: their new routine wasn't as nice. The redevelopment was taking forever, what with all those men on strike, standing around doing nothing. The wasteland, once an Acacia Avenue, a Primrose Close, a Rose Street criss-crossed by highroads named after the most noble of the land, was now a barren field of battle between the water board, the electricity board and the gas board, fought out with pneumatic drills and diggers and lorries raising clouds of contaminated air through which the Brunts had to trudge on their way to Tesco and the post office, their eyes running, their throats clogged. 'I'm getting very chesty,' Maisie complained.

———

Even though it was expensive to shop in Badger's Green, sometimes they did, after making elaborate excuses to themselves and each other for their recklessness. 'I think I'd rather go without something than do that walk this week. I've noticed your shoes have become very worn, Reg.'

'They have: they need a lot more polish these days.'

'It's awful! What with all our footpaths gone and the trees, it'll take ages for new ones to grow. D'you think they'll put in plastic ones?'

Both Reg and Maisie longed for the safety of tarmac. 'The market's a proper disgrace. Who buys all that stuff from China? Don't we make things here anymore? I wouldn't even buy my tea towels there. And all the veg is either stale or rotten. I prefer Ahmed's.'

'You're right, dear!'

'Why d'you think they've left the laundrette standing with all the windows broken and the machines gone – probably stolen? They've left wires all over the place! That's dangerous, with the kids around having nothing to do after school. I see they've taken greater care with the off–licence, what with its iron bars and padlocks.'

'I think we should try the post office in Badger's Green next week, don't you?'

'Oh! Reg, you do have such good ideas!'

'Brighton was yours, Maisie!'

———

Miss Corringer was not eating. Ahmed was at his shop's front, arranging aubergines and avocados in open boxes, when he saw the Brunts approaching. He greeted them warmly; it was he who had first alerted Reg and Maisie – as he had Miss George – to the fact that Miss Corringer was becoming increasingly absent-minded in her ordering and was throwing away more food than she was consuming. (Ahmed was distantly related to

Gita, from whom he learned more about Miss Corringer than he felt he needed to know.) Miss George had taken the news calmly: old people tend to lose their appetites, and so long as the Brunts continued to visit regularly and do little jobs for the old lady, she was happy to leave arrangements as they were. What were the alternatives? Miss Corringer was not going to agree to being moved into a care home; Miss George had had that conversation with her on more than one occasion, and knew exactly where the old lady stood on the matter.

Reg popped in to Miss Corringer's, intending to remove the chain and bolt from the front door. Earlier in the week, using Uncle Harry's keys, the Brunts had failed to get into the house because the old lady had gone back to her earlier habit of attaching both at night, forgetting that she had been party to the new arrangement. Having successfully detached the chain, and unscrewed the bolt, he put both in the kitchen drawer. He then tiptoed from room to room looking for Miss Corringer. He did not like to call out for fear of giving her a shock. But the shock was his: he found her prone by the side of her bed, her sticks tidied in the great Chinese vase at the other side. She had obviously got into bed conscious and subsequently fallen off.

Was she dead? Unconscious? Or just asleep? Had she had a fit? And how to find out? Reg felt a mixture of uncertainty and embarrassment, for the old lady's skirts were bunched about her waist, she was barefoot and there were holes in her stockings. Such of her face as he could make out under her mass of hair had turned a funny colour. He looked at her hands and saw how the raised veins ran to disgorge themselves at the delta of her knuckles, and how the skin was so dry and transparent it rose as if unattached from the flesh beneath. He leant over and whispered, 'You all right?'

'I may have had a little blackout,' she said, but when Reg finally managed to rouse her and pull her to her feet she brushed herself down and assured him she had not hurt herself and was quite all right. 'What a good thing you were passing, or I might have got cold,' was all she ventured.

Victoria Terrace was a damp house and Miss Corringer had started to feel uncomfortably cold in it. When winter came round, the Brunts decided she would be best served confined to a single room, with added warmth supplied by a paraffin heater. The night storage heaters worked, but provided less heat during the day than Miss Corringer needed at her time of life. 'Too much heat would not have been good for the inlay on some of the tables or the pictures,' she explained in defence of her parents, and as an excuse for their not having installed central heating. It was decided that her sitting room should be converted to a bedsit, and that she should use the downstairs lavatory and basin as her bathroom, given that they were adjacent. The Brunts would move into her bedroom (on those occasions when Miss Corringer's state of being demanded) and use the bathroom.

Miss Corringer agreed to this arrangement, for it had been a long time since she had been able to swing her legs over a bath. The move took days to complete because she proved very fussy as to which of her most treasured objects were to be brought down into her already overfilled sitting room and, as with a pathological hoarder, it was difficult to persuade her to leave anything behind. 'I must have everything from the bed-side table!' she told Maisie. 'All the little bottles of coloured sand, the photos, the postcards, the menus and my diaries.'

—

It took half an hour to walk south from the prefab over the wasteland to Badger's Green and on to Victoria Terrace. As Miss Corringer's needs increased – Maisie liked to serve her breakfast in bed at eight and her supper past nine – she and Reg found they were spending more and more nights in Miss Corringer's double bed. And they were enjoying it. An unfamiliar pleasure had entered the couple's life.

'Oo! Isn't this lovely!'

'It certainly is, dear.'

A visitor to the house in Victoria Terrace would have been hard put to work out the relationship between Miss Corringer and the Brunts. Were they a devoted couple in service, or was the house theirs and had they invited an elderly acquaintance to pass her final days there?

Miss Corringer rarely spoke. She had relinquished herself to her carers and seemed to have no objections to what they did for her, no wishes of her own unmet. She tended to gaze past Maisie when she entered with a tray, as if she were not seen. If Maisie made an attempt to gain her attention, Miss Corringer's face could contort and tighten, as if stung. If Maisie could not find her place in any monologue which erupted, she would stand back in bewildered silence. Even when Miss Corringer's voice rose questioningly, the old lady did not wait for a response. Nor did she voice any remark to which Maisie, in her habit of assent, could respond.

The Brunts instigated a new routine around Miss Corringer's needs. On the day she was collected by the community bus to be taken to the memory clinic, they felt free to go to Oxford Street and the shops, 'just to look, mind you!' or to the bingo hall that had opened recently a short bus ride from Badger's Green. Maisie took it upon herself to accompany Miss Corringer to the clinic at the London Hospital, to help her in and out of her clothes and interpret for her when she was at her worst. Reg went back to the prefab on a Tuesday to polish the commemorative plaque and see that no one had broken in. He had turned off the immersion heater, put rolled newspaper on the window sills to catch the condensation and stopped the milk and the Sunday paper as soon as they decided to move out. 'We might just as well make economies where we can.' Maisie preferred not to accompany him.

'Why's that, dear?'

'Can't say, really.'

She tried to work out why for herself and found she had rather turned against her old home. She was certainly not going to confide that to Reg. It would hurt him deeply.

———

Maisie had not been able to resist opening Miss Corringer's bedroom cupboards. She took out dress after dress and tried them on. She particularly coveted ones similar to those her mother had made from curtain material during the war. 'I'll ask her, shall I?'

'She probably won't understand what you're about,' Reg said. 'But it's best to ask.'

'Strange to think she was once my size. That must've been a long time ago. I'd prefer to ask her permission than just go ahead, but I'm afraid she'll go into one of her mumblings and get all distressed.' And so Maisie returned the tempting garments to their hangers and put the whole subject out of her mind.

Meanwhile, she moved round the house luxuriating in Irish linen sheets, Egyptian cotton bath sheets, French porcelain and Swedish glass, purchases made, Miss Corringer told her, 'when I was home-making', since when she had been making do with a mug and an old plate for her needs, and had put away the 'best'. But under Maisie's regime she appeared to accept her tray being laid with the 'best' cups and saucers, accompanied by a linen napkin.

In time, Miss Corringer became unresponsive and uncooperative. She neither answered Maisie's questions nor initiated requests, and she so thrust about her arms that Maisie became bruised from her efforts to blanket bath the old lady. When she placed a bowl of something sweet and easy to swallow on the bed tray, Miss Corringer swiftly swept it to the floor. Maisie could have done with some help with her, but thought it would be unseemly for Reg to see Miss Corringer in her nightdress, and Reg reinforced this nicety in Maisie. 'Best call the doctor, dear.' The upshot was that within days of the GP's visit, Miss Corringer was put on a geriatric ward in the London Hospital, where Maisie visited her daily until she died.

Maisie did not know why it was she suddenly felt a mixture of sadness and vexation. It was not like her to feel either. She did not want to confide this to Reg, but as they always felt the same, she imagined that he too was unhappy at the turn of events.

'Well, we don't have to go for a while, dear.'

'No, that's true. But I don't think I shall feel more like leaving Victoria Terrace in a week's time.'

'But it's not ours, dear. We would never have had the money for a house like this and all the old things and the garden. And we were very happy where we were and we'll be happy there again once we've got over the shock.'

Maisie was not too sure of that, and she wondered if Reg was absolutely sure himself or whether he was saying so to encourage her. That's what he usually did.

'Shall we put back the things the way they were before we made her the bedsit?'

'Yes. That'll give us something to do.'

They returned each item to its former place. Reg went back to the prefab on several occasions to test the immersion heater and throw out the rolls of paper he had made to catch the condensation, which year after year blemished the window sills. He bought a bunch of pinks for Maisie and placed them on the sitting room table in the milk jug he had won for her at a fairground when they were courting. He told himself that everything would be all right, but it would take time: it's not that they had liked the old lady much.

'When we get back, we'll have the telly again, and you'll like that, dear.'

'Yes,' Maisie agreed uncertainly.

—

Just as they had decided to turn in one evening, the door bell sounded. 'Who could that be?'

'Well, we won't know until we've opened up.'

'Is it safe at this time of night, Reg?'

'It's only nine o'clock, dear.'

A tall young man with very blond hair introduced himself as Miss Corringer's great-great-nephew from Australia. 'May I come in?' he asked.

'Well, I suppose so,' Reg said, his eyes focused on the young man's suitcase.

'You've heard, I suppose: the house is mine now. Muriel left it to me in her will. I was told you were here, not you personally, but that there were caretakers and that they were about to move out, so I flew over as soon as I could. Didn't want to leave the place unattended with all its valuable bits and pieces.'

'Well, we were not thinking of leaving tonight,' Reg said.

'No, that's all right. Tomorrow will do. I'll sleep in Uncle Harry's room tonight.' Keith set down his suitcase. 'I'll take a look round, if you don't mind!' he said, and Reg mumbled something to the effect of that being quite in order, and disappeared into the kitchen.

Meanwhile, Keith pushed open the door to the parlour and then to the sitting room, before joining Reg in the kitchen. 'All a bit past its sell-by date!' he observed, laughing. Continuing his exploration, he took the stairs two at a time, threw open Miss Corringer's bedroom door and peered into her bathroom. 'Oh my, there's a lot needs doing here!' he said to no one in particular, but conscious that Reg had been following in his footsteps.

'This is Uncle Harry's room,' Reg said, pointing. 'It's not been cleaned for years. I think Miss Corringer was waiting for Uncle Harry to come back.'

'What a mess! Looks like a museum installation.' Keith called down the stairs to Maisie for some clean sheets and blankets. He was tired after the journey and wanted to kip down as soon as possible. 'But there must be more to see.'

'Well, yes, there's Miss Corringer's assistant's flat in the attic. I'll get the key.'

'What's it like?'

'I can't say. I've never ventured into it. I felt your aunt didn't want us to go there for some reason. I think it brought back painful memories because, so far as I know, she never went up there herself.'

'I expect it's where she kept her most valuable treasures.'

Reg handed Keith the key and turned to go back downstairs. Maisie left a pile of linen on Uncle Harry's bed and followed Reg. Keith tied the key in the attic door and found it stiff, as if turning had not been required of the lock for a long time. Finally it gave way, and he stepped inside the room and turned on the light.

After a short time inside the room, Keith closed and re-locked the attic door and slowly took the stairs one by one. He had seen something with which he was going to have to deal, but not now. Tomorrow, or the day after tomorrow. The police would have to be informed, so too the solicitor. Hard to imagine where it might all end. He had read of such things, but always thought them far-fetched.

Reg and Maisie had heard Keith on the landing and were waiting in the hall to meet him.

'I've changed my mind,' he said. 'I'll not be staying over-night. I am sorry to have disturbed you.' He picked up his suitcase and opened the front door.

Reg closed it silently behind him.

The Talking Cure

'Why don't you talk to me? You never talk to me!'
Gregory Brewer shifted uneasily in his chair. It was impossible to gauge whether he was planning to rise out of it, whether he was irritated or his trousers were scratching his thighs. Certainly Daisy could not tell. 'What – now? You want to talk now? I thought we were listening to Michael Berkeley and what he has to say about Hildegard of Bingen.'

Well, Daisy informed him, she wasn't listening, wasn't in the least interested in Hildegard of wheresoever. She wanted to talk.

Gregory stretched across to the radio and switched it off, managing in so doing to express a lack of grace he had refined to an art. He settled back into his chair and asked his wife what it was she wished to talk about, and on being told 'just anything', said she would need to be more specific. What was on her mind? Was there something particular she needed to discuss?

But Daisy did not wish to discuss, she wanted to chat. She wanted to chat about this and that, things that interested her.

After eight years of marriage, Gregory had no idea of anything much that interested Daisy, apart from the little feminine matters beloved by women's magazines. Not that Daisy was to take from the reflection that he despised her preoccupations; had he wished to marry an historian, with his own passion for ancient Rome, there was nothing to stop him. Having got that straight, Gregory settled back in his chair, stretched his neck and stared into the past, where opportunities lay thick on the ground.

His wife had nothing more to say and was uncomfortably conscious of the silence he had wrought. Because she was staring at his legs stretched out over the carpet, she could see a hole in his left sock, and was reminded of a pile of mending waiting to be done.

'Well?' asked Gregory in the silence that ensued. 'Fire away!' He suggested Daisy might care to outline her day to him and, gratified by this sudden inspiration, he rubbed his hands together as if soaping them prior to performing surgery.

Daisy felt more diminished than ever. What had she done that day that could possibly interest her husband? She had escorted three old-age pensioners to podiatry, organised Mrs Rudge to clean the oven and the floor in the utilities room and done the week's shopping at Sainsbury's. This she relayed to her husband in a single breath, wondering what on earth would be his reaction.

'Oh, more shopping!' in a tone he satisfied himself was neutral. He paused to savour the ease with which he appeared to have entered into the spirit of things. Daisy had shown no disapproval, boredom or irritation. Well done! he thought to himself.

'But you'll be cross when I tell you what I did next,' Daisy warned, lowering her eyes.

'I don't have the energy for cross,' Gregory said, barely audibly. And so Daisy told her husband what she had been up to in Bond Street: she had bought a coat, a yellow cashmere coat from Armani.

Gregory gazed out of the window into the garden, as if to acquire some spiritual beneficence from the trees. Wasn't the combination of cashmere and Armani a dreadfully expensive one? he asked.

'One thousand, three hundred and thirty-six pounds in the sale, to be precise,' Daisy informed him, adding that he was quite right: Armani was not cheap, nor was cashmere.

Gregory appeared to be trying to swallow, but a convulsion overtook his larynx. Where had Daisy acquired such a sum?

Daisy had charged the coat to their Barclaycard and when Gregory saw the coat, saw his wife wearing it, he would agree it was money well spent.

Gregory doubted this. He found no beauty in contemporary fashion and could not afford to dip into his savings for such a frivolous purchase. Didn't Daisy already own four coats? Maybe they were not utterly up to date, but they were surely serviceable? She looked perfectly presentable in each, had no need of another and certainly not a yellow one. For what occasion would she wear yellow? Who in their right mind wore yellow, particularly someone with such a pallid skin tone?

Gregory did not so much shake his head as submit to a tremor taking hold of it. He closed his eyes for a second or two while he gathered his forces, and then launched into an

attack on Daisy revolving around his salary as a senior lec-
turer at Gower College, at the University of Slough, her lack
of financial independence, his economies, her profligacies. 'It
makes me feel positively sick, the way in which you take for
granted that I am here to provide you with luxuries of this
kind. Yours are the exhorbitant demands of a child.' He turned
in his chair in order to face away from his wife, and spat out
the word 'sick' as if her behaviour had provoked a seizure to
be evacuated in the wastepaper basket without delay.

Daisy thought it best to hold her tongue. It was Gregory's
indifference to her life as an individual, his tight fists in particular, that had led her to this purchase, but she refrained
from saying so.

Gregory continued his rant, reminding his wife of how
many times he had told her not to overspend, how he could
not abide the purchases of the exotic plants he had had to
watch perish in the variable atmosphere of their flat, cream-
filled Belgian chocolates that upset his digestion, the garish
Italian silk ties appropriate, no doubt, for a night-club manager, but not for an academic ... Then, unable to call to mind
all of Daisy's ill-timed, ill-chosen redundancies, he altered tack
and appealed to her pity. 'You married a poorly paid historian,
Daisy' – he dropped his gaze in a gesture of apology, cod
humility - 'not an armaments manufacturer. You should have
foreseen the implications of your decision.'

In her defence, Daisy argued that she only bought things
she thought he would enjoy, that would cheer him up. She had
noticed that he was not constitutionally a happy man.

'There are deeper things to strive for than happiness,'
Gregory told her. 'I don't pursue happiness, I seek fulfilment.'

He admitted that it was thoughtful of his wife to want to cheer him up but that she was maladroit in the performance. Certainly, her choice of sundries was not his, and surely by now, should she not know what gratified him? The threat of having to find over one thousand pounds for a coat she did not need was certainly not calculated to promote his happiness.

'The only thing that really cheers you up, gratifies you, as you put it, promotes your happiness, is to sit there with your flies open, your dick out and to have me suck you off.'

'Daisy!' A flush of embarrassment burnt Gregory's cheeks, while beads of sweat soaked the wisps of long, colourless hair combed across his balding head. His face contorted in a rictus of distaste. 'You have the most extraordinarily vulgar tongue!' His raised voice struggled with phlegm.

Daisy felt galvanized, in charge. 'But you have never complained of its efficiency. You've always admired my technique. What sort of a tongue would suit you better? I cannot imagine a decorous one would do much for your appetites.'

'I am not going to sit here under attack. If this is what you mean by talking, it's no wonder I am inclined to choose silence. You are trespassing on my time, Daisy. Find something to do, child. Don't depend on me to amuse you!' Gregory struggled out of the chair that had been holding him against his better judgment and left the room. But he was in a rage, and there was nothing he wanted to do more than defend himself. The flat was small, the kitchen Daisy's domain, the bedroom quite the inappropriate place to conduct this afternoon's upset. There was only the large sitting room that served as his study when he was at home, and so, after visiting the bathroom (which would provide the excuse for his precipitate exit), he returned to take up where he had left off.

But he hadn't bargained for the extent of Daisy's dissatisfactions. She was not finished with him.

'We never do anything together. We don't share things. Other couples talk to each other.'

'Can you be sure of that?' Gregory wondered what couples spoke about after so many years together. Could there be anything left to discuss? 'You must know that I am not one of those men interested in the preparation of food or the rigours of household management. I am not going to reflect with you upon the relative merits of Alan Bennett and Michael Frayn. I expect the critics to lead me to the worthier box offices, you to organise the kitchen, and I leave the weather to the almighty and the meteorologists. What else is there to talk about?'

'I just want to chat, you know, nothing important . . .' Daisy's voice trailed off. There was a pause that made her feel uncomfortable again, and then she asked her husband what he had done that day.

Gregory loosened his shoulders, picked non-existent fluff from his trousers, faced his wife aggressively and started. 'I went first to the library, where I read a Latin treatise on military strategy. I went to the George for a spot of luncheon, back to the library and, having thought over luncheon what it was I wanted to communicate, wrote up my conclusions relating to tactics that might have saved a particular Roman legion from decimation four hundred years before the birth of our Saviour. I caught a number 24 bus and came home. Now, is that the sort of conversation you wish to share with me?'

'That's not conversation, it's a report.'

'But evidently more to your taste than listening to Michael Berkeley on Hildegard of Bingen? Perhaps you have something to tell me in greater detail than heretofore regarding your day. You only provided me with a report, as you put it. You told me that you drove the pensioners, gave instructions to the cleaner, shopped for provisions and bought a coat that you are going to have to return. Anything else?'

'I had tea with Justin Lewis. We talked.'

'Really, I wonder what induced you to do that? I always found that young man an unprecedented bore. Perhaps you have discovered depths I overlooked?' Gregory leant across his desk and picked up a large volume into which he had inserted thin slips of paper to mark pages. 'Now, since we are no longer listening to the radio, since early music does not have the power to detain you, let me proceed with my work. I have things to prepare for tomorrow's seminar.'

'You see! You just won't talk to me. You are so bloody self-absorbed. You have no idea what interests me. You take it for granted that if by chance something does, it will be contemptible. Don't you think that having chosen to marry me, little me, out of all the other girls with whom you had an "understanding", as you put it, you might actually want to entertain me once in a while? After all, I spend just about all my time attending to you and your needs. I make you comfortable, I provide you with a peaceful, tidy background for your work. I don't get a salary for what I do. Even a dog gets taken to the park and a servant gets a day off. When did we have a holiday that I wanted, that was not to visit Roman castles, Roman battle grounds, Roman any and everything?'

'Do you have your period, Daisy?' Gregory raised his eyes over his bifocals. 'I suggest you run yourself a hot bath and throw in one of those stress-relieving unguents with which you line the bathroom shelves. Take a sedative! Have an early night! You'll feel quite restored by morning and we shall be able to resume the peaceful life we normally enjoy. By the way, while I think of it, my brown boots need re-heeling and I would appreciate it if you would pop down to T&A and have them pick out some solid-coloured poplins for me to choose from; my shirts are looking tired. Bring back four pairs of those socks with the clocks that I like! And as you'll be in that neighbourhood, return the cashmere coat. They'll credit the card if you do it without delay. Tell them your husband says he can't bear yellow on you.'

Daisy made the mistake of asking Gregory when he would be coming to bed, and he took advantage of her mishandling by saying when he had finished what he was doing. Daisy made the further mistake of reminding him that even a few months ago he would not have chosen his work over her at this time of day. But since her husband had found consolation with the brilliant Albertine, 'who dresses like a spinster gym mistress, doesn't shave under her arms and doesn't talk about anything other than the Romans', sex with his wife was apparently not as enticing as it once had been.

Gregory threw aside his book, watching in horror as twenty or more markers fell to the floor: 'Look what you've made me do!' He was as near to tears as he had been on hearing of the death of Princess Diana a month ago. He clapped his hand to his head and clutched at the few straws of hair. For how much longer was he going to have to endure this?

Daisy was feeling tired. She had lost interest in the topics of conversation she had herself initiated. Her mind filled with images of escape. Suddenly she realized that she wanted to be anywhere, or with anyone who wasn't Gregory. She gazed out of the window. Dusk had gathered in the dun-coloured grass and the dead particles of lilac on the tree outside. The mournful light added to her own gloom, and the monotonous hum of traffic in the main road beyond fatigued her hearing. She would never escape, never reach any sort of independence. Was being a prisoner of wedlock the price she had to pay for status, security, and perhaps for tuition? She had made the terrible error of marrying for things other than passion and friendship; even tuition required those foundations. She felt paralysed. To move from where she was standing, with her back against the bookcase, and leave the room, would be to obey her husband's exhortation. But if she were to stay, there would be further recriminations. And she was not past making them herself. She had a lot more to say about Albertine, for starters.

Gregory, still seated, held his head in both his hands, his eyes closed. Like a child, he imagined that because he could not see Daisy, she could not see him. Why was it, he wondered, that even though his arguments were so much better reasoned than his wife's, they achieved nothing? How had he failed to explain himself to her? He unbound his face and stared into hers. 'What is it that makes you think that because I married you, you have the right to assume my whole purpose in life is to become your pleasure? That not only must it be focused on your good self alone, but is bound to be entirely satisfied by you? And why is it that of all the women with whom I have enjoyed a measure of, shall we say, understanding, it is poor Albertine you so resent? You appeared quite unfazed when I took up for a while with little Chloë. You made no objection, so far as I can recall, over my liaison with Paula in Rome. I think you agreed that these little peccadillos positively enhanced my libido to your advantage. But for reasons I simply cannot fathom, Albertine brings out something acid in you. I need to impress upon you how very sensitive Albertine is. She feels things at a deep level, and to nourish what might be described as avalanches of feeling, she has to have an assortment of relationships. I am her only lover. She's no threat to you, Daisy; she positively eschews marriage. She gets proposals on a weekly basis, but like the foot fetishist would be thoroughly disorientated by the prospect of the whole leg.'

'And I provide her with a permanent object of contempt to share with you. When you have had sex, and are finished with the Romans for a bit, you can bitch about my inadequacies together. Why did you need to tell her I'd failed as a singer? What business is it of hers?' Daisy rocked herself back and forth against the bookcase. 'You betrayed me! You don't love me, you are not the least interested in me. I wonder whether you even like me!'

'Don't be childish, Daisy.'

'And don't you patronise me! You stay with me because you'd be lost without your housekeeper and your home, that familiar spot where you strew your dirty washing, pick up the occasional message, eat well-prepared food and get your dick serviced when one or other of your "understandings" is out of town. You might find me hard to replace.'

Gregory was uncertain as to whether he should look towards his wife or return his face to his shuttering hands. It was true, wasn't it?

'But what really gets me is that you have encouraged Albertine to believe that sleeping with her is being unfaithful to me, and that your being unfaithful to me gives her *carte blanche* to criticize me to you and for you to confirm her criticisms. Albertine takes fucking altogether too seriously and our marriage altogether too lightly. I suppose that comes from her not knowing much about either.'

'That is *so* perceptive of you, Daisy!' A strange sensation was overcoming Gregory. His pride was being assaulted. A woman undermining him! Since when did women set the rules? But his cheeks were engorged with fury.

'I don't in the least mind that you fuck Albertine, I mind that you talk to her!'

'Is that really any of your business?'

'Probably not, but I still mind, and I'd like you to stop. Talking to her, I mean.'

'Well, my dear, there are many situations in which we find ourselves that displease us, or fail to come up to our expectations, and there's nothing much we can do about them. I, for one, have found that this marriage has not brought the rewards I had counted upon.'

'Why stay in it, then?'

'Because I believe that in life one must make the best of one's hand, not just chuck it in on impulse.'

'That's not the reason! You stay because you've got it all here under one roof!'

'In some ways that is true. I have. But to suggest that I do not even like you is hysterical.' He looked up into Daisy's face and managed the simulacrum of a kindly smile. 'I do like to know you are always here, at home. Our home.'

The moment had passed when Daisy might have left the room, left Gregory to stew a bit. She would need to wait for another suitable opening and it might not arrive for a long time. She was stuck, looking down on her seated husband with his wispy, lacklustre hair, the little nicks on his florid cheeks where he had cut himself shaving, the spot on his thin nose. How unappetising he was. She thought the hands resting on the library book could have been those of a butcher and the broken nails those of a mechanic. Yet this was a man who had never so much as carved a joint or mended a bicycle tyre.

'Albertine would like to be your friend.' Was he whining? Or did he imagine he was cajoling her?

'She wants it all, doesn't she? If she's short of a friend, why doesn't she take up with one of your other, more knowledgeable girls? I don't think it's a friend Albertine wants in me, it's a confessor. She feels guilty. Well, I'm not going to be both the despised wife and the mistress-sympathiser. I'm sure it's the dual role you would most like me to adopt, but it's just not going to happen.' Behind those small brown eyes Daisy detected the absent expression of one who was saying one thing and thinking another, someone who had lost the thread of his excuses and was, despite the appearance of calm, desperately trying to put together his defence. Some new defence. 'Perhaps if Albertine knew what you really crave, a maiden at each orifice, she'd be less enchanted by you.'

'And what makes you think I don't share my fantasies with Albertine?'

'Oh, so she knows, does she? Well, why doesn't she go ahead and set things up for you? You have something of a gift for getting women to do what you want.'

'You have such a tasteless manner of expressing yourself, Daisy!'

'That must come from the tasteless manner in which you behave towards me.'

'In which you have concurred . . .'

'Yes, it has come to that.' Daisy twisted her wedding ring round her immaculate finger. She had been corrupted by him. Why was he serially unfaithful? Why did he need to be? And why had she acquiesced in accommodating his needs? What was it that he had to offer? It's not that he was good-looking. Perhaps he was able to exert some charm for a short time. His 'understandings' came and went quite rapidly. Only Albertine stuck it out.

Gregory's spectacles dangled from his mouth by their arm, giving him time to stall. And then he put them away in his top pocket, signalling that he was not going to continue the conversation. Why on earth had he allowed Daisy to know about his intimacy with Albertine? Why had he repeated to her their conversations? He could so easily have concealed the affair. What was it that had made him share his infidelities with the one person who could make objections? Had he confided in a colleague, he might have enjoyed some kudos. No, it was Daisy he wanted to tell: tell all. It gave him a rather nice feeling talking about Albertine with her. See! He did talk to her. Typical of a woman to object to what she so feverishly desired.

Daisy tried to remember what had led her to marry Gregory. She couldn't, not really. Was it rebelliousness? Was it the fact that she had failed academically and had become a cook? Or that her parents had vetoed the boy she had really loved as being unsuitable? Here was an older, educated man who wanted her despite her lack of education, despite her failure. Maybe it was that? When they had started going out together, Gregory had taken her to Shakespeare and Aeschylus at the National and several times to the Museum of Roman Antiquities. She recalled with a horror that made her blood run cold a talk by some German professor on the relationship between weather and skirmish. All in all, she had been bored out of her mind by it all, if flattered. She had not dared to suggest other distractions, ones she might have preferred. Their goings-out became less frequent, their stayings-in more so. She would cook a meal and then they would retire to bed. In many (different) respects it suited both of them. But it set a pattern, set it in concrete. Her first reaction to Gregory when he had stopped her outside the dry cleaners was to feel sorry for him. On acquaintance, she had thought he was clever. He remembered dates and numbers and temperatures. At first she had shared in the odour of satisfaction he gave off, but it was not long before she found it dank. What good did he put all these facts to? How could he be so certain of everything? And why did he write in violet ink, drum his fingers on the desk when he was searching for words? Did he need to take four sets of supplements for his health or was this hypochondria?

Gregory suggested that once they were married, Daisy might give up doing dinner parties for the smart set in Islington and Hampstead, and this pleased her. She was sick of the wives passing off as their own confections dishes she had laboured for weeks to perfect. 'When I entertain my colleagues at home they admire you in your cook's apron. There is something so comforting, yet so up to date, about a woman in an apron serving three-star-restaurant-quality food.'

Though they had vetoed her true love, Daisy's parents had not been entirely happy about Gregory either. What would her mother say now if Daisy suggested coming home for a while? And how could she put it to her mother that she needed respite care from marriage? Avril had been lonely since the death of Cyril. Perhaps she would welcome Daisy's company? Just a sorting out period, a spring-clean of things marital . . .

At the same time, Gregory was trying to remember what had got him into marriage with Daisy. It was that splendid dinner at Professor Cartright's. He remembered saying to him as he was leaving, 'Do give my compliments to the cook!' and Cartright's offering that he thought the cook would appreciate it if he gave them to her in person. Gregory had caught up with Daisy just as she was leaving via the basement door. In what amounted to an epiphany brought on by such prettiness and such capability, he saw how perfect she might be for his career: a pretty young thing on his arm, rather in the mode of a charm on a bracelet, about to serve splendid food to his superiors. But he had never come to fully care for her. How could he? She was thick. Should he stop pretending? He had been attracted to a body that could never satisfy his mind. He was not a practical man, couldn't mend a fuse, bleed a radiator, unblock a sink or drive a car. And he was tired of not knowing from where his next fuck would come.

Daisy would be an asset to his career, so long as he could get her to hold her tongue. In the small but beautifully self-satisfied world of the University of Slough, his colleagues preferred their own company, so would probably not engage in much conversation with Daisy at the social occasions that went with the territory.

No, Gregory had not married Daisy for social advancement. Indeed, it was Daisy who relied upon him for status and security, and he who had always planned to have a woman who would owe her existence to him. He told her, 'Daisy, you need me to lead you in the dance that is life!' The *fact* of her failure made her fear failure of any sort, so she committed to nothing serious. She was a ripe victim for domesticity. He had married her for the promise of a life of unbridled sexual passion, delicious meals, fragrant linen sheets and flowers arranged *à la japonaise*. For style, that was it!

The trouble was, Daisy lacked all emotional and intellectual depth. He realized now, too late, that he couldn't change any of that; learning is organic, and she had not put down roots at the proper time. On the bright side, however, she had not been contaminated by women's liberation. Women talk to no purpose; men require a purpose to talk. Daisy knew full well, for he had often told her so, that his pleasures resided in his head (she would find a vulgar retort to that were he to utter as much), whereas hers were all over the place. The corn would never come to ear in her.

'Albertine understands my emotions,' he objected, as if referring to a public monument of undisputed aesthetic value. 'They are subtle, modulated and awakened only by art and ideas. I channel them into my work – they are too precious to be squandered on the daily round.' Gregory was now affecting to be dreaming his words, as if the beauty of the source of his emotions lay quite outside the real and actual. 'But you are mistaken if you think I am unaware of your gifts and feelings. You are one of those practical souls who make the world go round. Because I am not, I am an intellectual, I need your ministrations to keep me balanced and healthy. I work so hard, Daisy!' Gregory pleaded. He shook his head from east to west, troubled by the memory of the strains he had to endure.

'So you need me? It's not that you love me, you just need me. Like a baby who can't walk and needs to be carried, or an old lady who can't reach the top shelf in the supermarket, and needs someone to fetch the packet down for her. Well, thanks a bundle!'

'Now Daisy this conversation must stop. I simply don't have the energy for altercation.'

'Has it ever occurred to you that I, too, have needs and may have feelings?'

'Indeed it has. I know all about your needs. They are many. And I know about your feelings; they lie shallow and are easily offended.'

'What you need is a housekeeper and a call girl! You would convince yourself that by paying both you wouldn't need to consider their feelings. But you are so mean, you wouldn't pay for two women when you can get one for nothing.'

'My! My! Daisy, how bitter we are today. But you are right. I should never have married, only made use of other men's wives on a temporary basis. Desire is always more excessive than fulfilment. I should have foreseen that. You, Daisy, are incapable of seeing things as they are, only as you are, without settled purpose and from a thoroughly bourgeois perspective. You are a Pinner person!'

'Are you suggesting I should go back to where I belong?'

'No, not precisely, but I am suggesting that you might find a niche for yourself somewhere and with someone with a similar mind set – New Zealand, for example. I am led to believe that New Zealand is much like Pinner but with a better climate.'

'So you want to get rid of me? But you're always saying how much you love me!'

'I was in love with you, or my assessment of you, at first. But falling in love is part of a process, and the initial stage only lasts so long as the beloved keeps her mystery.'

There! It was out! He had admitted he did not love her. She wouldn't know how to deal with the truth and that would give him the opportunity to recuperate from her.

'The only company you really value is your own. I should never have opened my heart to one who has none. It's just words, words, words with you, nothing from the heart!' Daisy pushed her bottom hard against the bookcase that had been supporting her and launched herself into and out of the room in a single dash. She was not going to emigrate to New Zealand. And she was not going to board and bed this man a moment longer. The worm had turned.

'Hallo, Justin, it's Daisy. Yes, I know, but I hope not too late? Good! Yes, I'd love to come round for a chat. About fifteen minutes. Ciao!'

Who She?

A licia Clark lived in two rent-controlled rooms off Oxford Circus, within walking distance of the office where she typed and filed. Her only friends were the six women with whom she worked. She had been raised in Scunthorpe, and her school friends had not needed to uproot to London, as she had. She had never thought of marriage, and no man had thought of marrying her.

Her elderly parents had christened her Mavis Dora, and as soon as she was old enough for it to be legal, she exchanged this misfortune for Alicia Aida. On the rare occasions she found herself among strangers and was asked what she 'did', she answered, 'I help the police with their enquiries,' and made it clear she was not open to further questioning.

She had but two loves: her cat and her clothes. For Pearl she cooked and cared, for herself she shopped and sewed.

Although she subscribed to *Vogue* and *Harper's* and picked up an Italian women's magazine on her way to work, Alicia was not a follower of fashion but a devotee of transformation. To this end, she cut out and filed pictures of clothes she would interpret when and only when they were out of fashion. She liked to coordinate the long past and the more recent past with the present, and took pride in not being a slave to the modern.

What she needed in the way of dresses, coats and skirts she found in charity shops and car-boot sales. For their embellishment – lace, feathers and flowers – she rummaged on market stalls. And for her jewellery she visited ironmongers, whose variety of chains and curtain rings she rescued from their more mundane functions to hang at her neck and from her ear lobes. Permanently on the alert for some discarded item of use to herself and Pearl, she always carried with her a plumber's bag or a satchel.

Alicia's colleagues were confused by her confections and sometimes found it impossible to conceal their dismay. She would appear one morning in a navy schoolgirl's tunic cut to the thigh, fringed with feathers, thick orange knee-highs and cowboy boots, and on the next in a full-length lace evening dress teamed with a leather waistcoat sprinkled with buttons and badges. She wore long-sleeved thermal vests under boob tubes, and faux fur held in place with nappy pins. On one exceptionally hot summer's day, she arrived in a bathing suit under an open cotton cardigan with goggles on her head. She liked to finish an outfit with headgear: a veil, a cloche, a fisherman's cap or a flower. (The goggles had been unexpected.) She dyed her hair and painted her nails to match and clash with her outfits, sometimes marigold, sometimes beetroot, often black.

Alicia was shortly due for retirement and looked forward with excitement to a bus pass that would take her, for free, to outlying suburbs whose charity shops and markets she confidently believed to be veritable Aladdin's caves.

One late November day, she decided to walk to work via Great Marlborough rather than Wardour Street so as to pass Liberty's celebrated window display. She gauged the time badly and had to rush past the windows, impeded by her tango footwear. In her haste, and only from the corner of her eye, she spotted models in sparkling gowns dispensing champagne. In the split second it took her to feel overawed by glamour, she was brought down sharply by the shadow of an old woman rushing from one corner of the window display to the other, apparently attempting an escape. Haunted by the woman's predicament, Alicia returned to Liberty's on her way home in the dusk. To her relief, the old woman had evidently got away. The window display was brilliantly, theatrically lit and far outshone the yellow street lights outside. Alicia examined everything closely: a yacht sailing on the Mediterranean, three models in silver lamé accompanied by three others in midnight-blue velvet tuxedos, standing by a table piled with sequinned stockings and satin and lace underwear nestling between bottles of perfume.

As she wandered home, Alicia remembered an old velour dressing-gown at the back of her wardrobe. She would cut it short, bring it to life with a shower of sequins and the length of fox she had inherited from Granny Clark.

In December Alicia took the Great Marlborough Street route to work again, remembering that the windows would be dressed for Christmas: a Dickens-inspired fairy-tale showing a family – grandparents, parents and children – seated round a table groaning under the weight of abundance. There was a bronze turkey, a ham joint studded with cloves and a curled ox tongue, there was plum pudding garlanded with holly on a dish of lighted flame, there was steaming mulled wine and there were crackers, and small children knee-deep in boxes and torn wrapping paper, a scene as unfamiliar to Alicia as the previous scene had been. She let her wide-eyed gaze slip beneath the table to where a cat was sleeping. When she raised her eyes from the familiar, she noticed a bent old woman dressed in an army great coat, her shoulder-length hair hanging in strings from under a cloth cap, staring out with an expression of utter dejection.

'I caught sight of that poor old woman again,' Alicia told her office friends. 'Looked ever so sad.'

'D'you think she's been put in there by Shelter, you know, as a reminder it's not the festive season for everybody?'

'No, Liberty's would never allow that. It would turn away customers.'

'Once they put a naked man in a fish tank in a shop window. Called it art, they did.'

Alicia spent Christmas Day transforming the winter coats she had picked up from a skip in Kensington Close. She cut the sleeves from both and sewed the red ones back on the orange coat and the orange back on the red. Then she unwound odd knitted garments that had accumulated under her bed, and dipped some in green dye and others in red. 'Quite Christmassy,' she murmured to herself.

Some time after New Year's Day, Alicia thought she'd see how Liberty's had brought in 1982. Two large windows had been decorated for a scene of partying on the Embankment. At the front, the Thames flowed black while fireworks sparkled on a pale winter sky, and at the centre of the scene beautiful young men and women dressed in furs gathered laughing round a spit where a sucking pig rotated. Alicia stood close and stock still. Little by little, she noticed the poor old woman staring at her from the shadow of the Thames. She had not been invited to the party, she was not wanted there, but how was she to escape? As Alicia moved away, seeking an explanation from the pavement, the old woman appeared to accompany her, her head lowered, her eyes searching the waters of the river.

Haunted by the old woman's predicament, Alicia felt it her duty to do something for her. On a subsequent day, she dressed carefully in what she considered to be her 'best' and with purpose in her steps, she walked to Liberty's. Just beyond the entrance, she found herself in a high domed hall given over to the display of scarves, some hanging like cobwebs in the air, others gracefully poured over sculptures. She tried to attract the attention of an assistant, but was ignored in favour of the folding and repositioning of silks and satins. She left them to it and wandered into a room of cabinets filled with gold and silver jewellery. A single assistant stood penned behind a counter.

'I would like to see the manager,' Alicia said.

'He is not available,' the assistant answered.

'In that case, his deputy.' Alicia had no difficulty in standing her ground and faced the assistant doggedly for what seemed an eternity, during which the assistant refused to meet her eye. Eventually, outstared, the assistant asked what Alicia wanted to see the manager about.

'There's a poor old woman gets trapped in your window displays. I've seen her there often and I'm most anxious about her. How can Liberty's permit such a thing? And where does she go when she's not on display? She doesn't look very well fed. And as to her clothes, they're a disgrace!'

Alicia's voice rose on a tide of indignation. She did not notice the assistant's hand slide under the counter to the panic button.

Just One of Those Things

At first she could not identify the sound. It was not quite human, nor was it animal. It was hybrid, that of a man-beast emerging from the grumous depths of a damned experience.

His head was thrown back, his chin thrown forward, dislocated. His eyeballs rolled, their seeing elements quite vanished. His face was drained of colour – not pale, not yellow, but colourless. Around his mouth was white foam streaked with red.

The penetrating sound-complaints were growing louder. His limbs were acquiring a life of their own, his legs thrusting forward in spasm and his arm rowing the air.

She was transfixed, imprisoned in a carapace of shock. While she sat silent and motionless facing the windowless, doorless walls of her cell, he thrashed the unseen army with the untamed vigour of his fit.

'I'm here, my beloved!' she murmured, knowing he was not.

In the eternity that is time stood still, they walked together on the bilberry hills and wandered along the scented banks of the river. They were free and did not know it. Only now, sentenced to life on the precipice . . .

'Please come! Come quickly! My husband is so ill!'

Without her supervision, in the minutes it had taken to dial 999, he had fallen from his chair. He lay awkwardly, his head caught between the felled table legs. She was not strong enough to disentangle him, extend his tortured limbs and roll him on his side. And so she slipped to the floor beside him and cradled his head in her lap. But with his alien fit-strength, he fought off her protection.

His face was swollen out of recognition, his cheeks and chin described a circle. Perhaps this time he would die, his whole system shaken and dilated to disintegration, his blood in spate having burst its banks, his frame as pervious as the crust of the earth when its boiling bowels erupt.

All suffering responds to sweetness of some kind. His kind was located in a plastic box in the refrigerator. Useless to fill the Leeds creamware bowl with wood strawberries, or scoop out a Charentais melon and fill the cavity with macerated currants. His needs would not be met by beauty or fragrances. It was not his sensuality that was waging war for a bounty of sweetness: it was his blood.

She had managed to ease him on to the kelim and pull the rug into the emptiness at the middle of the room. She had left him for no more than ten seconds, rushing to the refrigerator and back. Now she must sit and still her shaking. She would take in six deep breaths. He was safe by her side; there were no jutting edges on which he could injure himself.

Where were her spectacles? There was no time to look for them: they might be anywhere. She must remember to follow the procedure. She must hold the vial containing the liquid on the point of the needle, upside down. She must draw up the pure liquid into the tiny syringe and then inject it into the second vial, where the freeze-dried sweetness lay. She must shake it well before drawing the mixture into the syringe . . . She must avoid damaging the needle; supposing it snapped in half, it was so fine . . . And there was something else. She knew there was something else. Yes! Above all, there must be no air bubbles. She peered; without her spectacles it was a little hard to be sure.

His groans echoed round the room as he rolled back and forth on the rug at her feet. His shirt had parted company from his trousers, leaving an expense of bare flesh. She noticed he had not wet himself, and she was relieved; when eventually he established peace again, it must not be clouded in humiliation. She sank to her knees beside him and thrust the needle into his flesh. How tough is flesh, how resistant!

And then the doorbell sounded.

'You're quite sure it's an insulin reaction?'

'Quite.'

'It's happened before?'

'Yes, several times.'

'What's his name?'

The two young men sat on the floor beside her husband. One removed his shoes and the other held his hand. She watched Mary Magdalen and the mother of the crucified man at the deposition.

'James! Can you hear me?'

They lifted him on to the bed.

'James! Can you hear me?'

The groans were sounding at longer intervals, the tossing to and fro had ceased. James was curled in the foetal position, reciting numbers. Starting at 80 – always 80 – he counted back to 34 or 20 before returning, obsessively, to 80. What did it signify?

'Will you telephone his doctor? We can't get him down your stairs.'

A locum arrived an hour later.

'Is his brain damaged?' the woman asked nervously.

'Just inflamed,' he said. And then: 'Your stairs: they're sheer murder. Whatever made you put them in? I wouldn't have them as a gift!'

Really! How interesting . . .

'Is this fit different from others he's had?'

Not really, she remembered. Perhaps a little less severe. He had not bitten through her finger or given her a black eye this time. But of course, by now she knew how to defend herself from his unnatural strength.

In her childhood, the family doctor had been a friend, a cultured man, dedicated to healing patients and tending roses. He was always available, even-tempered and reassuring. This half-pint technician, disfigured by acne and a mind hypnotized by its own concerns, instilled no confidence in her. Why had he not paid as careful attention to ridding himself of his spots and his unfortunate manner as he had to the selection of his matching shirt, tie and socks? She wished he would take his beastly hands off her husband.

'There's nothing I can do for him, of course!'

———

She was glad to be alone with her husband.

'I feel so sick.'

'You always do, after an attack. But it passes.'

'What happened? When? How long was I out for?' And then again: 'I feel so sick!' He had stopped counting. Instead, as he slipped from unconsciousness into semi-consciousness, he asked the same three questions over and over. She had poured *eau de Cologne* into a bowl of warm water, and with a new flannel she bathed his face and hands. Between her ministrations, he raised himself on his elbow and threw up foul-smelling vomit into the garden bucket. Following each ejection, he sank back moaning, and repeated his questions. Her replies never satisfied him. It was as if the questions he posed were more important than any answers he might receive, for his questions established his existence, made tenuous by the emptiness of time passing but barely experienced.

For her part, she felt a surge of pleasure placing his head on the freshly laundered linen pillowcase and settling a hot water bottle at the small of his back and the cashmere car rug over his feet.

'What happened?'

'You had a hypo. Don't worry! It's all over and there's no harm done.' And now she must test his blood. She tried to prick his finger with the Autolet but he withdrew his hands.

'Please! I have to do this.'

'Why?' It was useless to attempt an explanation. By the time she had explained he would have slipped back into unconsciousness.

'I need your cooperation. Could you sit up?' And she pressed two pillows behind his back. His blood-sugar level was rather low. She could not risk injecting him with his usual nightly dose of insulin without ensuring that he first took in some sugar.

'Would you drink orange juice if I made it fresh?'

'Why?'

She did not reply. She would squeeze four oranges and, she judged, he would drink the juice because he felt hot and sticky and the oranges, coming straight from the refrigerator, would taste cool and fresh.

'I'm going to give you your injection.'

'What time is it?'

'Two in the morning.'

'I never inject at two in the morning!' He showed real fury. And there followed a stream of questions, uttered emphatically: What had happened? When? For how long had he been unconscious? Who were the men who had been in the flat? Which doctor had come?

'Never heard of him!'

When he was peacefully asleep, she rose quietly and picked the books and papers from the floor where they had fallen when his uncoordinated limbs had upturned the table. She mopped up the flower water and replaced the roses in the rose bowl. The room itself had acquired his chaos. She would make order in the morning.

'I feel terrible. I ache – all over. My legs! My arms! And I think I've done my back in. And look!' He thrust out his tongue and she saw that he had bitten through it on the right side.

'I'll run you a bath. It'll relax you. And you'll feel altogether better when you feel fresh.' He leant on her, shuffling into the bathroom. While he lay in the hot bathwater she had scented with bergamot oil, she scoured, polished and dusted, threw open the windows, and tidied.

She covered a tray with a piece of her embroidery and laid it with pottery. She placed a vase of buttercups beside the freshly boiled eggs and crustless fingers of brown bread.

'I feel ghastly,' he mumbled.

'You will for a few days, but rest always restores you.'

'Where's my radio? What book am I on?'

Having found his radio and his book, his wife wondered if a short walk might do her good. She knew the signs: any minute now and he would become contentious. But she had waited too long making up her mind.

'I've got a very important meeting on Wednesday. When's Wednesday?'

'Tomorrow!'

'Then I've got a very important meeting tomorrow!'

'I'm afraid you just won't be well enough to go.'

'Then I'll go without being bloody well well enough!'

She walked ten minutes to the park and sat down on a bench. She always carried food with her for her husband, in case of emergencies. She fed half a marmalade sandwich to the sparrows. She reflected that she could not refuse to care for him because he did not care for himself: she loved him. It would be much harder to withdraw her care than provide it in the face of his obstinacy. But should she reveal to him that she knew what had triggered his hypo? They were a metaphor for his life's behaviour. He always cut off when he was not getting his own way.

'When was it that you were going to Florence?' he enquired when she handed him his mid-morning coffee.

'Today.'

'Oh, my God. I've ruined it all for you!'

'It's not the end of the world.'

'Will you lose all that money?'

'I've not thought about that.' And she drank her coffee. 'Why d'you think you had a hypo, this time?'

'I've really no idea,' he said thoughtfully, between gulps of coffee. 'Just one of those things.'

The Unexpected Marriage of
Vanilla to the Stars

P lanet Earth was dead. The blistering Sun had all but expired, taking with it the milky Moon. The Stars looked down in despair, for their view had been eclipsed. Falling through the Void, shooting from one to another and sparkling for themselves alone had lost its charm. In lively exchanges, they struggled to remember how long they had hung disconsolate in the great Void of Thead. They beamed in excess of twenty-digit numbers across the electric highways, and as each made its calculation, having agreed a figure of time just short of infinity, they reckoned it might still be just possible to galvanize Planet Earth into life.

The regeneration of Planet Earth became the *raison d'être* of Stardom. It was urgent on two counts. First, the aesthetic: they had had nothing to view for eons; secondly, the gastronomic: their populations were bored with their diet of thin air. Archaic wisdom had it that unlike their species, Human Beings supported their existence by ingesting material from beneath their feet, from creatures that trod and from slimy, silver softnesses gathered from the oceans. The Great Chunks, star elders who ruled, and the Shards, their minions, had maintained stony acceptance of their lot until recently, when the Shards had expressed some dissatisfaction with nothing to gaze at, nothing to savour. *Jouissance* was no longer a factor of their existence. Perhaps there was something to be learnt from Planet Earth?

The Sun retained a few tepid embers among its clinkers, the Moon a flickering memory of its days of contemplation and its nights of teasing itself into segments, lowering and raising the light of the night sky, drawing the tides back and forth. But both Sun and Moon were old and tired. Neither one could muster the energy to support the other, and together they indulged in pitying complaint against their erstwhile collaborators, the Cardinal Winds, who had abandoned them.

The Stars harmonised in the Great Void of Thead. The Great Chunks spoke in the name of their population of Shards. Regeneration, they said, could not be accomplished alone; the cooperation of the Winds was essential. But this would not be easy to arrange. The Winds had become unruly, with a tendency to continuous dissent. One could no longer appeal to the better nature of the Soft Breeze without the Raging Tempest gathering momentum. One could not, however courteously, demand a little cloud formation with a following shower, but a Hamsin would ensue. The Great Chunks agreed: the Cardinal Winds were vain. Perhaps they might be flattered into consent?

And so it was decided to lure them with the promise of an EVENT in their honour: a one-off light and music extravaganza such as had never before been seen, to which the Winds would be invited to lend their formidable energies. They should get their cast together! Thunderbolts, Tornados, Tsunamis and Typhoons: all would be welcome.

A circle of the Greatest Chunks approached the Cardinal Winds, dozing in the Void of Thead, but the Winds proved impossible to rouse. One or two forced open an eye and appeared to listen; one or two raised themselves on a little pillow of squall and listened, but inattentively. Most slept on, apparently in dream. The Great Chunks were affronted. Their plan, an excellent one, had undeniably failed.

At the time of their omnipotence, the Stars had controlled the Winds. They must do so again. But entreaties fell on deaf ears. Flattery had no force. It was useless to persist in cajoling such fickle, mutable energies. The Winds would have to be overtaken, captured, made prisoner, tied in knots according to the temperament of each and then unleashed as required. The Great Chunks had taken the decision for the Stars. It was for the Shards to take the prisoners.

The Great Chunks themselves felt no need for the stimulus the Shards craved. They were the founding rocks, stolid, dense and impermeable. They had existed since the echo of creation, nourished their rock-hard selves on the elements of their conception. The Shards, on the other hand, were in the process of becoming: splinters cast off from the Chunks, their lean, pitted forms dependent upon thin air passing through them. They had unfulfilled yearnings for *jouissance* which, left unmet, might create unrest. It was this that prompted the Great Chunks to suggest that a contingent of Shards should gather and form in the most efficient configuration for a launch to Planet Earth, there to see for themselves whether the merest inbreathable ingestible had survived the unawakened death of the host.

The journey was hazardous, the view in eclipse. The Shards clung together in a stream of their own light as they shot through the Void.

The breathing world was dead, the surface of the Planet a dust bowl. No human being, no four-legged creatures, nothing emerging from the debris. Planet Earth, a midden, was shrouded in the dirty brown texture of indifference. The Shards dragged themselves over the unstable surface, the interstices in their rough-cast forms clogged with the foetid air of death and decay. Meanwhile, other Shards accompanied prisoner Winds to the Sun and Moon. One lot unleashed a Hamsin on the Sun and ordered it to work its monstrous bellows furiously to stoke the flickering cinders. The Sun was unresponsive. Another lot accompanied a Great Blizzard and unleashed it on the Moon, but the torrents of hail they delivered quickly melted. The Blizzard recoiled. All Shards reporting back to the Great Chunks confirmed that the Sun remained cold and colourless and the Moon tepid and unlit. Heavenly bodies no longer had influence.

A Hurricane unleashed to rage over Planet Earth dispersed the dust and a Thunderstorm's deluge laid the debris. The Shards, optimistic at first, waited expectantly, but all that confronted them was undulating brown sludge stretching in sullen uniformity into infinity. Weakened, they felt their mental concentration slipping away. They remembered nostalgically the immaculate, silver domain they had left behind. They were tempted to give up and return to the Stars, but to admit failure was too dire to contemplate. With the terrain cleared, albeit corrugated, it was just possible to drag themselves across the surface of Planet Earth, and while so doing, to *think*. What, they wondered, lay *beneath* the surface?

They sent back to the Stars for Meteorites to rip through the crust of the Earth and penetrate to its interior. When it was done, Shards gathered at the rim of the crater and peered into the bowels of Planet Earth.

The landscape was unlike anything they had seen or imagined. They had no names for what confronted them. For a long while they hesitated, frightened to probe the chasm; all they could make out within were hollownesses, caves and cells, shadows and other manifestations of concavity. They took measure of what lay ahead against their own size and that of the Great Chunks and found it awe-inspiring.

A few Shards moved cautiously towards the rim. Little by little they dropped down into the great bottomless hollow, drawn by uncontrollable forces, prompted by something in the air.

Pale flares beamed from individual Shards did nothing to light a pathway, and so they gathered together and moved in clusters, led on hypnotically, deeper and deeper towards the centre. The air that had previously clogged their breath had given way to something permeable and alluring, something that excited them to explore.

More and more Shards plunged through the Void of Thead and into the chasm, sent by the Great Chunks to report back on the findings made by the expeditionary team. But the Shards returned no messages, for each successive group had fallen under the same spell. As soon as they had inhaled a single breath of the air in the chasm, all thoughts of their domain in the Stars evaporated.

While the mercurial Shards gathered in pleasure, the Great Chunks agonised in stasis, their habitual stance in the acceptance world shattered. Had the Winds turned against their captors? Had the Shards found nourishment and vision and failed to return their bounty to the Stars? Were they injured, their lights permanently extinguished?

The Shards continued to lower themselves and sometimes, in their haste, fell towards the source of the spicy fragrance that aroused within them an unfamiliar gratification. With no thought of their safety in this alien world, no thought of how they might get out and return to the Stars, they plunged on, ever deeper, their enjoyment intensifying.

At last, they found themselves in a warm, moist atmosphere. Their precipitous fall gave way to drifting and they came down gently to luxuriate on a bed of fleshy stems and leaves dotted with small, greenish flowers. In the silence of the dark chasm, they thought they could make out the repetitive buzzing of bees and the humming of birds.

At the centre of Planet Earth, the Shards had discovered the long lost echo of the sacred Vanilla, a plant with a mission to delight, a mission of such unique significance that when the Sun, Moon and Planet Earth died, it alone was given a role in eternity.

Every Shard dispatched from the Stars to find and return their fellows to the Heavens became intoxicated with the sacred fragrance, and in response, they watered the Vanilla with their *sputum lunae* and lived on in eternal *jouissance*.

The Final Journey

A strikingly handsome Swiss student was travelling by train with his cousin from Geneva to Paestum, where he was to sketch the Greek columns. Noticing that an elderly man was having difficulty opening the carriage door at Milan, he quickly rose to unfasten the catch, help the man to his seat and set his suitcase on the rack. His eyes did not dwell on the old man's face but his mind focused on the infirmities of old age, hence his solicitude.

After less than one hour, the old man prepared himself to alight. Again the young Swiss rose to help him with his case and the obstinate catch on the door. The student did not register his spontaneous deeds, so automatic were they. Concern for old people was second nature to him. And then it was Paestum, back to Geneva where he parted from his cousin, thence to Paris where he took up his studies.

Six months passed. The seventh brought a letter from his cousin enclosing a cutting from *Le Matin de Genève*. It had been placed among the personal advertisements and requested that 'the young man of courtesy, travelling from Genève to

Paestum on the 18th April contact Herr Professor Gautmann with a view to accompanying the Herr Doctor to the Greek archaeological sites of Sicily'.

'It is most certainly you who are being sought! I myself was struck by your solicitude that day towards the old man.'

The student considered the offer. He was troubled by it. Was the Herr Doctor a benefactor, a *deus ex machina* who had noticed his poverty? Did he see in him a talent that would waste for want of the nourishment that only funds might provide? Or did he have impure designs on him? He supposed that he and his cousin had been discussing Greek antiquities and had shown themselves to be knowledgeable. Did the old man feel he had something to learn? Or was it that he was lacking a son? If he were rich enough to fund a complete stranger, how was it that he had no friend or valet to accompany him?

The student wrote back to his cousin: did he remember the subject of their conversation in the carriage in front of the old man? His cousin replied: 'Paestum and Pompeii, of course!'

After some weeks of agonising, the student decided to accept the good Herr Doctor's offer. He would travel to Frankfurt (on a ticket provided) and the two would leave together for Sicily the following morning.

It was a wise decision to meet at the Doctor's house. The student would otherwise have had difficulty in recognising him. In the event, he was shocked by the old man's appearance. He was truly ugly. His thin face was the colour of parchment, his frame so insubstantial in his coat as to remind the young man of a wizened hazel, loose in its shell. His handshake was bony and chill.

The student carried more bags than he was accustomed to lug, not only because his host appeared to be travelling with all his worldly possessions, but because he had almost none of his own. During the journey he spoke to his host untiringly and easily, in an informed manner expressive of his knowledge and graciousness. He helped him on and off with his coat, assessed when to wrap and unwrap him from his travelling rug, saw to it that the old man was provided with food and drink, and met all his other needs.

Once in Taormina, his host's pallid face gained a little colour, and with such agreeable company with whom to share his food, his very bones appeared to put on flesh. His gait quickened with his enthusiasms for the sites laid before him by his young companion and he gathered force enough to insist upon carrying the guide book and the water bottle himself.

A conviviality persisted for ten days and was mutually rewarding. The old man neither burdened the younger with his frailty nor with his greater scholarship and the young man neither took advantage of the generosity of his host nor expressed himself with servility. However, on the eleventh day, while examining some rock-hewn tombs of the first Siculan period near Palermo, the student suddenly became aware that the skin on Herr Professor Gautmann's face had become tightly stretched across his cheekbone, yet lay in folds around his mouth. The legs of his trousers were slipping over his shoes, scraping the dry earth, and his coat sleeves were hanging over his gnarled hands. A peculiar smell emanated from him.

Herr Professor Gautmann asked his companion whether he would regard it an imposition if he were to take his arm or lean on his shoulder. It was with time and difficulty that the student managed to pick his way safely over the loose stones and lead his host back to the carriage that stood waiting a quarter of a mile away at the foot of the hill.

The Italian physician was forthright. 'Herr Professor Gautmann must have been suffering from his cancer for many months . . . he must have known his condition was serious. This is hardly the time to be touring archaeological sites.' And he expressed his regret that 'your father is not going to enjoy the comfort of dying in his own bed'.

Throughout his life, even when he was old, the student remained haunted by what had happened. 'From time to time,' he wrote to his cousin, 'I make a conscious effort to recall Professor Gautmann and the risk he was prepared to take to control the circumstances of his death. Sometimes, and I can't account for why, I regard his as a courageous act, sometimes as selfish and foolhardy.' He knew nothing more of the German's history than that he had never married and had devoted his life to the study of Greek civilisation. And after all those years, he still didn't know what to make of him. What accounted for his behaviour? Perhaps the old man had been looking to realise a fantasy at a moment in his life when he would not risk being prosecuted for it. Perhaps, in his final days, he was released from desire in order to discover the rewards of disinterested companionship. Did Herr Professor Gautmann die happy, despite the lifelong burden of his unusually ugly appearance and lonely soul? He wished someone could explain.